Praise for Janis Hallowell and
The Annunciation of Francesca Dunn

"Provocative and suspenseful . . . Hallowell offers no easy answers as her various narrators incisively trace the intricate connections between divinity and madness, faith and reason."
—*People* (four stars, Critic's Choice)

"Janis Hallowell writes with lucid grace of madness, divinity, and the tender watershed between the two. Brave and compelling, *The Annunciation of Francesca Dunn* delves into the characters who yearn for the holy with very human hearts and reminds us that we must struggle with belief until a blessing is evoked."
—Donna Gershten, author of *Kissing the Virgin's Mouth*

"A first novel that unfolds with the certainty of a summer blossom . . . uncommonly moving and well told."
—*Tampa Tribune*

"[An] ambitious first novel. . . . Hallowell challenges the reader to think in new ways. . . . There's a lot to admire in the complexity of issues [she] raises—and in her lack of easy answers."
—*Kirkus Reviews*

"Hallowell's characters . . . are eccentric without being caricatures. Everyone in the story has dimension and importance . . . all contribute mightily to a tightly woven fable."
—Amazon.com

Valari Jack

About the Author

JANIS HALLOWELL has been a potter and a graphic
designer. She was awarded an associateship by the
Rocky Mountain Women's Institute to write this book.
She lives in Boulder, Colorado, with her husband and
daughter.

THE

ANNUNCIATION

OF

FRANCESCA DUNN

Janis Hallowell

Perennial

An Imprint of HarperCollins*Publishers*

Grateful acknowledgment is made to reprint the following excerpt by Mirabai, translated by Jane Hirshfield, used as an epigraph, from *Women in Praise of the Sacred* by Jane Hirshfield, editor. Copyright © 1994 by Jane Hirshfield. Reprinted by permission of HarperCollins Publishers Inc. For additional territory contact Michael Katz, 173 Tamalpais Avenue, Mill Valley, CA 94941.

This book is a work of fiction. The characters, incidents, and dialogue are drawn from the author's imagination and are not to be construed as real. Any resemblance to actual events or persons, living or dead, is entirely coincidental.

A hardcover edition of this book was published in 2004 by William Morrow, an imprint of HarperCollins Publishers.

HarperCollins books may be purchased for educational, business, or sales promotional use. For information please write: Special Markets Department, HarperCollins Publishers Inc., 10 East 53rd Street, New York, NY 10022.

First Perennial edition published 2005.

Designed by Betty Lew

The Library of Congress has catalogued the hardcover edition as follows:

Hallowell, Janis.
    The annunciation of Francesca Dunn : a novel / Janis Hallowell.
      p. cm.
    ISBN 0-06-055919-5
    1. Schizophrenics—Fiction. 2. Homeless persons—Fiction.
3. Teenage girls—Fiction. 4. Miracles—Fiction. 5. Cults—Fiction.
I. Title.

PS3608.A5485A83   2004
813'.6—dc21   2003051265

ISBN 0-06-055920-9 (pbk.)

05 06 07 08 09 ❖/RRD 10 9 8 7 6 5 4 3 2 1

FOR ZOE

for the divine in all of us

Only those who have felt the knife
can understand the wound,
only the jeweler
knows the nature of the Jewel.

—Mirabai, sixteenth-century Hindu mystic,
translated by Jane Hirshfield

One

CHESTER

People who live in houses never get it, but street people know: Fall begins on the fifteenth of August, at the exact moment when summer's at its peak. It happens like breath, the exhale being the seed of the inhale. There's the first yellow leaf. A tiredness comes over the green. The smell of snow rolls down from the mountain, and your bones remember the cold that's coming. It was that night, the night summer slipped into fall, that she became the Virgin. Before, she was just a girl who worked at Ronnie's Café on weekends, handing out free food after hours. There had never been anything about her to suggest divinity. No trace of roses lingered around her; there was no holy brightness. But all of that changed with the season.

That night, as always, I waited until dark to look for a place to sleep. There was a spot in the bushes by the river that I often used, and after I smoothed the dirt with my hand, I gingerly pulled my sleeping bag from its sack, trying to keep the goose down from leaking out of the many small rips in the fabric. I aligned the bag north to south because I can't sleep crosswise to the earth currents, and then I checked to make sure it wasn't visible from the road. You see, when the season changes, it brings the college boys back to town. They come, all suburbs and sex, looking to show their frat-boy friends how to kick bums trapped in sleeping bags. They never got me, though. I knew their ways from teaching them, long ago. And from being one of them before that.

I sat and ate my supper, a splendid ripe tomato pinched from a backyard garden. With the tip of my knife, I saluted my unknowing benefactors. They of the white picket fence and cozy kitchen. When the tomato was gone, I put away my knife, wiped the juice out of my beard, and turned up the collar on my coat. I didn't take off my boots. As much as I hated the dirt going into my bag, boots tend to disappear if they're not on you, and boots can make the difference between staying alive and not.

I had settled in, hoping for sleep, when there was a commotion above the water. I opened my eyes, and she was there. She was a vision, a visitation, a sighting, a hallucination. All words for the same thing: the moment that imprinted itself on all the remaining moments of my life.

She hovered over the creek, swirled in ambrosial light. The water coursed around her feet, but her dress stayed dry. She held the baby close. Her mouth moved, but I couldn't hear the words, so I made my way to the edge of the water. She was the girl from Ronnie's, only with eyes as deep as the universe and wrapped in a cloak of glory. The smell of roses, the velvety ache of them, lured me in. She smiled at me and said, "Yours will be a magnificent role in the coming of my son."

I'm no newcomer to strangeness. I've had it all my life. It's my curse and my blessing that I can smell things other people can't. I can pick up the rotten sweetness of infection from across the street. Anger coming off a person is an acrid, mustardy thing, not unlike the odor of ants, and lying has a cloying, soapy smell that makes my mouth pleat. In the past, when social workers and do-gooders discovered my gift, they sent me to shrinks who gave me the latest antipsychotic. I tried to take them, but the drugs always made me go dead inside. Each time I ended up deciding to carry on intact, smells and all, rather than live in that pharmaceutical twilight.

I had been smelling things forever, but I had never had a vision before. And this was the real deal, complete with singing angels and rapturous awe. I knew instantly who she was. I hadn't been to church since I was a little boy, but I knew. I recognized her by the roses and by the blue of her robe. And before I realized what was happening, she reached between my ribs and took my heart in her hand. It settled there like a tame rat, trembling at her touch.

I don't know how long she was with me, but when I came back to myself, I was waist deep in the water and she was gone. And I knew that this was what I was supposed to do: find her in the flesh and serve her.

SID

Francesca and I became friends the year before, on the first day of seventh grade, when we were both new at I. F. Stone School. Our homeroom teacher, Martin, who became our history teacher in eighth grade, made us tell the whole class what we were interested in and why we "chose" Stone School. I mean, what did he expect us to do? Say why we couldn't make it in public school? Because even though the official line was that Stone School was for "exceptional teens," we all knew it was for losers.

Francesca said she was there because her parents got divorced. But everybody knew there was more to it than that. I learned later that she had stopped eating and wouldn't get out of bed in the morning.

I was there because I got caught cutting. With my Swiss army knife. On my thighs. It wasn't this big sick thing that people think. I didn't get all grotesque about it. It was just something I did. I can't explain it very well, but letting out my own blood calmed me down. Too bad if people didn't understand. I was careful. I had it under control. Nothing ever got infected.

They sent me to a shrink, of course. Which we couldn't afford. He had a thing for stroking his tie with his hand. He said that cutting was symbolically offing myself. So I asked him what he thought yanking on his tie was all about. After that I stuck to cutting a few select places on my feet, where no one would ever know, and he stopped interpreting my life for me.

I didn't say all that in class that day. And I sure as hell wasn't going to say what I really wanted to be, which was a doctor, a surgeon, if you can believe that. Fat chance. A kid like me, going to medical school? So I made up some feeble bullshit about wanting to be an artist, just like everybody else at Stone School.

Francesca didn't. She sat up straight and waited for everyone in the room to pay attention, and then she said she was studying to be a concert cellist. And she said it in this way that people didn't think she was a bitch either. She made everybody wish they were studying to be cellists, too. She had the kind of beauty that made boys freak out so bad they couldn't deal with her at all. They just got all stupid when she walked by. But not with me. Boys never noticed me.

It was the biggest thing in my life, that she wanted to be my friend. I was happier than I'd ever been, even though my mom was working nights and sleeping days and our apartment was a pit. We were always at Francesca's. Francesca had to practice the cello for hours, so I read books or hung out with her mom. Anne was cool. She was more like a big sister; she wore clothes like us and everything. If I hadn't liked Francesca so much, I would have hated her for having such a great mom.

Their next-door neighbor was Ronnie. She was a funny little woman with a squishy body and red poodle hair. She had this restaurant, Ronnie's Café, where they served breakfast and lunch, but what was really cool was on weekends she gave free meals to the homeless guys.

"I just like to feed people," Ronnie always said when anyone asked her how she managed it. "Everybody deserves to eat. There's always enough, somehow." People left bags of produce on her back step. Grocery stores donated eggs and meat. Her suppliers always gave her extra, and customers stuck dollars into the can by the register to help out.

The summer we were fourteen, me and Francesca got our first jobs at Ronnie's. We always worked the bum breakfasts because we didn't have to make as much money, being underage and everything. Ronnie paid us in cash at the end of every shift. I saved three out of every five bucks I made. By the end of the summer, I had four hundred and thirty-eight dollars saved up for the car I intended to buy the minute I turned sixteen.

We worked Labor Day weekend, Saturday and Sunday. Ronnie unlocked the back door as usual, and the bums shuffled in. I was used to them; they didn't shock me at all. And now that the mornings were starting to get nippy, there were even more of them. I got busy with the coffeepot, and Francesca started to deliver loaded plates. The place filled up fast.

When we first started working at Ronnie's, I was surprised that lots of the homeless looked pretty normal. You wouldn't even know they needed a free meal. And then there were the loonies, the ones who fit the stereotype, who would be in mental hospitals except that they couldn't afford it. There was Cristos, who was totally sweet and afraid of everything. He'd taken some bad LSD, and now he just stared at his shaky hands all the time. And there was Mary Lein, this scary woman who hollered every few minutes at no one in particular. With them was Briggs, an old guy with one eye that was scarred shut.

Chester sat at the far end of the counter talking to Ronnie. He'd been missing the past few weeks, and Ronnie said he'd had an episode. Now he was back and looked weirder than ever, moving his big body around in his dirty coat as if it were a bag full of raw eggs. Still, he was the best of them, and I was glad to see him. He always spoke softly, and he mostly said things that made sense. He helped the others when one of them needed something. He was kind of their spokesperson.

He and Ronnie always talked about books. He wrote down books for her to read, and she checked them out of the library. That day he was waving his hands in the air, going on about something, when Francesca came through the kitchen door carrying three plates of hot food. His hands froze like he was in a stickup.

She headed for him through this beam of sunlight, and when she got near him, the whole place went quiet and people turned and watched Chester and Francesca. It felt like we were all in a drop of water between two slides, like in biology lab, squashed flat so that nobody could move, so that everything could be seen, and we were about to be put under a huge microscope.

For that flattened-out moment, I could see what they all must have seen, what Chester must have been seeing: Francesca, a perfect jewel, standing there with her braid in a twister tie, holding hot plates on her arm. Her cheek was curved like the moon. Something bright seemed to burn around her head. Chester slid to his knees, and Francesca froze.

"Come on, Chester, get up," Ronnie said, like he was a big two-year-old on the floor. Like, no big deal.

Chester didn't listen. His face was all lit up, looking at Francesca. He grabbed the hems of her jeans, and I thought she was going to drop those heavy plates right on top of him.

"Chester, let go," Ronnie said, irritated with him now.

"Give me your blessing," Chester said to Francesca. It creeped me out.

Ronnie tried to pull him up, but he was a big guy, and he didn't budge.

"Bless me," Chester said.

Francesca's eyes were wild. People milled around. Briggs muttered loudly. Mary Lein whooped and cussed. All in all, it was getting way too crazy and they were crowding in way too close.

Ronnie got this set look on her face, and I could tell she was afraid and mad at the same time. She took the plates from Francesca and banged them on the counter.

"Do it," she said.

"What?" Francesca said, kind of freaking.

"Bless him. Put your hand on his head or something," Ronnie said. "And then he'll get up, won't you, Chester?" Chester's head bowed lower to show that he'd heard her.

Francesca's hand moved slowly from her side to the space over his head. She hesitated and looked over at me, like, What should I do? I shrugged. I meant, Do what Ronnie tells you to do. I would have.

Her hand floated down gently, barely touching his matted hair. The room went quiet.

"Bless you," Francesca whispered.

Chester let go, and I could hear the breath rush sharp and fast into the lungs of every person there.

CHESTER

Early Sunday morning Ronnie woke me, standing so that she shaded my face, her head framed by leaves and sky. I sat up, alarmed. I'd never seen Ronnie outside the café. I didn't think she knew where I slept. My heart clunked in my chest. It had to be about the Virgin.

"Don't *ever* touch her again," Ronnie said. I smelled the rancid sweat of fear over her usual mild, grassy smell. "You scared her. You're acting crazy, okay? Do you need to see someone? A doctor or someone?"

I shook my head. I was beginning to realize I'd messed up.

"She's Francesca," Ronnie said. "What's the matter with you? She's just a kid."

I realized two things. One: The Virgin's name was Francesca. I wondered how I never knew it before. And two: I had messed up bad. I shouldn't have touched her. Out of respect for her, I shouldn't have touched her. It suddenly seemed obvious to me that her new holiness made her vulnerable to the desires and needs of everyone around her. Instead of grabbing at her and demanding her blessing, I should have been protecting and serving her.

"I'm sorry," I said, ashamed of myself. "I won't do it again."

Even though I'd bungled the day before, the Virgin was back at Ronnie's on Sunday. The place was laced with her sweet rose smell. I don't know much about women, but her stomach didn't look all that pregnant to me. It was early, I guess. But her eyes already carried worlds. The people received her blessings unknowingly, along with the sausages and toast. I watched her goodness enter them when they ate the food she served.

I had talked about my vision. Some of us, Mary Lein, Cristos, Briggs, Lou, and I, were hanging out by the river, passing a bottle, and I told them. Cristos listened with eyes wide. Briggs scuffed the dirt with his boot. Mary Lein twitched and laughed and took a swig of wine. "Bring it on, is what I say," she shouted. Lou just reached for the bottle.

Whether they believed me, and spread the word, or they didn't, and it was just a coincidence, there were nearly twice as many people as usual at Ronnie's. Briggs sat next to me, following the Virgin with his eyes. He was red and blurry from his night in the cold and the years of drink. His smell was always electrical, but that day it carried an undercurrent of rot. A bad heart. I knew he had pills to put under his tongue, but they didn't do much. Maybe he was ready to believe me about the Virgin, because he was close to death.

I watched her move around the restaurant. I wouldn't touch

her, but I was ready to help if she needed me. When she filled Briggs's cup with coffee, I could see a pale green vein pulse in her wrist. But she moved on, purposely leaving my cup empty. I closed my eyes and made a silent vow to win her trust.

From the next stool, Briggs jerked hard and brought me back to myself. He smelled like an overloaded fuse. His hand went to his left shoulder. Concerned, the Virgin turned and set the coffeepot down. Her long braid of hair swung over her shoulder and bonked him on the chest. Right where he was grabbing. The smell of roses filled the place.

"Are you okay?" she said, leaning over him. It seemed to me she was asking about his whole life. He looked up at her and began to cry. His color improved. So did his smell.

"It feels better now," he said, straightening up, amazed, as if somebody had given him a hundred bucks.

Ronnie came over. "What's going on? You okay, Briggs?"

"Yes," Briggs said, and he grabbed the Virgin's hand and tried to kiss it.

"Not you, too," Ronnie groaned.

The whites showed around the Virgin's eyes. She was ready to run. I saw how to use what I had learned. I pulled Briggs away.

"Not like that, Briggs. You can't touch her." The Virgin blinked. Her hands held on to each other. She stepped back so that I was between her and Briggs. I was proud that she did.

He looked stoned. "I feel better," he said. "The pain is gone."

"The rest of you go on back to eating," I said, waving away Mary Lein and Cristos and the others. Francesca and Ronnie went into the kitchen. The other waitress filled cups and served food, trying to get things back to normal. I smelled the starch of nervousness and excitement in the room. I was ready to do a jig on the countertop. She had let me know that she wanted to do her works quietly. And that my job was to take care of her, to intervene. I thrummed with purpose. My wish, my prayer had been granted.

ANNE

I spooned cereal into my mouth, staring at my calendar, rear-
ranging weeks of lectures, research, and museum deadlines, while
Francesca paced the kitchen speed-dialing her father's phone
number in Italy.

"He's not there," she complained.

"Give him a few more days. He's not even past the jet lag
yet," I said, making a note to reschedule our dentist appointments for October. "And why are you calling him now, when we
have to leave for school in five minutes?" I counted on my fingers the eight hours ahead to Rome time. Seven o'clock here was
three o'clock there. "It's only afternoon there. On the weekend
you can get him in the evening."

Peter was having the year in Italy he'd always wanted. That
we'd always wanted. When Francesca was little, he was home
with her a lot. Being a paleobotanist, I had to travel at least
three months of the year. I had digs all over the world: India,
Australia, Europe, Mongolia, North America. I missed both

Peter and Francesca terribly at first, and then somehow I didn't. Now she was fourteen, Peter had a girlfriend to take with him to Rome, and I was traveling less, though I still went out in the field three or four times a year. Most recently I'd been working on an exhibit of fossils from North Dakota. I was planning to go in the spring for one last dig to round out the specimens from ten to twelve meters below the K-T boundary, but the museum director called over Labor Day and changed everything. She said the exhibit scheduled just before mine, something from Russia called "The Jewels of the Czars" had been canceled, then reinstated, and then canceled again. It seemed the borrowing of national treasures was a delicate, political business. Our deal with their Ministry of Culture was subject to the whims of government officials who came and went faster than black-market electronics. After meeting with the other forty-five members of the exhibit department and the curator of anthropology, the director had made her decision.

"We're going to move on," she said. "We can't operate with this kind of waffling from the Russians. Anthropology doesn't have another exhibit they can move into the slot. Your Hell Creek fossil exhibit is ready to go. Let's move that up to the spring." So I was left to rearrange my whole life to make it happen.

Francesca turned her back to me and pressed redial. I heard the electronic beeps rush over themselves in the same configuration as before, and I returned to my calendar problems. I flipped the pages from September to May and back again. I had been planning to stay home the entire winter. I wanted to spend time with Francesca, teach, and work on a paper I needed to finish. Now the exhibit was on the calendar for May 21. I didn't have any problem with getting the lab work done and the exhibit designed and installed over the winter, but as I looked at all the boxes representing the months ahead, I realized that I couldn't get out of a trip to Hell Creek before winter. There was an alarming gap in the data, and if we were exhibiting in the spring, I needed to go before the whole thing froze solid. As soon as Francesca got off the phone I would call Ronnie next door and see if Francesca could stay with her for the two weeks I'd be away.

Already I was aware of the buzz, the heady preexpedition excitement. Once we were at the site, life would narrow until it became only a matter of the dig, and, I confess, I was craving that simplicity. Late September, early October were beautiful in the badlands of North Dakota. Mornings would be cold. My team would chip through frost, but it would melt off by eight, and we would work in shorts under the wide sky until the sun dropped early, at three-thirty or four in the afternoon. The work would be bone-wearying and dirty, and my crew would be sick of each other by the end of two weeks. But we were an efficient machine, an organism whose task was hacking through rock until we'd harvested the fossils we needed. I would simultaneously love and loathe being out there, that's how it always was for me, but I would come home feeling wise and fit and with renewed faith and wonder in the world.

Francesca put the phone back in its cradle and slumped into a chair.

"I don't see any way around going on this dig right away, Francesca."

She shrugged. "If I call him after school, it will be eleven or twelve at night his time, right?"

I went on, "I'm sure Ronnie will be happy to have you. It's just for two weeks." I sounded guilty as hell. She looked wretched sitting there, and I didn't know if it was my leaving or not reaching Peter or something else.

"Anyway," I said, taking the bowls and coffee cups to the sink, "you have your school trip this weekend, don't you?"

"So?" The one-syllable weapon of fourteen-year-olds.

"So you'll be away and having fun."

Francesca was already heading for the front door, swinging her backpack onto her shoulder. I followed with the dish towel in my hands. She pulled open the door and froze on the threshold, her arm on the doorjamb blocking my way onto the porch.

"What is it?" I said, peering over her shoulder.

Directly in front of the door on our worn wooden porch was an intricate pattern, about two feet by two feet made entirely out of flower petals. There were golden orange marigolds and magenta asters and lemon chrysanthemums, which I thought I recognized from the city plantings in the park across the street. Someone had arranged them in a bright concentric pattern of squares and circles, with watermelon seeds providing the black outline between the shapes. Like a Tibetan sand painting, it must have taken hours and a steady hand to arrange the flower petals and seeds just so. I looked around the porch. There was no note or signature of the artist anywhere among our bicycles and recycling bins.

"Beautiful," I said. "Who made it?"

She stepped over the mandala as if it were the morning paper and tossed me an indecipherable look.

"How should I know?"

"I don't have an admirer, so this must be for you."

She rolled her eyes. "Come on, we're late," she said, but I noticed her cheeks were flushed and her eyes were bright.

Maybe this school year would be all right after all, I thought, dropping her off at school. I felt sure that some sensitive boy who wanted her attention had left the flowers. He wouldn't be the usual high-school kind of kid, all sweaty palms and Nintendo-mania. Not the maker of this flower poem. Maybe this rough patch between Francesca and me would smooth over as her attentions turned to a new friend. Her first boyfriend.

That evening when I got home, the flowers were dried up and scattered, walked on and blown around until they were just more debris on our porch. Francesca and Sid were in a circle of light at the dining-room table, bent together over some project. I liked Sid. She was tough, but she was smart, and she wasn't goofy about boys the way a lot of girls get. The truth was, I saw a lot of myself, back in high school, in Sid.

"Did you find out who left the flowers?" I asked as I walked through the room toward the stairs.

"Flowers?" Sid said, lifting her head.

Francesca's face tightened, and she bent closer to her note-book paper. "It wasn't exactly flowers."

Sid looked at me, waiting to be included, a laugh ready around her mouth. Francesca glowered, silently forbidding me to say more. I put down my bag and crossed my arms.

"What's the big deal, F?"

"It's not a big deal," she spat. "It's not anything."

"Tell me," Sid said, urgent and gleeful, delighted at Francesca's embarrassment. I was surprised by the force of it myself.

When you have an only child, you find yourself uneasy but also relieved when sibling-rivalry-type situations occur between your child and her friends. You realize it's a chance for her to learn something, to experience something important with a peer instead of with a parent or a teacher. It's a chance to stop being so singular. It forces her to have to share, to take the ribbing or fight, like other kids. That's what I was thinking, if I was thinking at all. Or maybe I just wanted to prod Francesca a little myself, tease it out of her and satisfy my own curiosity. Or maybe my motives weren't at all clear; maybe I was worried, a touch resentful, a bit left out, and I wanted to take the side of her friend this one time, to see what would happen. In any case I broke the first rule of a parent. I spilled the beans.

"Oh, somebody made a design out of flower petals this morning and left it on our porch," I said lightly.

Francesca half rose from her place at the table. Her mouth shaped itself for reproach, her eyes hardened. She was formidable.

Sid grabbed her arm. "So who was it?"

Francesca shrugged, miserable now.

Sid wouldn't let it go. "Come on. You know. You just don't want to say."

"It was beautiful, Francesca," I put in, trying somehow to undo what I'd done. "You shouldn't be embarrassed."

"Shut up," she cried.

She turned to leave the table, her face rigid and mean. She

spun around so fast that her long hair flew out in a wide circle, and the blunt, abrasive tips of it grazed my cheekbone.

That night I stayed up, long after I had apologized and been grudgingly forgiven, long after she had talked to Peter on the phone and gone to bed. I sat in the dark and worried about leaving her for Hell Creek. I watched to see if her suitor would come again. I waited and watched and worried and thought about the vulnerability of women. With all our perishable eggs in our two ovarian baskets, we are unprotected from love's biological counterpart: the urge to reproduce.

Francesca was certainly a virgin, but now she was one large step closer to being a woman simply because she was the object of a boy's admiration. I knew that the most powerful thing in the world was the urge to mate. It was stronger than friendship, stronger than ambition. Stronger than parent-child love. If it could have been harnessed somehow, it could have powered spaceships. Imagine a rocket fueled by sex. Not love. Love was something else, also powerful but different from this biological urge. Love was the urge of the soul, in spite of the body. It involved acts of will, even sacrifice. Sex would have none of that. The cells of the body couldn't give a shit about loyalty or duty. They just screamed what they wanted until they got it. And nobody's cells screamed louder than a fourteen-year-old girl's.

I told myself to slow down. A boy's gift of flowers didn't mean she would be having sex with him. With luck there would be years of courtship and friendship and the gaining of experience. Very late, I fell asleep on the couch, having decided that this boy who painted with flower petals was probably exactly what Francesca needed.

In the morning the front porch was a study in blue: veronica, pansies, scabiosa, delphinium, and bachelor buttons arranged in a wave pattern, with small white rocks meticulously placed around the edges. He'd layered and blended the petals so that the shades of blue graduated from dark violet to palest sky.

"Oh," I cried from the door. I would have been completely won over if it were for me, but my daughter was made of tougher stuff. Francesca wore her poker face and didn't give away a thing, but I noticed when we left that she was careful not to step on any part of the offering.

FRANCESCA

The hot water holds Francesca, covers her. It is heavy and slowing. Her arms float upward, knees splay outward. Her breath deepens.

She hears her mother typing on the computer in the next room. She hasn't said anything about the things that have been happening at Ronnie's. How Chester had done that weird thing. He got on his knees. He asked for her blessing. She was afraid when her leg was caught in his grip. And then the other one, Briggs. And the people crowding. She saw the fear on Ronnie's face. On Sid's. She can still hear the howls of Mary Lein over the blood pounding in her ears.

But there is something else. The thing she is most acutely aware of. Embarrassed of. Which causes her to pull up her knees in the bath and cover her chest with her arms. When she had her hand on Chester's head, when Briggs tried to kiss her hand, when she saw the flower mandala on the doorstep, the surge that went up her spine was not simple fear. It was the rush of crossing a finish line. It was acing algebra. It was like a perfect cello performance. She touched them and something passed from them to her. It went jolting into her bloodstream. She would never, ever say so, even to herself, except in the confessional of her bath, hidden by steam, softened by water. But in fact, she had nearly liked it.

She runs her hand, the blessing hand, down her slick skin, avoiding the breasts, which have become swollen and sore. It is the same hand that held the hand of the boy in California. An older boy she never told her parents about.

She'd kissed him. It was her first, which she tried to hide by pretending to be cool about it. And after the kiss they saw each other every day. But it wasn't like he was her boyfriend. They didn't talk; she hardly knew him. They just walked and kissed, and she learned she could make him want to kiss her. Eventually they stopped in some hidden place, and she found she could make him crazy to kiss her. This coy game was what he liked. The last night she was there, they lay on a blanket in the dark, and their kissing grew more complicated. His hands were inside her swimming suit. He touched her and pressed hard against her. And she liked it.

A blush prickles up her neck. Her body goes hot at the memory and the shame of it. She had her swimming suit on the whole time, she tells herself fiercely. Nothing really happened.

She closes her eyes. She listens for quiet. She is aware of an odd sensation in the pit of her body, deep inside, an annoying ticking coming from someplace behind her pubic bone. And she finds herself praying, though she was raised without religion. "Please God, don't let this be happening to me."

Two

ANNE

Natural selection was the God I believed in. I saw Him as a slightly psychotic Rube Goldberg. He was out in the garage with a cigarette dangling from His lip, drinking a beer and tinkering. His was a rigged-up junkyard full of life, held together with spit and baling wire. Oh, sure, He gave us vertebrae. Then He made arms and legs from fish fins to get us to crawl up out of the water. Sometimes, over the long course of evolution, life improved. (The prehensile thumb was a good idea.) But sometimes I imagined that God got up the next morning with a hangover, and while He scratched His ass, He wondered what the hell He could have been thinking.

Take the day after He added the whirligig that gave us reason. Four billion years and one hundred million species, and *Homo sapiens* somehow developed the ability to understand. That must have been some morning after. It was a risky thing to give to a bunch of monkeys. And we promptly went and thought up

all kinds of perversity. Like foot-binding and slavery. Like eth-
nic cleansing. Like recombinant DNA.

It was my job, I told myself, as I packed a flannel shirt and
several pairs of wool socks in my duffel bag, to try to figure out
one tiny sprocket in the thing. And my sprocket was the K-T
boundary, the stratum in the earth that divides the fossils from
before the dinosaur extinction and after. This was the slice of
time, 65.51 million years ago, that I had made my life's work.
It was my job, along with other scientists around the world, to
figure out what had happened then, why thousands of plants and
animals, among them the dinosaurs, were wiped out and why
other species stayed in the evolutionary game. It was important
work. I didn't need to feel guilty about doing it. But I did.

"Don't forget to practice," I said, knowing that I shouldn't
remind her. The one thing I was sure Francesca would do was
play cello. Since Peter and I had divorced, I made an effort to let
Francesca be casual about the cello. Knowing that she drove herself harder than we ever could, I didn't monitor her practice the
way he did.

I loaded my tools and ropes into the back of the truck and
secured all of it under a tarp. Francesca stood on the sidewalk in
front of the house and chewed her thumbnail with a look on her
face that said I was the stupidest person alive.

"Okay," she said.

"You'll water the plants at our house?"

She nodded.

"Every other day, right? And you'll get to bed on time?"

She rolled her eyes. "Yeah, Mom."

"Okay, then," I said, and moved awkwardly toward her,

wondering whether she'd squirm away if I tried to touch her. Sometimes she hated my affection, and other times she was still like a little kid, needing to be held and kissed. I opened my arms for a hug, and to my surprise she squeezed me hard; so hard that it was difficult to get a breath.

"I'll be back in two weeks," I said when I could fill up my lungs.

She walked backward up the walkway, turned around, and went into Ronnie's house. I loaded the last of my stuff into the truck, my sleeping bag and duffel, my camp stove and thermos and food for the road.

I started the truck and put it into gear, trying to abolish the guilt. It was old guilt, I knew, left over from all the other trips. I let out the clutch and rolled down the street, stuck a tape in the player to get my mind off leaving. Francesca would be fine with Ronnie, I told myself. School would occupy a lot of her time. She'd play her cello. Sid would be around every day. And there was the mysterious admirer, the flower-petal guy. She'd be so busy she'd hardly know I was gone.

SID

"Life is like pastry dough," Ronnie said, furiously chopping butter into flour until it looked like sand. She didn't bother to look up to see if we were listening. She didn't care if we liked what she said. Ronnie was cool; she didn't care what anybody thought. She went on talking, more to herself than to us. "Every piecrust is different. You have to add more water when it's dry and more flour when it's raining. If you're sad, you have to add more butter. If you stretch it too much, it'll tear, but if you leave it thick, it'll be tough."

Francesca and I rolled our eyes at each other. We were used to Ronnie's long speeches. We were staying with her while Anne was in North Dakota. My mom didn't care. She knew that if I was with Francesca, I was okay. We liked being at Ronnie's because she treated us like adults. She respected us and trusted us. She acted like I was as important as Francesca. She let us do stuff that Francesca's mom never would. One time she took us out to a big field and taught us how to drive her 1972 Volkswagen Bug. I was pretty good, but Francesca sucked. She ground the gears every time. When she finally put it in the ditch, I almost peed my pants laughing.

What I found out after we started staying at Ronnie's was that Chester had taken to sleeping at Ronnie's, too, but outside, in the bushes. And Ronnie didn't make him leave. At first I thought, How disgusting. Then, when I got to know him, there was something about him that made me wish he wasn't homeless. I mean, he was gentle and nice, once I got over how he looked. He had these intelligent eyes, just like the big brown eyes of a really smart dog, all loyal and true and everything. He sort of became Francesca's bodyguard, ever since Briggs popped his top and went all devotional on her.

During the day Chester hung out on Ronnie's front porch or in the park across the street. He had a thing about houses. Like, he freaked out if he had to sleep inside. When we were at school, he took off and did whatever homeless dudes do, but he always walked home with us. Well, not *with* us. God. We would have been *so* embarrassed. He stayed on the other side of the street or a half block behind us, but he was always there.

On one of those fall days that are so bright it makes your head ache, we were sitting on Ronnie's couch having a piece of cheesecake and doing our homework.

"'What is the meaning of the conch in *Lord of the Flies*?'" I read out loud. Francesca thumbed through the book, frowning. This was the kind of thing she was really dense at. You know, the metaphorical stuff. It was the kind of question I could answer even if I hadn't read the book. I could always bullshit my way through a question about symbolism.

"They want us to say it was this symbol of power or leadership," I said, watching her read as though the book itself would tell her that. "Or maybe order. It was probably a symbol of order. Like a flag. Or like a microphone. When they had the conch, it meant it was their turn to speak." Duh. Of course that's what it meant.

"I hate this book," Francesca said, tossing it facedown on the couch.

"Me, too," I said, taking a big mouthful of cheesecake. But I didn't. I mean, it was pretty nasty, but it really got to me. We weren't even halfway through it, but I thought about those kids stuck on that island a lot. I worried that they were going to kill each other, and I kind of dreaded reading the end, because I could tell it wasn't going to be good.

A car without a muffler pulled up in front of the house. We both got up in time to see this fully beige-looking woman get out of this banged-up boat of a car. I mean, the car was huge and packed to the top with stuff, and the woman was so pale, with dishwater hair and pants that used to be white. Nasty. She went around to the passenger side of the car and pulled out a sleeping kid, draping his arms and legs around her.

"Oh, my God, it's Rae," Ronnie said, coming into the room. She opened the front door as the woman walked toward us holding her kid.

"Ronnie!" the woman said, like she was surprised to see Ronnie here in her own house. Like, what a coincidence, bumping into you on your own front porch. "I can't tell you how great it is to be here," she went on. "Seems like Jonah and I have been driving forever." She glanced at the sleepy kid's face on her shoulder.

Jonah was cute. He was one little peach-fuzzy, cowlicky

angel, clutching a beat-up old stuffed puppy in his fist. I saw him there, and I just fell in love. He was the little brother I had always dreamed about. He was the kid I wanted to have some-day. He was way too gorgeous to belong to Rae, even if she was Ronnie's sister.

"I thought you took a vow," Ronnie said, reaching for Jonah. "You said you were taking a vow of silence at that ashram in Tennessee."

"Didn't you get my message?" Rae surrendered the kid and smoothed her grungy pants on her thighs.

"What message?" Ronnie put her cheek on Jonah's and closed her eyes, all blissed out from holding him.

I nudged Ronnie. "Let me hold him," I whispered. His thick black lashes rested on his cheek and his tiny hand patted Ronnie's soft face.

"Hello, darling," Ronnie whispered to Jonah, ignoring me.

Jonah opened his eyes. "Aunt Ronnie?"

"The message I left on your machine last week," Rae sput-tered. "The message I left saying I was coming."

"Excuse me, sir," Ronnie said to Jonah. "Have you seen my nephew Jonah? He's a lot littler than you are."

Jonah sat up in her arms, sleepy but grinning. "I'm Jonah. I'm four, and you know it, Aunt Ronnie."

Ronnie smooched his face. "My Jonah."

Rae began rubbing her shoulder. "I think my shoulder's in spasm. Girls, would you help me unpack the car? I don't think I should lift anything." She waited for us to nod, and then she smiled this sucky smile at us while she sat on her ass and watched us work.

The huge backseat of the car was packed to the top with clothes, plants, cookware, plastic toys, and even a small rocking chair. We moved the clothes in first.

"How long are you planning to stay?" Ronnie asked, following Rae into the second bedroom, where Francesca and I were sleeping. Without being told, we knew we would have to give it up. We picked up our stuff and put it on the couch in the living room. We watched Rae manipulate Ronnie. I hated her already.

"Ronnie, I'm so disappointed you didn't get my message," she said. "I left it all on your machine. I'm going to live here. Everything I own is in that car. Oh, don't worry, I'll get a job and a place for me and Jonah. I thought you wouldn't mind if we stayed here until we got settled." She pouted mightily. "Jonah loves you more than anything, but if you want me to, I'll get us a motel room. I have enough money for a week or so." Of course Ronnie wouldn't tell her own sister to leave, though she should have.

Jonah sat on the floor and played with Legos. He had a way of concentrating that made him look old and wise. His quick hands turned the pieces, searching for just the right one. I sat with him, wanting to eat him up. Jonah made even Rae worth putting up with.

"What are you making?" I asked.

"A double helix," he said seriously. "You know, like DNA."

"God. Are you some kind of genius?" I asked. He kept working on his spiral.

"Probably," he said.

There was junk everywhere. Jonah's toys were all over the

place. Rae's plants crowded the coffee table, and boxes of clothes and dishes sat piled up against a wall. Francesca and I made up the fold-out couch in the living room. By the time we were done, it was dark outside. The lights in the park flickered on. I hadn't seen Chester, but I was sure he was out there, keeping an eye on us.

"I made tea," Rae announced, coming into the living room from the kitchen. I guess her shoulder felt better. She moved some plants and lit a couple of candles on the coffee table. Four of Ronnie's good teacups sat around a teapot that could only have been Rae's; it was handmade and leaden-looking, with a broken bamboo handle across the top. A disgusting smell came from it. Lucky Jonah had a cup of milk.

"This is my own blend. It will balance your *chi*."

Ronnie sipped from her cup and looked like she wanted to throw up. I didn't even pretend to drink mine; I just left it there on the table. I didn't care what Ronnie's sister thought about me, no way was I going to drink it. Francesca put her cup to her mouth and sipped. She didn't look grossed out at all. She actually smiled at Rae.

When Ronnie and I were washing up in the kitchen, she made a face while she poured the nasty dregs of the tea down the drain.

"How's your *chi*?" I asked.

"Smells like dog shit," she whispered.

"Dude. You drank it."

She did an elaborate Ronnie shrug. "She's my sister; of course I drank it."

Being an only child, I hated it when people talked like that about their sisters or brothers. Like it was some kind of club

they were in and the whole world should understand how special they were to each other.

"Bullshit, Ronnie. You'd do anything your sister said?"

She considered. "Not anything. But she's my only family.
And she's had a hard life. I've had a much easier time of it than
Rae. So I'd do a lot for her, yeah."

It sort of hit me right then, that I felt the same way about
Francesca. We were closer than anyone. We were like sisters.

I had my Swiss Army knife in my pocket, and I rubbed its
smooth red surface the way Jonah rubbed the ear on his puppy.
I had rubbed it so much over the last year that the tiny silver
cross on it was nearly rubbed out. I was like a smoker who puts
an unlit cigarette into her mouth but doesn't light it. I held the
knife and sounded myself. I was okay. I was with my best friend
in a house that didn't smell like booze and refrigerator grunge.
Even with Rae around, it was better than home.

I wanted to cut, the urge was always there, but I didn't need
to cut. Not tonight. I concentrated on the sound of Jonah's little voice in the next room and Francesca answering. Ronnie
handed me a soapy cup, and I had to take my hand out of my
pocket, off my knife, to rinse it. I realized I felt safe. My heart
was beating slowly and evenly. Right then, at that moment, on
that one night, everything I had added up to just about enough.

CHESTER

At the southeast corner of Ronnie's house there was a bush with arching branches that created a place big enough for my sleeping bag and me. The dirt was dry and clean underneath. I was well hidden from the street, yet I could see the front of the house and around the south side, too, if I positioned myself just so. Nobody told me to sleep there, but I knew it was my job to keep watch. And I was determined to do it well.

I lay under my bush, in my bag, catching the smell of roses that told me the Virgin was inside. Light and the faint sound of voices leaked through the window glass. The front door opened, and Ronnie walked around the house toward my bush. She had a heaping plate that she held carefully level while she knelt, knees cracking, by my bag.

"You know, this would all be a lot easier if you would just eat inside with us," she grunted, handing the plate to me. I smelled melted cheese and corn tortillas and green chili. I saw beans and tomatoes and a folded tortilla with butter running out of it. My stomach made a fist, and I couldn't help but get out from under my bush and start filling my mouth with the food. Ronnie shifted her hips and sat on the grass with her legs to one side. Little frizzy hairs stood up from her head and shone in the light.

She watched me eat. My attention was on the food, but after a while I looked up at her and was surprised by what I saw. Her face, in the light from windows and stars, was naked and beautiful. I stopped chewing, midmouthful. I'd known Ronnie for years. I'd eaten breakfasts at her café every weekend. We had talked about books. Her particular smell was familiar and mild, like prairie grass in the rain. But never had I noticed her this way before. She was suddenly strong and noble, more Hera than Persephone. Not the beauty of convention and not divinely beautiful the way the Virgin was, but still, beautiful in her own right.

"You like those enchiladas," she said, with some satisfaction.

I nodded, looking back down at my plate, hoping she hadn't seen me admiring her. I sopped the tortilla in the green chili. I could tell she was working up to say something difficult. She spoke slowly, as if to avoid making a mistake.

"I've seen you keeping your distance from Francesca and getting the others to leave her alone, too," she said. "That's good. And you know you're always welcome to eat here and sleep in my yard or whatever." She waited until she caught my eye, and then she fixed me with a powerful gaze, and again I was caught by her solid beauty. "But not if you're going to get freaky about Francesca again." She held me in her vise-grip stare and then let me go. She shifted back into her everyday self. Gone was the earth goddess. And I admit I was relieved. I focused my eyes on my empty plate.

"Freaky? What kind of word is freaky?" I said, sounding more schoolteacherish than I had intended.

"You know what I mean," she said, taking the empty plate from me and getting to her feet.

FRANCESCA

Her cello sits among the laundry and boxes of kitchen junk from Rae's car. She lifts it, in its hard black case, up and away from the mess, and takes it to an armless chair in Ronnie's room, where she checks the tuning. Ronnie and Rae are at the park with Jonah, and Sid is at her own home for once, giving Francesca privacy to practice. The familiarity of the preparation, the rosin on the bow, the adjustment of the end pin, gives her comfort, like a repeated prayer. But it also stirs up anxiety and intimidation. For Francesca the cello has always held this mix of drive and defeat, desire and failure. From the beginning it has been this way.

She didn't start her relationship with the cello the way other children did, lost in a school orchestra with a shabby rented instrument. Her father's Uncle Randolph played the cello with the Boston Philharmonic, and Peter was determined that Francesca would play. When she was ten, he bought her a three-quarter-size cello, small enough for her child's frame. It was of better quality than anything her schoolmates played, but much lesser quality than the cellos Uncle Randolph owned. At the time she wasn't sure if she even wanted to play, but it wasn't optional; it was expected. So she began to study with Keith Jacobson, the best cello teacher in town, and she did well. She practiced at first because she had to, but halfway through the first year, she began to like it. And soon after, her father and Uncle Randolph used the word "talent" when they talked over the phone about her progress. She graduated to larger instruments as she grew. Keith began to prepare her for competition.

When she was twelve and a half, the same year her parents got divorced, Uncle Randolph died and left her one of his fine cellos. She went to Boston with her father to bring it home.

"Randolph wanted you to have this cello," Great-aunt Althea had said, gazing at Francesca with hooded eyes, holding the cello out of reach until she was good and ready to allow Francesca to touch it. "This cello has its own personality and soul. It cannot be neglected." And so it became Francesca's cello, and she understood that it was a very fine, very expensive one and that she was expected to show her gratitude by becoming a great cellist.

Uncle Randolph's cello was made in Vienna in the early twentieth century. The finish is smooth and hard under the fingers in a way that the finish of newer cellos only imitate. Its tone is as rich and redolent as its color. Ever since it came home with them, occupying a third seat on the plane, she has felt inferior to it.

The bow is another matter. It is entirely her own. She tightens the hairs and pulls the bow over the C string, sounding the first low E of the Brahms sonata. She loves her bow. She adores it. It's from a bow maker in San Francisco who showed her bows made of brazilwood, ebony, ironwood, and teak. They had bows with ivory, mother-of-pearl, and gold on them, but the one she chose was a simple octagonal bow made of pernambucco, with a German-silver-mounted frog and a nickel-silver tip. She liked it because it felt good in her hand and because she had picked it.

Soon after she got Uncle Randolph's cello and her new bow, she began working on her first important competition: auditioning to be a "young artist" with the Boulder Philharmonic. The prize was a thousand dollars and a solo performance. Even two years later, she cringes to think of it. The judges and the other contestants watched while she botched the Boccherini concerto that she'd worked on for months. The piece that she had performed perfectly, time after time, for Keith and at home eluded her at the audition. She missed notes, she lost her place in the music. She felt as if she had no strength in her arms to bow. She plodded through to the end, her training wouldn't let her quit, but when she was finished, she ran off the stage in disgrace. She's tried to compete since then and even got second place once, but she always freezes up. She has never played her best for judges, and she hates to do it.

Playing the opening measures of the Brahms, she wills herself to bow slowly, with measured control, letting the horsehair draw the sound out of the cello. She concentrates on pulling a strong, even legato, from the strings, finding the notes and playing them dolce, with sweetness. The top edge of the cello rests against her breasts as it always does, except that today they seem hard and sore, and the cello's pressing into them is uncomfortable. She shifts position, bringing the cello closer and more upright, then tries it lower and at a wider angle. Neither adjustment helps much. Both alter her technique, making it difficult to play. The tenderness is constant and alarming; it is with her all the time now. The pain and its accompanying dread creep into her sleep at night, causing her to wake up worried, scanning her body for signs that it might be returning to normal. She feels "off," as her mom would say. One thing that's wrong is that she hasn't been able to practice enough at Ronnie's. Three hours a day, Keith Jacobson says. She's lucky if she can get in an hour. And she hasn't competed this year.

Her father still acts as if she's going to be a great cellist. He still thinks she'll be touring and concertizing and making recordings. But she knows it isn't going to happen. Keith has a real prodigy now, a twelve-year-old boy with pimples and dust-colored hair who has been winning competitions all over the country. Keith is taking him, not Francesca, to Europe next year. She knows she's not good enough. She's slipping closer to mediocrity all the time. Keith hasn't said so, but she knows he thinks it, too.

As she works her way into the Brahms, pausing now and then to correct her fingering, she hears herself as if from the outside. She should be able to concentrate, alone at last, but the sound she's producing is hollow and pale. She closes her eyes, searches inside for the passion, the spark she hasn't felt in months. She undulates her body with her cello, trying to find the rich communion she used to have with her instrument and the music.

She works through the first movement, playing hard but not well. When Rae and Jonah and Ronnie come in, she stops, exhausted and sick of playing. Her bow hand rests on her knee, and she's breathing heavily, as if she's been running. Shame sits in her chest like wet cement.

CHESTER

We entered a brief time when the Virgin was left in peace. Briggs still sounded off about his healing, but most people in the larger world chalked it up to his being whacked and homeless, and anyway, they thought it was impossible. A few from the café understood who she was, Cristos and this guy Lou, but they didn't make problems; they just honored her. They allowed her to be divine, and they were happy to be near her. They ate in the café and accepted her blessings and didn't bother her much.

It was that rich season when the earth gives up her last and best. At night the trees layered on gold until, by day, the world looked completely gilded. Like other animals, I soaked up the last of it and denied the approaching end to warmth and plenty.

I knew that the presence of the Virgin among us wouldn't remain the secret of a few. I sensed that I would be called upon to actually protect her soon, but the day it happened, I was as surprised as anyone.

We were eating Sunday breakfast at the café. Ronnie's sister and the kid were in the booth by the kitchen door. It had been a cold night with a hard frost, and everybody was hungry. The place was almost packed. A man came in and sat down at the other end of the counter and accepted the plate of food that Sid handed to him. It happened sometimes that someone who had a home came in for the homeless breakfasts. Ronnie always served them, no problem.

"Anybody who needs to eat and shows up here is welcome to it," Ronnie said on those occasions. "If they have a million dollars in the bank but they need a free meal, that's their business. I'm not going decide who eats and who doesn't. I just cook it and serve it up."

This guy had a home. Of course he did. He smelled like someone who slept inside and avoided public toilets. He had the air of someone with status in the world, a guy who expected a certain respect and got it. No way was this guy one of us, though he wore a moth-eaten sweater and had about two days' growth of beard. The sweater was clean, and he had gone to great lengths to mess up his hair. I smelled the tang of an impostor.

He forked the pancakes into his mouth and followed Francesca with his eyes. He had heard about her; I could tell by the way he watched her. I shifted in my seat to keep an eye on him.

Cristos and Lou came in together, smelling of the park and the river, and I caught the cold aluminum smell of pain. Cristos's eyes were wild. He had his WILL WORK FOR FOOD sign around his neck, and his hands cupped his ears. Lou led him to the back booth, across from Rae and Jonah, the blind leading the blind, so to speak, and sat him down. The Virgin had a coffeepot in her hand and made right for them.

"He's lost his hearing," Lou said, too loudly.

Ronnie looked up from across the room. Mary Lein craned her neck.

"Shit, fuck," she called out involuntarily, and went back to eating. The impostor at the counter could see as easily as I could. Cristos fell down to his knees and pulled out a medal of some kind that was hanging from his neck. I walked over to intervene, knowing that the impostor at the counter was watching, but it couldn't be helped. Cristos lifted the chain over his head and held it out for Francesca. I intercepted, taking the St. Christopher medal from him.

"Sorry, man. You can't touch her, you know that."

"He just wants her to bless his medal," Lou said, still on high volume and causing anybody who hadn't heard him the first time to stop eating and stare. "His ears are killing him." Francesca kept her eyes on Cristos, who writhed before her. She held out her hand for the medal, and I gave it to her, letting the chain run like water from my hand to hers.

Ronnie appeared next to me, wiping her hands on a towel. "It's probably an ear infection," she said. "Lou, you should take him to the clinic."

"No, wait," Rae said from her seat. Her face was lit up.

Francesca dropped the medal back into my hand as Lou and Ronnie pulled Cristos up to his feet. Cristos rocked with pain, his hands over his ears. I gave him the medal, and his hand went back to his ear. He rocked forward and back, causing the little St. Christopher to swing from his hand. Lou lifted a steaming cup of coffee to his lips, but Cristos turned away from it. A few seconds later, he was screaming high and sharp like a cat, then stopped as suddenly as he started, and his hands slid down from his ears. A slow, stoned smile came over his face. It was the first time in all our years on the street together that I'd ever seen him relaxed. His forehead unknotted, and his top teeth stopped grinding into his bottom ones.

"It's gone," he said.

Several people started talking at once. Rae made a beeline for Francesca, preventing anyone else from getting to the Virgin and allowing me a few seconds to check out the room. Mary Lein stood up. "Fuck, fuckitty, fuck," she chanted. The impostor at the counter was standing up, too. And he had a big enough, serious enough camera for me to realize that he was a professional. He was clicking away at Cristos and Francesca and the whole scene, but when I went to stop him, he turned and slipped through the crowd. They let him pass, but they grabbed at me, shouting out their questions and excitement. I saw the photographer run out the door and disappear, but I couldn't follow. My first responsibility was to the Virgin. It couldn't be helped. I had to go back inside and see to her safety. The photographer would get away and tell the story to some newspaper, and either they would think he was a crank for hanging out with the likes of us or they would run the pictures. Nothing I could do now would change what was going to happen. I made my way back through the chaos to where Cristos was weeping and Mary Lein was whooping. I looked for Francesca, but she and Rae had slipped out the back door, just as surely as the journalist had slipped out the front.

SID

The I. F. Stone School (we called it the I. M. Stoned School) had this September tradition where everybody was supposed to go on a camping trip all together. Stone School bonding. Our history teacher, Martin, had this family land that some uncle bought; hundreds of acres that nobody ever used. It had these old mining cabins on it and that's where we went, all twenty-five students and ten teachers bouncing into the woods in four Jeeps and one big pickup truck, down a road that was more like a riverbed. At the end of the road, the cabins huddled in the crease of a hill. A fast-moving stream made so much noise that we had to yell in order to hear each other.

"Let's go," I said to Francesca, dragging her out of Martin's Jeep before it had come to a complete stop and before the two retards in the backseat, Lawrence and Skip, could beat us to it. We ran toward the five small buildings, pathetic huts, really, but hey, it was home for the next four days, and I meant to claim the best one. I charged through the backlit aspen that everyone else was gaping at and checked out the cabins. In the late-afternoon sun, I suppose there was a little bit of charm there, but mostly they looked like shacks. The first three had seriously funky bunk beds and brutal-looking vinyl chairs and stuff. No thank you. The fourth one didn't have any beds at all and only one window. It smelled like piss.

"Here's yours," I shouted to Lawrence and Skip, who were already hanging out with the other slackers, standing in a sulky group by the river, smoking cigarettes in the gathering dusk like it was going to be their life's work.

The fifth and last cabin had a bunk bed, a cot, and one big bed in it. It had nice windows that looked out on the river, and best of all, there was a stone fireplace and a wood cookstove.

"This is ours," I said. Francesca and I had been sleeping on Ronnie's fold-out couch, so it was no big deal to take the big bed together. Besides, we were a unit. We were best friends. I think that was the first time I actually said those words to myself. But we were. I'd never had a best friend before. We threw our stuff on it and went back out to find two other girls and the required female teacher to share it with us.

After we ate the nasty stuff they called dinner, we had a campfire and everybody hung out, talking and singing and stuff. We sat on a log and toasted marshmallows on sticks that I cut with my Swiss army knife. I have to admit, the camping-trip bonding thing was working with me, because I did not want to leave the circle around that fire and wander even a few feet into the dark to take a pee alone. I made Francesca go with me. She had no problem pulling down her jeans and squatting on the ground. It wasn't so easy for me. She held the flashlight while I leaned against a tree and peed on my boots. All I could see was the circle of ground where she pointed the light. Everything else was blacker than shit.

"Do you think there's poison ivy here?" I asked, feeling something tickle my butt. Or maybe it was spiders. The breeze blew on my skin, and it felt like I was exposed to the whole world. I was sure that anyone from the campfire could see me if they turned this way.

"I don't think there's poison ivy this high, but I'm not sure," Francesca said, flipping the flashlight beam back and forth on the ground.

"Stop it, you're making me dizzy." I zipped up, careful to step over the spot where the pee was.

She shut off the light. The blackness came right up and smacked me in the face.

"Hey, what the fuck?"

"Look up," she said.

I did. Above us, in and around the trees, there were zillions of stars. More stars than I had ever seen in my life.

"Do you think there's anything up there?" she asked quietly.

"Yeah. The stars are up there. Planets."

"No, I mean God. Do you believe in God?"

What with the stars, the dark, the mountain air, and tipping my head back the way I was, I suddenly felt *really* dizzy, like I was falling backward into the star dust up there.

"Whatever," I said. "Turn the light back on."

"My mom says that if you keep your eyes level with the horizon, you can see in the dark."

That was the kind of thing Anne would say. It sounded like poetry. The closest my mom ever came to something like that was one time when I couldn't find my coat and she said from the couch, "Open your eyes."

I turned my head from side to side, looking for the horizon, but I couldn't even see the trees that I knew were in front of my face. The only thing I could see besides the sky above was the light from the campfire and the silhouettes of the others sitting around it. I wanted to get back there. This talk about stars and God made me nervous. It made me feel more exposed than I did with my pants down and peeing for the whole world to see.

"You better watch it with the God talk. You'll start sounding like Chester and the rest of them," I said.

She didn't laugh.

"How'd you get rid of him anyway? Isn't he your devoted slave?" I lurched around, imitating Chester.

"Ronnie took care of it."

"You know, you do sort of encourage them," I said softly.

"What?"

"You do. You don't *dis*courage them. You let them think you're special."

She was pissed. I could tell by the hard silence.

Suddenly I was aware of the aspen trunks standing out against the lighter shade of the sky. I found that if I kept my head level, I could see the line of the mountain making a third shade of black. I began to see that none of it was really black, that everything was actually made up of soft colors this side of black, and they were as richly textured as the pile of sweaters on

Francesca's closet shelf. If I stared at the place where I thought the sky met the ground behind the hill, I could see several feet ahead.

"Wow," I said, holding my head as still as possible so that I wouldn't lose the angle.

Francesca took off through the trees, probably thinking she was leaving me to freak out, but I followed her to our cabin, amazed at how much I could see.

The bed in the cabin was lumpy and damp, and we put our sleeping bags side by side on it without speaking to each other. Francesca let me sleep on the inside, next to the wall, and she took the outside, turning her back to me. I settled into a half sleep, aware of the cabin's moldy smell and my nose turning numb in the cold and the rest of me warm in my borrowed down bag.

Sometime later, when the dawn had washed the grays a shade or two lighter, Francesca slipped out of her bag and went outside. I was crawling out of mine before I had a chance to think about how cold the floor would be on my bare feet with their various scabs and scars in progress. The boards burned against my skin, and I hopped across them and out into the frost-covered aspen leaves. I was planning to tell her I was sorry for making her mad. I was hoping she'd say to forget it.

The sun hadn't come up yet, and the stars were all but gone. The aspens flickered silver over the black ground. Glowing in her white long underwear, Francesca was bent over next to a tree, one hand braced against her knee, the other holding back her hair. She breathed heavily a time or two and then puked on the ground. She looked up as I came closer.

"Go back to bed."

"Are you sick, F?" I said. Like, duh.

She shook her head, still leaning on her knee, waiting to hurl again. And even in the soupy dawn light, I could see her brows knitted fiercely over her eyes, which were staring right at me.

"Don't tell anyone," she said.

CHESTER

"Make them go away," Ronnie said, standing in her living room between me and the closed door. "I mean it, Chester. Tell those folks to leave her alone." She made a shooing gesture toward the closed door. On the other side of it, across the street, Briggs and Cristos and five or six others were hanging out just to be near Francesca. What Ronnie was saying made my arms and fingers twitch; it made me shuffle my feet and look at the door and wish it would open.

I wanted to help Ronnie, I did. She gave me food. She was good to me. She was my friend. But I couldn't make the people go away. They recognized the Virgin for who she was, and they had as much a right to be there as I did. They were in a public park and not breaking the law. Now that the Virgin had made herself known to them, it wasn't for me to send them away. Her authority was higher even than Ronnie's.

I pulled at my jacket, and my bandanna was suddenly tight around my neck. The air was taking on that already-been-breathed texture. I could smell the mouths and throats and lungs of many others. I inhaled shallowly and as little as possible through my mouth, in order not to take in too much.

"I want you to talk to them. Tell them they can't follow her around. Explain to them that she isn't what they think. Jesus, Chester, call them off, will you?"

I was trying to think how to explain to Ronnie that she was putting me in a terrible predicament. I was trying to make the sentences in my mind first so that I would say it right, when the telephone rang. Rae, who even in the next room emitted a smell like the shower at the shelter, picked it up. Ronnie and I could both hear her.

"Yeah, I'm telling you, word is spreading fast. If you want in on it early, you better catch a plane and get out here." There was another pause. "Think of it like this: If you knew Christ was living, wouldn't you drop everything in order to follow Him? What could be more important?"

Ronnie flew into the bedroom, leaving me at the door, sniffing the burned starch of her anger.

"Who are you talking to?" she yelled. "Don't be telling people that. You know there isn't anything going on here except some desperate people who want to believe in anything."

Rae's voice came as loud as Ronnie's. "Excuse me, I'm on the phone."

"Well, get off."

Rae spoke quietly to the person on the other end of the line. "She doesn't understand. I'll have to call you back."

Her voice rose several notches when she spoke to Ronnie again. "I would think even you couldn't go untouched by what is happening right here in your own home. Pretty soon the whole world is going to be here hoping to get a glimpse of her."

"I'll tell you who's 'touched' Rae, you are. You're insane if you think this is going to be any bigger than a local incident. An embarrassing, stupid, local thing."

I stopped looking at the door and began focusing on the window instead of their voices. I trained my eyes on the street, where Briggs was talking to a man, a clean-shaven man, who, it dawned on me, was the photographer who'd pretended to be one of us the day that Cristos was healed. Briggs was waving his arms around, telling his story. The photographer pulled a little notebook out of his pocket and scribbled in it. Ronnie rematerialized next to me.

Rae's voice followed her from the other room. "I happen to know a lot more about spiritual matters than you do."

Ronnie rolled her eyes. "See what I mean? My sister is as Jewish as I am, and she's saying she would drop everything and follow Christ? Normal Jews don't expect God to speak to them. Just Rae. Even God has to answer to Rae."

I couldn't think while standing inside a house with the door shut. I needed to see the sky, to breathe the air, and then maybe I would be able to know what was expected of me. I waited as quietly as I could for Ronnie to tell me we were done talking, but she went on about her sister. I tried to follow, to pick out what I needed to know, but I couldn't sort it out. My feet shuffled the throw rug into an accordion. The little boy, Jonah, appeared in his pj's and stared at me.

"Spiritual, schmiritual," Ronnie shouted into the other room. "Next you're going to be saying you saw Moses in a tortilla."

"Do you want to go outside?" came Jonah's voice from somewhere near my knees.

I nodded.

"It's okay," he said solemnly. "You can."

But I couldn't. I couldn't reach out and turn the knob. My hands were moving and trembling in my pockets, and I couldn't get them out. Any minute the ceiling might start coming down, even though I was standing up and not trying to go to sleep. Sometimes that happened. Especially if I was nervous.

Jonah reached up to the doorknob and turned it. "Here," he said.

It was that easy. The door was open, and clean air washed over my face as I bolted through. I took big gulps of it, walking quickly down to my place by the gate. Across the street in the park, Briggs was nowhere to be seen, and the photographer had disappeared. Cristos and a few others sat on the grass.

I breathed in and out, filling my cells with fresh air and emptying out the stale house air. I had to keep my eyes and nose on what was important. I was letting myself get confused by Ronnie and Rae. I was becoming infected with the wishes of the people who were showing up outside. I needed to focus. The Virgin had to be my only guide, the only one to tell me what to do. And because she never said otherwise, I had to assume that all of this was the way she wanted it. There had to be a divine and cunning plan that included photographers and even Ronnie's sister. I told myself again that the Virgin knew what she was doing. I tried to stand up straight, like a person free from doubt, but the weight on my shoulders wouldn't allow it.

SID

During the two weeks at Ronnie's, Jonah turned five. Ronnie said that for his birthday dinner, Jonah could have anything he wanted; he didn't have to have any vegetables or fruit or milk. We made all his favorite stuff: lasagna, french fries, cookies, banana cream pie. Francesca and I baked a chocolate cake. Jonah sat at the head of the table and crowed, eating as much as he could. Rae nearly ruined the party. She had to sit next to Francesca at dinner and didn't pay any attention to Jonah.

Ronnie lit the candles on the cake. Jonah had his eyes squeezed closed, his forehead wrinkled in concentration as he made his wish. It was his moment. He was about to blow them out when Rae said, "Francesca, shall I run a bath for you after dinner?" Jonah opened his eyes and blew out the candles, but he'd lost his concentration, and one candle stayed lit.

I volunteered to put Jonah to bed. I carried him into the bedroom and shut the door. Then I dropped him on the bed the way that made him giggle. I put him under the covers and tucked his puppy into the crook of his arm before I pulled the blanket up around his chin so that he looked like a little smiling head on a pillow.

I didn't know what else to do. I mean, I wasn't into baby-sitting, and I never had a brother or sister. But I wanted to do it right. I found myself wanting to make up for his mom.

I said, "What do you do for a bedtime story, recite the periodic table of elements?"

He was deadpan. "No, my mom tells me stories. Aunt Ronnie sings. But you have to get in bed with me." He moved over and opened the covers for me. I looked around, but of course nobody could see us. I knew it was all right, though I felt strangely guilty and embarrassed. But I got in. It was warm and smelled like juice and kid sweat. He wriggled against me, snuggling in. I put my arm around him and waited for him to quiet down. I tried to think of a lullaby, but I didn't remember any. Parts of stupid songs from my mom's oldies station kept coming to mind: "God didn't make little green apples, it don't rain in Indianapolis," and "Knock three times on the ceiling if you want me." Finally I hit on Christmas carols. I launched into "Silent Night," having to start over twice to get the beginning low enough so that the high part wasn't too high. By the time I got it right, he was snoring along with the crickets.

The next day was warm and sunflowery. On our free period at school, we went around the corner to the 7-Eleven for a Coke and a smoke. Francesca was wearing this dress that I would have died for. It was long and green and had something embroidered around the neck. I wished I could hate it, knowing that it had to cost at least a hundred dollars, but I couldn't. That dress rocked.

Francesca tapped her Coke can with her nails. "How do you know if you're pregnant?"

I'd been waiting for something like this ever since I saw her hurling on the camping trip. I knew it wasn't the flu. I was impressed, though, by how she never talked about guys. I mean, she'd obviously been doing it with some dude over the summer. You'd think she'd talk about him a little. I mean, that's what best friends are for, right? But I let go of my own hurt feelings and got right down to business.

"Have you missed your period?"

"I think so, but they're irregular anyway. I've missed it before."

"Sore boobs?"

She nodded. We both drank from our Cokes.

"It doesn't sound good."

Her forehead creased in the middle.

"But what about, you know, actually getting that way?"

I didn't get it. I couldn't believe she might be asking what I thought she was asking. "*Excuse me?* You mean, how do you get pregnant?"

"No. I mean . . . well . . . can it happen if you don't actually, you know, do it?"

I tossed my Coke and lit a cigarette. "What are you saying? You didn't have sex, but you think you're pregnant? Or you don't know if you had sex?"

"Sort of both."

I snorted smoke out of my nostrils like a dragon. This is why we were best friends, because I could explain these kinds of things to her.

"Okay, dumb-ass, you can't get pregnant unless there's a penis involved, you know? A woody. A stiffy. Whatever you call it at your house. There has to be actual penetration, you know? Believe me, if there was penetration, you'd know it. It hurts, girl." I wasn't speaking from firsthand experience, but I knew all this stuff just the same.

She wasn't satisfied. "What if the sperm was right there, like, really close? Could it swim up there or something?"

I cracked up. I felt older than my years and very wise. "Forget about it. You're not pregnant. You're just a prude. You'll get your period."

We walked back around the corner. There were people out on the grass in front of the school. I didn't think much about it, just assumed it was some lame I. F. Stone class like Basket Weaving for Cretins. But I could see that the crowd wasn't entirely Stone students. There were fifteen or maybe twenty people, including some in wheelchairs and a few moms with kids and some regular old people like you'd see at the mall. And then I saw Mary Lein and Briggs and Cristos. And Rae. I got this cold feeling in my stomach.

They faced us all together. I swear it was like something in a movie, the kind where there's a giant lizard about to eat the earth and all the people flee in horror. I looked behind me to see if I was missing something, but nothing was there except a stop sign and a mailbox. Francesca didn't bother. She stopped and took a deep breath. She knew they were there for her.

They were around us then, and all of them were trying to touch Francesca. They pawed at her dress and her hands and her hair. One poor loser got down on the sidewalk and touched his head to her shoes. A woman put a baby in Francesca's arms, and even I could see that there was something wrong with it. Its little head was bald, and its skin was too smooth and tight and kind of yellow. It gave me the creeps.

I was slowly being edged to the outside of the group. They milled around her and called her "Mother" and all kinds of other weird shit. They stopped traffic. Somebody was taking pictures; I could hear the camera clicking and advancing. Kids came out of the school, openmouthed. I saw the principal standing on the lawn looking totally useless. Francesca gave the baby back to its mother.

Right about then Ronnie drove up in her old VW Bug with Chester stuffed into the passenger side. She laid on the horn and edged through the people. Chester got out of the car, and they made way for him. You kind of had to; he was so big, and he just took up all the air. He put his arm around Francesca like she was a rock star and walked her to Ronnie's car and helped her get inside. He closed the door and turned to them, spreading his arms and pushing them back.

"Don't crowd her. It's hard on her. Go home now."

A woman put her hand on Francesca's window as if to touch her through the glass. Francesca put her hand on the glass, too, the way prisoners in movies do. Then they were all doing it, all of them were touching Ronnie's car. The VW rocked on its wheels.

"The police will be here in a minute," Chester warned. Some stepped back when Ronnie inched the car forward. I could see Francesca's face in the window, looking at me as if she were going off to jail. Ronnie must have seen her chance, because suddenly the car shot out and sped down the street, leaving me with all the loonies.

Inside the school everybody was blabbing about it. The faculty had an emergency meeting where they must have gone into collective denial, because they wouldn't answer questions about Francesca or what happened out there in the street. They acted like anybody who asked was completely mental. Finally I couldn't take it anymore. I raised my hand and asked to go to the bathroom.

I shut myself into the first stall. My breath was sort of missing. I mean, every time I tried to breathe, my ribs would move, but I didn't get enough air. My heart was doing reggae. Those people out there, they hadn't all been bums from Ronnie's restaurant. Most of them had homes and lives. The people in the wheelchairs and the woman with the sick baby, they were just people. This thing about Francesca wasn't just a few cases at Ronnie's. It was bigger than that, and it was spreading.

What about me? That's what I wanted to know. Ronnie and Chester didn't even think about me out there in that mob. Just Francesca. Just the saint.

I pulled out my Swiss army knife, my little red friend, yanked down my jeans, and looked at a place on my hip where there weren't any scars. A virgin site. For the Virgin. I had been only opening up old wounds on my feet, feeling proud that I wasn't actually cutting. But now the pain inside was so bad I knew I would cut. It was the only thing that made this gnawing hurt feel better.

With the small blade, I cut. A thin line of blood appeared. I knew from years of experience that it was too clean to make a good scar, and I wanted this one to last forever. I cut again, this time turning the blade so that it gouged and brought skin and tissue with it. Calm smoothed through me as the blood flowed. I was able to breathe out completely, and then back in. I thought about those old-time doctors with their leeches and chipped bowls of blood and how maybe they weren't quacks after all. I mean, relief came with the letting of blood, and I wasn't the first person in the history of the world to figure it out.

FRANCESCA

She huddles on the couch in Ronnie's living room. She is jangled by the sensation she can still feel, of hands reaching out to her, wanting to touch, wanting a piece of her. She is exhausted by their eyes demanding her attention and making her care.

She knows they will come, the people who organized themselves and found her at school today. They will come to her as sure as night. And she will give them what they want, somehow. She knows this, too. She will go out among them and let them touch her and suck life from her, if that's what they need. It's as good as already happened, that's how sure she is. She's on a steep slide, and there's no stopping it. She will be propelled by her own weight, plus gravity, plus whatever started this whole mess, until she hits the bottom.

Jonah kneels on the floor, drawing complicated geometric patterns with his fat-tipped little-kid markers, uninterested in Francesca. Ronnie is at the window watching the front yard, where Chester stands at the gate.

She should practice the cello. Keith Jacobson would say, "The only constant thing in life is to practice every day." But he is touring with his prodigy, and she can't make her legs take ten steps across the room to pick up her instrument.

The back door opens with the sound of something coming unglued. Rae slips into the room.

"Mama," Jonah says. Rae ignores him. She goes instead to Francesca. She kneels on the carpet at Francesca's feet. Francesca pulls her feet back, away from Rae's hands. She tucks them under the orange-and-green afghan on Ronnie's couch.

"How long have you had this power?" Rae asks, the same way a doctor would ask how long she's had a cough.

Francesca doesn't want to answer. She doesn't want to acknowledge that she knows what Rae is asking. She shrugs an exaggerated teenage shrug.

"I don't think I have any power, but stuff has been going on for three weeks or so," she hears herself say.

"Not before?"

"No."

"Do you know how it works? Can you do it whenever you want?"

Francesca shakes her head. Tears sting her eyes. It's not fun, this thing she has. She hasn't actually tried to do it. It just happens. She wishes someone knew what was wrong with her. She misses her mom, but she knows that her mom wouldn't understand anything about this. "Religious horseshit," she would say. Her father might do better. He might have a simple explanation. Maybe he could make the frightening sliding feeling stop.

But he hasn't been home in Italy when she calls. He hasn't

answered her e-mails either. She looks at the clock and counts ahead eight hours. It would be ten at night there; he would be in a restaurant eating a late supper with his girlfriend Stacey.

Rae takes Francesca's hand and strokes it. Her palm is surprisingly dry and soft. She speaks in a soothing voice. "You have a kind of divine innocence. Did you know that you can be completely enlightened and not even know it? You can. It happens all the time. But those people, your devotees, they see who you really are."

"What nonsense are you telling her, Rae?" Ronnie says from the window. Rae keeps stroking Francesca's hand, talks softly in her ear. "It's okay," she says. "You're not crazy. This is supposed to be happening to you. We'll take care of you."

The familiar lump of sickness rises in Francesca's throat, and she struggles clear of Rae and the afghan to run to the bathroom, where she is quietly sick for the second time that day. She has cultivated a hidden talent for throwing up without making any sound. When she flushes and comes back out, Ronnie clears her throat. "Francesca, why don't you go into my room and lie down? Don't let Rae's *meshugass* get to you."

Francesca does what she is told. She drags the afghan with her into Ronnie's room and shuts the door. She lies down on the bed wrapped up in the afghan and drops backward onto the wheel of sleep.

A few hours later, she wakes to the sound of singing coming from beyond the dark window. It takes her a minute to recognize "Amazing Grace." It has the strangest pull on her. Her skin seems to move on her flesh. She hears Ronnie and Rae talking softly in the other room. She makes out snatches of their conversation.

"Blessed Mother" and "holy" and "complete fucking bullshit" and "divine" and "pregnant." She hears Rae say "savior."

She picks up Ronnie's phone and punches in the many numbers to get to her dad in Italy. She has no idea what time it is there. It doesn't matter. She needs to hear him say he misses her. Maybe they will plan her Christmas visit. Skiing in Switzerland. That's what he said the day he went away.

"*Pronto?*" Peter answers on the first ring. His voice is thick with sleep.

"Why haven't you been answering my E-mail?" Francesca hears herself say, sounding bratty. She is so glad to hear his voice that she starts crying.

"Francesca, it's four o'clock in the morning here."

"Sorry."

She can hear Stacey say something in the background. Peter sighs. His voice softens.

"How are you, sweetheart?"

She'd like to tell him that she's not good at all. She'd like to say how sick she's been and how worried and what strange things have been happening. But she also wants to be the old Francesca, just a kid on the phone with her dad.

"Did you get my ticket for Christmas yet?" she asks, controlling the wobble in her voice. Now they will make plans. Now he will say how much he misses her. "I have my passport."

He sighs again and clears his throat. "There's a problem."

She's not surprised. Her heart only falls an inch in her chest.

He goes on quickly. His voice is sad. "I have much more work than I thought, so my vacation is already shortened. You would just get here and then have to turn around and go back home. Do you see?"

She sees. She won't let him squirm, snared in his own guilt. It's always been this way; she can't stand to see him disappointed or sad.

"It's okay, Dad," she says.

"Really? It is?" He's so relieved to be pardoned that she actually feels sorry for his discomfort. She knows she has done what her mother calls "making it okay for Peter." But she can't imagine it any other way. She's always been aware of a fragility in him, a sensitivity that she can't bear to probe.

Now his voice is warm and buttery, coming through the receiver. It's her reward for letting him off the hook, and she takes it. He says maybe she can come over spring break. He talks about Rome. She closes her eyes and imagines the cobbled streets and balconies with flowers. She sees the curved ranks of marble saints and the crumbling columns. She hoards the sound of his soft voice so that she'll have some for later.

When they hang up, she feels better. Almost. Except for the arc of pain behind her eyes. And the panic that is rising in her throat almost as fast as the nausea. She makes it to the bathroom in time and then crawls back into Ronnie's bed. She spreads the orange-and-green afghan over every inch of her, even her head, and falls asleep to the sound of strangers singing her name.

ANNE

"How's Francesca?"

I spoke into the receiver of a phone bolted to the outside wall of a run-down Burlington Northern bunkhouse in Marmarth, North Dakota. It was the only option, because cell phones didn't work there. We stayed in Marmarth because that's where the Little Missouri River has cut down through the Hell Creek formation and exposed the layers of rock I was looking for. The pay-phone cord was too short, and since it was freezing out, I had my watch cap pulled down over my ears. I thought I heard Ronnie hesitate before answering.

"She's fine," Ronnie said, sounding sort of vague, or maybe it was just the bad connection.

I leaned into the phone and rubbed my left shoulder with my right hand. The summer of teaching and writing and staying home had weakened my digging muscles, and they were letting me know about it. But sore muscles made me feel alive. I was proud that at forty-two years old I had slept under the stars in both hemispheres and most continents and had thrived on it. It was staying home, trapped inside, that I couldn't handle.

It was dark and cold, and I wanted to get inside to eat my dinner. The rest of the team, two grad students, Hayden and Seth, and a girl named London, a Princeton grad whose father gave generously to the museum, were inside, drinking beer and eating fried potatoes from the local diner (fifteen varieties, THE LOIRE VALLEY OF FRIED POTATOES, the sign said). They were, as usual, laughing a lot.

"How about this one?" Hayden shouted. "Why did the rancher take his favorite ewe to the edge of the cliff?" I pulled off my hat to hear Ronnie better and blocked my outer ear with my hand.

"Everything's okay there? You're all fine?" Ronnie and I had been neighbors for ten years. She loved Francesca. I trusted her. It was the bad phone that made her voice sound so flat and tinny.

"We're fine."

"May I speak to Francesca?"

"Sure."

Francesca took the phone, and I swear there was a change in the quality of the static on the line before she spoke. I could hear her breathing. What was she doing? Was she sick? Was there something she was trying to hide from me? Jesus, when I was fourteen, my sister and I had plenty to hide from our parents: cigarettes, pot, boys we liked, boys they didn't like, sneaking out, rides in cars with friends who were older, drinking beer. That's what we did. I shuddered to think what kids did now.

"Mom?"

Hooting and laughing from inside the bunkhouse drowned

her out. London squealed like a sorority girl. I'd been wondering which one of the guys would end up sleeping with her. They'd both been courting her the entire trip, but she hadn't picked her man yet. My money was on Seth, the quiet one.

"Francesca? Is everything all right?"

"Yeah."

I could probably rule out broken bones and head wounds, but would she tell me about anything less obvious? I tried to adjust my position, but the short cord kept me where I was. My hands and ears were getting numb in the cold wind.

"How's school?"

"Okay." Ah. Torture by one-word answers.

"How is it at Ronnie's?"

"Okay."

"How's Sid?"

"Fine."

"Have you talked to Dad?" I hoped Peter had taken time out from Italy and Stacey long enough to call her. I switched the receiver from my left hand to my right.

"He said I can't come for Christmas."

Bastard. Now I knew what was wrong. "Ah, honey, I'm so sorry."

"Mom, it's no big deal."

I took a deep breath. Francesca was fourteen and very responsible. If she didn't want to talk to me about Peter, I had to understand it.

"How are things at Ronnie's?"

"You already asked me that."

"Are you practicing your cello?"

"Mm-hm."

I had run out of questions. I told myself that if there were something to worry about, Francesca or Ronnie would tell me about it. Hovering didn't work, especially by long distance.

"Okay, sweetheart. Anything else you want to tell me?"

There was a hesitation before she spoke. "I guess not."

I was freezing and exhausted. I needed to peel off my outer layers and get into my sleeping bag. I needed to eat. I couldn't do any more with this conversation.

"Then I'm going to get off. I love you."

"I love you, too," she answered.

"We'll be finished here in a few days. I'll be home as soon as I can."

The next day was cold and raw. We had been trenching the Bobcat Butte section for ten days, exposing sections of the Hell Creek formation, but now I could see an especially fossil-rich section at about twelve meters, which was exactly what I needed. The boundary itself is a half-inch strip of dusty asteroid fallout, but the fossils above and below showed the obvious demarcation between the diverse subtropical ecosystem from the end of the Cretaceous period and the contrasting lack of diversity in the Tertiary. Once we took measurements on fresh rock to later calibrate the age of the stratum, we began to dig for specimens. The wind whipped dirt into our eyes and chapped our hands into sandpaper, but we didn't care, because finally we were collecting the right fossils and the sandstone split beneath our picks like ripe watermelon.

"This is it," I yelled to the guys.

"Fuckin' A," Hayden crowed. Seth peeled off his fleece vest. They both moved in closer to get at the layer I'd exposed. The four of us dug out hundreds of fossils quickly.

It's one of nature's ironies that some rocks and fossils that have been buried for millions of years will melt away if they get exposed to moisture. And, of course, as soon as we were going hard at it and specimens were all over the ground all around us, the weather threatened to move in from a fretful-looking sky in the west. It's the paleo equivalent of knowing that as soon as you light up a cigarette in a restaurant, the food will come.

We knew what to do. Hayden and Seth and I kept whacking on rocks as if we were demented, knowing we might not be able to take them all. London numbered and wrapped the fossils in thick layers of toilet paper. Then came a layer of newspaper and masking tape, and the specimens were ready to pack.

I gave up my pickax and helped London get the wrapped specimens into watertight containers. You haven't lived until you've packed and lifted fifty boxes of rocks, double time, into the back of a truck. I didn't think that London had the muscle or the grit, but she surprised me and kept up. Toward afternoon snow started coming down as if from a burst pillow, and it was beginning to stick. But we had our specimens; it was time to go.

"We're leaving tomorrow at daybreak," I announced. The three of them stood there grinning, too tired to cheer or get excited, but London looked up at Hayden, and I saw that she'd made her choice. Wrong one, I thought, as I forced my tired arms to lift the tools into the truck. Handsome, obnoxious Hayden might be fun, but Seth was the one to count on. Of course, remembering back to the mating decisions of my youth, I didn't have any business pointing fingers at London. I'd made the same mistake too many times.

I thought about Francesca's distant voice, and Ronnie's. I wanted to get home. I wanted to be there.

The next morning there was six inches of snow on the tarps, and it was still coming down. We swept it off and headed out to the highway. For the first two hours, I couldn't see more than about five feet in front of the truck. The ten-hour drive became fourteen, but the storm stayed out on the plains, and by the time we rolled into Denver, the sky was almost clear. We unloaded the specimens at the quiet museum, stacking them up next to the door in the lab, to be sorted out later.

"God, every muscle hurts," London said, taking a box from me and passing it to Hayden. "Even the muscles in my fingers are sore."

"Go home and take a hot bath," I said. "Use Epsom salts."

She shook her head. "No tub at my apartment, just a shower."

I saw Hayden's eyes flick toward Seth and then move in on her.

"I have a hot tub," Hayden said.

Seth kept his head down, pretending not to notice the look that passed between Hayden and London. When the work was done, we split up in the parking lot. Hayden and London left together. Seth got into his car alone.

I had to struggle to keep my eyes open on the way home. When I pulled up to my own house around ten o'clock, my arms and legs felt like rubber.

A small crowd in the park across the street didn't surprise

me. That summer we'd had more than a few incidents of college kids partying there. I locked the truck, just to be safe. I thought I'd just put my duffel inside and get out of my boots before I went over to Ronnie's. Two minutes to myself, was what I was thinking, before I had to shift gears and be the mom again. Out of habit, I flipped on the TV. It was the news, and I let it run, paying only scant attention.

I was stepping into my clogs when I heard the news anchor say something about Boulder. I glanced up, and there was Francesca on TV. It was the most amazing and disorienting feeling, to be in my house, thinking everything was fine, and then to see her on the news.

I couldn't make out what they were saying. It all sounded like nonsense, as if my ears were working overtime trying to hear it and so ended up with gibberish. Something about a cult. They showed a clip of Francesca in a crowd of people. All I could think was that she had been involved in a crime, that she was hurt. I ran out of the house and over to Ronnie's, my heart threatening to pound through my sternum. A big, hairy guy stopped me at the gate.

"No one is allowed inside."

He was big but soft-looking. I wondered how well I'd do if it came down to fighting him. My muscles were weak from exhaustion, but with the adrenaline pumping through me, I didn't feel tired anymore.

"I'm looking for my daughter." Each word stuck in my throat as I said it. I hoped Francesca was in there. He looked at our house, and I followed his gaze. Light was streaming out of my windows.

He said, "You're her mother?"

Was this bouncer person somehow connected with my daughter? I didn't have time to ask.

"Anne Dunn. Francesca Dunn's mother. Is she in there?"

He walked me to the door and knocked on it, but I wasn't going to wait another second.

"Out of my way," I said, and opened the door myself.

Inside, Ronnie jumped up and came toward me. There was another woman on the couch, but I was interested in only one thing: Francesca, on the rug, playing with a young boy.

"Are you all right?" I dropped to my knees and took her face in my hands.

There are moments that, even while you're living them, you know will be burned forever in your memory. I was aware of each eyelash, each pore, and the lovely combination of all the parts making up the flesh of my child. I felt a deep, resounding joy that I hadn't lost her, that she didn't appear to be hurt. She was sitting on a floor playing Legos with a little boy, and it struck me as the most beautiful thing on earth. It was a moment I will unfold again and again, but a moment is only as long as breathing in and out, and the next wasn't so joyous.

"God, Mom," she said in an irritated voice. "I'm fine." Now that I could see for myself that she was, I got a little pissed.

"Glad to hear it. Now maybe you can tell me what's going on?"

She didn't answer, so I turned to Ronnie. "What in hell is going on here?"

Ronnie turned red and tried to explain. "It's crazy, I know, but people are saying that Francesca is . . ."

"Is what?"

"Well, holy, I guess."

"Holy?" I couldn't believe I'd heard her right. "Holy? Ronnie, that's not a word we use in modern language unless we're in church. It is certainly not a word that applies to my daughter."

"I know, but some of the people at the café believe it."

"Believe what?"

Ronnie squirmed. "That they've been healed."

I couldn't take in what she was saying. I turned to Francesca. "Francesca?"

She shrugged. "Don't get mad. I didn't make it happen, it just did."

"*What* happened? What in God's name are you talking about?"

The woman on the couch spoke. "It does seem ridiculous, doesn't it? But I saw it myself. Two men were healed when she touched them."

The crease between Ronnie's eyes deepened. She fidgeted as if her shoes were too tight. "Come on, Rae. Those guys will believe anything if they're getting a free meal. Anne, this is my sister, Rae." She gestured to the boy with Francesca on the rug. "And that's her son, Jonah."

I looked around the room. Of them all, Rae was the only one who didn't seem to be afraid to meet my eyes. She seemed to be watching the whole drama with something like humor. But Ronnie was the one in charge, and I wanted answers from her.

"People believe they were healed, Ronnie? Who, specifically, says this?"

She finally looked at me. "Well, a guy named Briggs said his heart pain went away. And Cristos had an ear infection that stopped. They're both regulars at the café. But I really think it's over now, Anne."

I shook my head, trying to grasp it all. "And those people out there in the park, are they connected with this?"

Ronnie closed her eyes and nodded. "The police chased them away, but they came back."

I began to see how it was. A bunch of weirdos had some crazy idea about my child, and Ronnie, whom I had left in charge, hadn't been able to take control of the situation.

I picked up her phone, dialed 911, and reported the gathering. Then I collected Francesca and her things and opened the door. The big guy appeared. I stood my ground, glared up into his crazy face. I was almost a match for him with my filthy jeans and dust-filled hair.

"Get out of our way," I growled.

"Mom, don't be mean. That's Chester. He's okay."

I spoke to Ronnie over my shoulder. "I can see that letting Francesca stay with you was a serious mistake."

Chester said, "It would be better if you left by the back door." His voice was halting, though surprisingly intelligent and gentle. I looked around his bulk and saw flames from lighters bobbing in the park. They were chanting my daughter's name along with some other mumbo jumbo. The hair stood up on my neck. I wished the police would hurry up.

"Maybe you're right," I said, turning around again.

We went through Ronnie's house and out the back door. The properties ended at the bank of an irrigation ditch, and the fences were tall, solid wood, so it would be difficult for someone to get into the backyard that way. But, like Ronnie's, the front yard fence was hip-height picket, more of a garden decoration than a real barrier. It wouldn't keep anybody out. And from the front yard they could let themselves into the backyard. For all I knew, there could be people there now, waiting for us behind the fence. All of a sudden, I wasn't sure how safe we were.

There wasn't a gate between the houses, so we had to climb over the fence. Chester gave Francesca a leg up and handed over her suitcase and cello. I scrambled over by myself.

The yard seemed perfectly normal. The stripped patio furniture was where it had been when I left. A broom I had leaned against the house was still upright. All we had to do was get inside the house and wait for the police.

Without my asking, Chester stayed on Ronnie's side of the fence.

"I will be here, if you need me," he said, through the wood. I appreciated the man's generosity. However misguided, he did seem to have Francesca's safety at heart.

"No need for that," I said. "The police will be here soon."

"I'll be here anyway," he said. And I found it almost comforting to think of him waiting on Ronnie's side of the fence as I unlocked the back door to our house and turned on the lights.

The police came. They explained to me that the gathering, though not completely legal, wasn't exactly illegal either. Apparently the group had a permit to hold a demonstration in a public place, and the park was a public place, but they had to leave at dark. And they couldn't have candles. The police assured me that they would make sure the park was empty when they cruised the street throughout the night.

I hardly slept, knowing that a police car on the street wouldn't take care of the one or two stragglers who might be in the dark backyard. I decided to call my lawyer first thing in the morning.

I shut my eyes, but I was too wired for sleep. I tried to think of Mongolia, of India, and places around the world where I had camped and worked, but those memories didn't bring me any peace. Then I mentally went through each drawer in the specimen room at the museum, trying the monotony approach. Around dawn I walked through the house, checking doors and windows. A lumpy form lay on the lawn next to our porch, and I could make out Chester's head at the top of it. The park was empty. I went back upstairs and got into bed, more tired than I thought I could be. I fell asleep thinking of that big guy, Chester, out there in his bag, keeping watch.

Three

CHESTER

Word traveled. People came. It wasn't my doing. I didn't try to convince anyone of her divinity, and they didn't ask. After the first couple of newspaper stories, it became my job to keep them away from her. The irony of it wasn't lost on me. The people who needed her, the very ones she was here for, had to be kept back. The Virgin couldn't be pawed by greedy and desperate crowds of people. For a few, just being near her was enough, but most of them wanted something. They wanted a personal audience. They wanted a healing. They wanted a boon. They wanted her to do for them, and they didn't think about what the cost was to her, or to the one she was growing in her belly.

I could smell them all: a woman with the tongue-curling odor of persimmon; a man who had the stale, metallic smell of a motel ice machine; a college student who smelled like bread mold. And there were the ones who came every day, the regulars. Three women, sisters judging from their resemblance to each other, came every evening at sunset, exuding the bitter, smoky

smell of acorns and longing from underneath their veils of perfume. I watched them pray in the park together, and their
cumulative sadness made me ache until I felt sick. It got so that
the street between us wasn't enough to keep me from smelling
the very emptiness in their blood and the disappointment that
festered in their kidneys.

It took its toll, being the membrane, the filter through
which they all had to pass. I hadn't been quite so hyperolfactory
since graduate school, back when the smells were new. I was still
refusing my gift then, trying to fit into the world as it was,
according to other people.

It started when I was working on my thesis, day and night.
I was living and breathing Chaucer. I occupied a table in a dead-
end corner of the labyrinth on the second floor of the library.
There I immersed myself in the Wife of Bath and the Pardoner
and breathed in the heady aromas of book dust and moldy paper
with the words of great thinkers whispering to me from the
stacks.

Sometime in the second month of my thesis, I began to
notice the smells of living people, not just the books. When
someone happened to walk past my lonely spot, his or her smell
distracted me from my work. Aftershave, shampoo, deodorant
all wreaked havoc with me. It got to where I could distinguish
Head & Shoulders from Breck. Colgate from Pepsodent. After a
while, when I couldn't think about my work for all the Right
Guard and Dippity-do in the air, when I couldn't find the thin,
clean, honorable smells of the stacks for all the manufactured
stink, I got angry.

That level of smell, the most mundane, has always been the

most offensive. I growled like a caged animal when anyone came to my corner. Checking out a book required me to stand in line with people who exuded the stench of their last meal mixed with whatever mass-marketed poison they had sprayed and smeared on their bodies. Simply eating a meal became a problem. I searched out places to eat where the waitresses didn't wear perfume. It got to where I started covering my hand with my handkerchief before I gave them the money for my food. After a while I just started leaving more than enough on the table so that I wouldn't have to risk touching their hands and carrying their scent on me all day. Eventually I bought things to eat at a grocery store and ate them out of the cartons in my room, staying away from restaurants altogether.

I lost weight. The few friends I had started to avoid me, and I was glad for it, because it meant less olfactory input. I was supposed to be teaching, but I missed most of my classes because the smells were more than I could bear. I couldn't go to my adviser with my problem, because his office reeked of sex and minty mouthwash, and it nauseated me to be there.

And then the day came when I started smelling the deeper layers. It was both a relief and a curse. A relief to be able to tune out some of the surface stink. A curse because now I could smell fear, desire, hatred, illness in all their many subtle shadings. And with the greater perception came an empathy I didn't know how to use. What was I supposed to do with the sulfurous stink of an ovarian cancer coming from a woman who looked perfectly fine? How was I supposed to handle the information that came to me through my nose? Like this one's lust for that one's wife or that one's case of gonorrhea that whistled through my senses like a freight train full of rotting meat. One guy's suicidal urge had a rank sweetness, more potent than skunk, and I didn't know what to do about it.

Finally, one day in the dead of winter, I caught the scent of a person who smelled good. She was the first. Sitting in my corner of the library, I picked up a smell like fresh cedar. It was a clean smell that came from the core of a very pure person. I left my books and papers and walked the stacks, following my nose through groups of students at tables, scores of people sitting in lone cubbyholes. I climbed the stairs and took the elevators, sniffing like a basset hound, trying to locate the source of the delicious smell.

It was on the science floor, somewhere near the periodicals, that I found her. I came around the corner and there she was, sitting behind a stack of scientific journals. She was thin and pale, her face and hair almost the same color, and she hunched over her work so that her shoulder blades stuck out like wings. A silver chain trembled on her wrist as she wrote in her notebook or reached up to tuck a limp hank of hair behind her ear.

I hadn't planned what I would do when I found her. I didn't think I could approach her, talk to her; I was too ragged, too unpracticed at speaking to people. She wouldn't like me. I stood rooted to the floor, unable to go forward or turn around and leave. I was caught there, gaping like a fish. She looked up and saw me, and, as I could have predicted, she quickly packed up her things and left. But the next day, from my corner down in Literature, I could smell that she was upstairs again. And the day after. From time to time, I would sneak upstairs to catch a peek of her reading, but I never tried to approach her.

I worked steadily on my thesis, tuning in to her aroma and turning down the others. I knew more about her from her smell than I ever would if I fumbled through meeting her. I didn't need her words or her direct gaze; I had her essence.

But the day came when I couldn't pick up her scent in the library. I paced the floor, unable to work. The next day was the same. A week went by, and she didn't come in. I began to walk the campus. I roamed day after day, stepping into buildings to smell the air in stairways, looking for her. At night I walked beneath the dormitory windows, trying to catch a thread of her scent from somewhere within. Work on the thesis was no longer possible. Eating became a distant memory. Eventually I ended up in the hospital and found myself on my first round of Thorazine.

Since then, over the years of living with my "gift," I've encountered very few people who smell good to me. So once I found her, the white-rose smell of the Virgin guided me in all that I did. As a result of placing myself between the world and Francesca, I became the custodian of her following.

I got up each morning before dawn and took my position at the gate.

"We want to speak with her," her devotees said. "We want to see her. Take us to her."

Of course I couldn't do it. I tried to explain why and absorbed their sullenness when they realized they couldn't get in. Usually the mystery flower-petal artist had been there while I slept. Some days his offering was simple, a circle within a circle or a block of color with a feather on it. Some days it was complex, a complete painting. I had my suspicions about who the artist was, but it was weeks before I saw him in action.

One morning I was up so early that only the smell of dawn let me know day was coming. I took a piss in the bushes, and when I glanced at the house, there he was. Cristos. As I suspected. He was crouching on the porch floor, sprinkling something from a bag, working quickly and efficiently. I stayed where I was and watched him move with the grace of a sniper. When he was finished, he jumped the fence without a sound. Technically, once I discovered it was Cristos, I shouldn't have let him continue, but I knew Cristos. He had been touched by her. He didn't mean her any harm. I kept quiet and decided not to ruin his pleasure.

The entire fence and sidewalk area in front of the house became a shrine. People who had heard about her left bunches of flowers stuck between the pickets. They left mementos of their lives, along with candles and poems and pictures. Strange things appeared, like a single baby shoe and a ring box full of teeth. I kept it all tidy, ignoring, as much as I could, the stench of the people. I occupied myself with sweeping up the litter and dead flowers, making room on the sidewalk for more, because I still believed that she should be accessible, in some protected way, to anyone who genuinely wanted her blessing. They came with fantastic stories of healings they had heard about. One guy told me he'd heard that a child with cerebral palsy had gotten better because the parents left a picture of him on the fence. An old woman held out her arthritic hands and said they didn't hurt anymore, because the Virgin had answered her prayers. Every day someone would come up to me and ask to hear about Cristos and Briggs.

Some of the people who came were pilgrims by occupation.

Miracle whores. They told me tales of yogis who levitated and statues that bled. One of them handed me an article about a girl in Idaho who had been in a coma for nine months. People who came to her and touched her were healed. I was looking at the picture of the girl in her hospital bed when a man put his hand on my arm. I stepped back. I didn't like to be touched unless I knew it was coming.

"Hello, my friend," said a voice accompanied by a cloud of musk.

The man was egg-shaped and balding, a softly rounded person who earnestly held his pudgy hands in front of his chest. His new golf jacket and cheap shoes pegged him as a proselytizer. That and the con-man stink.

"The Reverend John Stucker," he said, sticking out his hand and standing too close to me. I kept the article about the sick girl in my hand so that I wouldn't have to touch him.

"We haven't met, but the Lord knows us both, doesn't he?"

"What can I do for you?" I asked, taking another step back. Now I was as close to the fence as I could be without actually bumping into it. He moved in after me and succeeded in making me feel trapped.

"We would like to invite your little girl to come worship with us," he said, handing me his card. It said "Church of the Redeemer." The raised lettering read NO SOUL SHALL BE LOST.

"There are many in my congregation who believe there might be something to what she's saying." His wet lips stretched into a smile.

"She's not saying anything," I said.

He smiled harder and coughed. "Well, I know that. But the

point is . . . well, does she accept Jesus Christ as her savior? Do you?"

I thought carefully. I hadn't gone to church since I was a boy. On the other hand, I had found the Virgin and knew myself to be blessed. I knew she was carrying someone who would save humanity from the disaster we were headed for. Was it Jesus? I didn't know. It seemed to me that the Messiah was something like the office of president. More than one person has been president. I suspected that there had been many messiahs.

I answered slowly. It was the first time I had said it out loud. "The unborn child in the Virgin's womb is my Savior."

"All right," he said, all good-natured hick preacher full of ersatz love for sinners like me. "All right, son, we can work with that, but I think you're mixed up on your Bible stories. That's the story of how Jesus was born in Bethlehem, and, friend, it happened two thousand years ago."

I stepped past him. I didn't want to debate it. His kind was always looking for a chance to flog the Bible. He called after me, "There's only one Jesus Christ, and He says unto you, 'I am the way, the truth, the life: no man cometh unto the Father but by me.'"

"You'd better leave now," I said, picking up my broom and sweeping around the offerings.

"Son, have you heard about the Antichrist? Many have seen the signs. He is the devil, and he is coming just as Christ is coming. I ask you, which one is in the belly of that girl?" John Stucker pointed his finger at Francesca's house. A half dozen people had gathered around us. He had a rich, resonant voice that demanded attention, and he knew how to use it.

"Go on now," I said. I knew guys like this. They hung around shelters and food lines, looking for easy marks for their soul-saving quotas.

He held up his hands in mock submission. He made sure that everyone was listening. "Watch out," he said before he turned and walked away. "You may be worshipping the beast."

ANNE

Carol Markowitz's brown eyes scanned me with sympathy and professional concern. On her desk was a rough and worn stone carving of a Hindu deity. Her hands played with a small elephant statue, rolling and turning the rounded bit of silver in her well-groomed hands, rubbing it like a worry stone. I had seen these in India, in every marketplace and temple and restaurant. To me they were just part of the cacophony of junk that made up the cities of India. But in her hands the statue seemed precious and meaningful in some way known only to her. I watched her fingers, and I wanted, for a minute, to know what she knew, what every vendor in Calcutta seemed to understand about this chubby elephant boy, dressed up like a prince. What did he do for them? In India it seemed there was a deity for every occasion, for every concern. Didn't they realize how they'd been duped? How religion kept them passive? Carol Markowitz was an attorney, a graduate of Yale and Columbia, and yet she caressed this pagan idol and apparently got some comfort or meaning from it. She did it openly in her place of business, and yet her reputation didn't suffer.

Carol had been our divorce attorney; she had facilitated our split with such grace and compassion that Peter and I were able to do the thing without going to court, in itself nothing short of a miracle. I trusted Carol. I knew her to be a person with a clear understanding of the world and a good navigator of the law. And yet she was religious, or at least spiritual, which didn't match my picture of a good lawyer. To me religion had always meant dogma, and spirituality had always meant unfocused wishful thinking.

For a second a sharp paranoia caught me. A lot of people seemed to know something I didn't. Maybe I was defective, spiritually handicapped. Maybe I was missing something essential. I shook my head to clear it. Carol may have been levelheaded, but those people who hung around hoping to catch a glimpse of my daughter weren't Carol Markowitzes; they were lunatics.

"There isn't a lot you can do," she said now. "Nobody is trespassing on your property. Nobody has threatened Francesca or you. People are allowed to believe in anything they want and scream it from the mountaintops, as long as they don't hurt anybody else."

"But what about the fact that Francesca can't go to school? What about the psychological damage from all this weird attention?"

Carol sighed and looked down at her silver elephant. "Well, who would you sue? The street people? The city? It's the same problem that celebrities and their families have. There isn't a law that protects people from their own celebrity. The police are patrolling the street. You're keeping the house locked. You aren't talking to the press. The law wouldn't see her as being prevented from going to school just because folks might make a fuss over her on the way. None of the employees of the school is harassing her. Of course, you can always change schools or find some alternative educational instruction. You can hire a bodyguard if you want. I'm sorry, Anne, but legally there isn't anything we can do at this point. My advice is to wait it out. Eventually they'll lose interest."

She tapped the silver elephant on the desktop, clearly finished with the consultation. I got to my feet. It didn't seem right or even possible that the law couldn't protect us, but since I had no other questions that would get me different answers, and since I was paying through the nose to hang around, I made my way out.

At home, the dusty fall light fading, I waded through the junk strewn on our fence and sidewalk. Chester stepped quietly between me and a couple of hangers-on, and they walked off as soon as he said something to them. He opened the gate for me, and I walked through it, too tired to know if I was grateful for his help or irritated by it. He did seem to be able to control these people far better than the police could. It occurred to me that no hired guard would have that kind of influence. Somehow Chester commanded their attention and respect.

Inside, Francesca was doing homework with Sid at the dining-room table and the red digital number on the phone machine read 21.

"About half of those are from Ronnie," Francesca said.

I felt my shoulders inching up toward my ears. I rolled my

head on my neck to ease the tension. I had been avoiding Ronnie, not returning her calls. I was pissed at her, to say the least. She should have told me what was going on when I called from Hell Creek. She should have told me to come home right away. Now even Hayden and the crew at the museum couldn't stop talking about it.

We had been unwrapping and cataloging the specimens from Hell Creek when Hayden turned to me with a smirky smile. "So when's Francesca gonna expand her clientele beyond the homeless?"

I looked up from the computer. "Shut up, Hayden."

He elbowed Seth, trying to goad him into the teasing. "No, really. She fixes up these bums. She should start healing some rich fuckers. Plenty of them with heart conditions and ear infections, too. You could make some good money."

Seth kept cataloging in silence, so Hayden turned to London. "It's a good scam she's got going, don't you think? A career opportunity, eh? Pretty soon Anne's gonna be able to quit her job and live the good life."

"Hayden, you're an asshole," Seth muttered.

I continued going through the motions at the computer and managed to get through the day. When I finally got home, I went out on the back deck to smoke my one daily self-allotted cig. I thought about calling Peter. But the thought of telling him that strange men believed they'd been healed by our daughter was more than I could manage. How did things get so out of hand?

"You should have nipped this in the bud," he would say. And in the end I would still be the one to deal with it all. Peter wasn't going to come home and fix things.

The sun melted in a pool of pink clouds over the mountains, and the yard was shadowed and quiet. Chester stood up from the far corner of the deck, unfolding his large body as if he were stiff or sore. It occurred to me then that standing on our sidewalk all day wasn't easy. I realized I never saw him eat, and except for this glimpse of him on the deck, I never saw him take a break from his post. I had tried to ignore the fact that he was sleeping in our yard. I suddenly wondered where he went to the bathroom, where he ate meals.

"Sorry," he said.

"No, it's okay," I said. "Please sit. You've been standing all day."

He sat.

I stood on the edge of the deck about ten feet from him and cleared my throat.

"Is there anything you need? Food or anything?"

He tilted his head to one side, considering. His mouth worked before he let the words escape.

"I'd . . . take a smoke."

I reached across the space between us to hand him the pack and the matches. He helped himself to one and lit it with curiously clenched hands. The air was just cold enough that our breath and the smoke together came out in satisfying plumes. His hands were clean enough, resting on thick army-surplus pants that might have been green once but now were stained and worn to a dark gray. He wore a thick coat when a sweater would do, and the cuffs were crusty with dirt. I realized that even if he were getting showers at a shelter somewhere, he didn't have a place to wash his clothes or money to take them to a laundry.

I knew how it was to be dirty, Lord knows. I'd been without a real bath for weeks sometimes, in the field. But I'd always been able to pay for a room in a town at the end of it and take a bath when I wanted one. I'd always been able to jump into my truck or get on a plane and come home, where I'd strip off the filthy clothes and soak in hot soapy water, dry myself in a fresh towel, and put on clean clothes. I got dirty and lived out of my back-pack by choice and was paid a decent salary to do it. I had no idea what it would be like to have no choice.

"Thank you for looking out for Francesca," I said.

He dipped his head in a queer, dismissive sort of gesture.

I said, "You've known Ronnie for a while, haven't you?"

He nodded once. "A long time," he said, and fell silent.

My cigarette was burning close to the end, but I wanted to get him to talk to me. My mind raced to find a toehold in the subject of my daughter and his connection to her. There was nothing I could say that didn't seem ridiculous, and yet I wanted to ask him questions. I wanted information. I wanted reasons. I wanted someone to explain the whole mess to me. My lawyer hadn't. The police hadn't. Ronnie hadn't. Francesca hadn't, or couldn't. As strange as it sounds, Chester seemed to be the person who best understood what was happening to us.

"Why Francesca?" I blurted.

I could see the cogs turning in his brain before his mouth formed the shape of the first word.

"She's the Holy Mother," he said finally.

"Now, see? That's what I mean. What makes you think that?" I demanded. "Will you please explain it to me?"

He closed his eyes and searched his mind. "I just know."

I stubbed out my cigarette, sending sparks into the grass. I was tired of pussyfooting around this entire weird notion. I had no idea how intelligent Chester was, but just because he "knew" something didn't mean I had to buy stock in it.

"No scientist would ever accept that," I snapped. "Neither would any grade-school teacher. 'I just know' isn't an explanation. It shuts down reasonable discussion."

I had expected him to get up and amble off to the front yard to stand guard and resume his religious fantasy, but he didn't. He blinked hard and pinched out his cigarette butt, and I could see him rolling my words around in his mind.

As a teacher, one of the first things you learn is how to tell the difference between people who are willing to think and people who live on automatic. Chester was willing to use his mind. I saw poverty and hard living and maybe even damage there, but he wasn't a blank. When he looked at you, you realized he had a brain and he knew how to use it.

"You're right," he said in his halting way. "It isn't an explanation. This simply can't be explained."

"Okay, okay. Some things can't be explained, I agree. Intuition plays a part in the best scientific work. Einstein had intuition. But he postulated a theory and backed it up with data. His intuition came from real knowledge. You might say that art can't be explained either. But someone has to decide if it's art, don't they? So in a sense it has to be defined, if not entirely explained." I knew I was talking too fast and skipping ideas, putting things together every which way. His eyes followed my mouth and hands, almost never my eyes. "This obsession with my daughter that you people have. You may not be able to explain it, but surely you can do better than 'I believe it, therefore it's true.' What is it that makes you believe something that goes against all common sense?"

"She came to me."

I stared at him. "Came to you? Francesca?"

"In a vision. I had a vision of the Holy Mother, and it was Francesca."

I shook my head. "Maybe it was indigestion. Maybe you were seeing something else, something explainable, and you *thought* it was a vision of my daughter."

"I don't think so."

"What about the others? Did they have visions of her, too?"

He shook his head.

"But why Francesca?"

He sat quiet and solid, and it was clear there would be no hurrying him.

"I don't know. It just is. People pay attention when there are healings. I think that's why there *are* healings, to get the attention of the people. You saw all the stuff they left on the fence. They all believe in her."

Now it was my turn to sit quiet with no response. When he saw that I wasn't going to say anything, he went on.

"It's understandable, your confusion. But like it or not, from now on, your daughter is the Holy Mother first and your daughter second." He watched my face as a person would watch an animal run out into traffic. "It's terrifying, isn't it?" he said softly. "I'm terrified for her, too."

FRANCESCA

Sweaters are in various stages of unfolding and falling out of the open armoire. The cello silently reproaches her from inside its case. She hasn't practiced in three days. It's the longest she's ever skipped. Not only that, her room is a pit, and she doesn't care. She stares at the sweaters and the cello. She's stuck there, sitting on her unmade bed. She's a prisoner, locked in a cell. She's a princess in a tower. It's a Sunday morning, and she's fourteen years old, and she's even famous, sort of, and she has to sit in her room.

It isn't fair. It isn't right. Sid can come and go as she pleases. Sid brings homework and news from school and stays for a while most nights on her way home, but she can always leave. She's free to go anywhere she likes.

From her room Francesca can hear her mom in the kitchen making coffee and reading the *New York Times*. She could go down and join her, but Anne would just start in on her again about what happened at Ronnie's. And Francesca would say that she didn't do anything to make it happen. She doesn't know why.

It's not her fault. She's told her mother these things many times, and it does no good. Anne still acts as if the whole thing is somehow Francesca's doing.

She hears the back door open and Ronnie's voice, along with her mother's answering murmurs. She opens her own door wider and stands in the doorway.

"You were responsible for her," Anne says, an edge to her voice.

Ronnie's voice is always louder than Anne's. "True, but I'm not responsible for the rest of the world. I can't help what people think."

"You could have done something."

Ronnie's voice rose higher. "Like what? What could I have done? Guys come into the café and say weird stuff all the time. I was supposed to know that anybody would listen?"

"But why didn't you tell me at least? I called home to check in, and you didn't say anything."

There's no answer from Ronnie. Francesca can imagine her little round frame standing across the kitchen island from Anne and Ronnie hanging her head so that her red poodle hair falls into her eyes.

"I should have," she admits. "I didn't want to worry you. I thought it would blow over." Anne says nothing. She's not about to let Ronnie off the hook.

Francesca knows the routine; her mother still says nothing. Until Anne gets an actual apology, she will wait it out. Francesca has watched her do the same thing to her father, lots of times.

Ronnie starts to cry. "I'm sorry," she says finally.

At last her mother will open her arms, and Ronnie will fall into them, grateful to be forgiven. And her mother will retain the upper hand, the "moral advantage," she calls it, the place where she best likes to be.

After a few minutes, Anne continues. Her voice is gentle now. "So how long is your sister staying with you?"

"I'm not sure," Ronnie says. "She's looking for a job."

Anne would be pouring coffee for Ronnie now, handing her a spoon and the milk and sugar. "Oh? What does she do?"

"She's going to work the evening shift at the café so that she can be home with Jonah in the daytime. I'll watch him at night."

Anne's voice sharpens with interest. "So she's home all day? Ronnie, until this mess gets sorted out, Francesca is doing her schoolwork at home. My lawyer says the less these folks see of her, the better. Eventually they'll get tired of the whole thing. But I have to work on the exhibit that I collected in Hell Creek, which means going to Denver three days a week. Do you think your sister and her little boy could be here? I would pay her, of course. Just to answer the door and the phone and make sure Francesca's all right. It would be a huge help right now."

Ronnie hesitates. Francesca wonders if she's thinking about telling Anne that Rae is no different from any of the "followers" out by the gate. Francesca holds her breath.

Ronnie says, "I'll ask her and let you know. I better go now. The café opens in an hour."

Francesca closes her door again and locks it. She turns around and sees the cello standing mute in its spot. From the window facing the street, she can see the park and the sidewalk below.

A few people are there, at the fence. A small group is sitting quietly in the park, singing. She can see the flowers and things meant for her. People have been leaving her letters and gifts, and she doesn't even get to look at them.

She leans on her windowsill and looks down. She used to climb out the window all the time. It was simple to walk along the shake shingles around to the side of the house and let herself down onto the fence and then to the ground. She glances back at the door. She can hear her mom running water for a bath. Anne will be in there for at least an hour, reading and soaking. Francesca loosens the screen, lifts it out of its track, and pulls it inside. Then she climbs up into the open window and perches there. She tells herself that she's just checking it out. She's just going to sit in the window and think about it. Not necessarily do it. She glances back into the room. She should go in and practice, make the damn cello stop its reproachful silence. But instead of crawling back into the house, she glares at the instrument and gives it the finger. Then she steps out onto the shingles, nearly laughing at the ease of it. When she drops to the ground, Chester appears at her side, out of nowhere.

"Come with me," she says. He doesn't argue or talk to her like other grown-ups do. He follows.

The couple at the fence don't look up, don't see her until she is standing next to them. The woman is tacking a picture of a baby to the fence along with an envelope addressed to Francesca.

"Hello," Francesca says.

They are startled, almost afraid at first. Then slow recognition comes over their faces, and she has the strange sensation that these people she's never seen before know her. In fact, she can see on their faces that they feel intimate with her in a way that she doesn't with them. They know what they want from her. They each take a hand. Chester moves to intervene, and she shakes her head.

"It's okay, Chester." He nods and obediently steps back.

The woman is worn and pale, her eyes bloodshot and raw, her hair heavy, unwashed. The man has dark circles under eyes that follow his wife.

"Is that your baby?" Francesca asks gently, pointing at the picture on the fence.

They nod. The woman starts to cry. Francesca watches their drawn and tense faces.

"He's sick, isn't he?" she says.

"Yes," the man says.

A piece of something inside Francesca breaks away and lodges in her chest. She can feel pain there, the awful, huge cloud of their grief about to come over them. The woman is almost crazy with worry and lack of sleep; that's plain to see. If the child dies, she will pull herself apart with guilt.

Francesca eases her hand out of the man's grip and takes the woman's hand in both of hers.

"It's not your fault," she says. "Stop blaming yourself."

The woman nods, tears washing down the flat planes of her face.

The desolation Francesca feels coming from these two people is more than she ever wanted to feel. She searches for something to say to them. It wouldn't do to give them a lie or a platitude. She closes her eyes, still holding the woman's hand. This is the moment they have been waiting for. They believe she can do something for their child, and it would be cruel to say otherwise. But she doesn't know anything about this baby. She suspects that he isn't going to get well, based on what she's seeing from them.

If she tries to get a sense of the sick baby, what would happen? She knows in a slice of a second. A tiny glimpse of daybreak opens up in the midst of the pain. He's a very sick baby, but she doesn't know if the relief she feels is his death or his recovery. Yet she finds that she knows what to say.

"Either way, he's going to be fine," she whispers before she extracts her hand and walks away, exhausted and saddened by the encounter.

The others in the park haven't seen her. It's as if they are so intent upon worshipping the idea of her that when she actually comes out, they don't realize who she is. She walks back around the side of the house, with Chester following. Her legs feel heavy and weak. She no longer has the desire to be out.

Chester has to give her a boost up on the fence. It feels like she has vinegar for blood, and it is leaching all the strength out of her bones. Somehow she climbs onto the roof, walks around to her window, and squeezes into her bedroom, where she immediately falls across the bed into a deep and multipatterned sleep.

SID

When she was drunk, my mom didn't pay me much attention other than giving me a lot of big wet kisses and calling me "girlfriend" and telling me too much about her sex life. She was boozing while I was at Ronnie's and couldn't have cared less about what was going on there. Then she decided to go on the wagon. It was no big deal; she quit drinking all the time. Every time she sobered up, she always made a show of parental disapproval. That was how I was supposed to know she cared about me. Every six months or so, she got sober, went to a few AA meetings, remembered that she had a daughter, and found a new job somewhere. She was a receptionist, a restaurant hostess, a clerk in a shoe store, and, when she really got desperate, a maid in a motel. Things would be good for a month or so. She would bring home the money from her job and buy groceries and start to pay off some of the bills. We would spend the evenings together, or, if she was working nights, the afternoons after school. We sewed quilts. My mom was an awesome quilter, when she wanted to be. We would piece together bits of bright fabric and watch TV, and I would get lulled into thinking I had a pretty good life.

Then she'd meet a man. A man who drank. And before you knew it, she would be drinking again, coming in late at night, sometimes bringing the guy, forgetting to buy food, missing work because of hangovers, and eventually she would lose the job. That's how it went for as far back as I could remember.

"I don't like what's going on over there at Francesca's," my mom said on a Sunday morning, sober and making us both suffer for it. She held her coffee with a trembling hand, sipped it with her mouth pursed against the heat. She was fully made up, her mask in place, but still wearing her faded turquoise bathrobe. Her hair was in a messy bun held with a clip. She was circling ads in the classifieds. I was waiting for Anne to come pick me up. She paid me ten bucks a day to bring homework to Francesca. Until my mom found a new job, it was buying the groceries.

"I saw something on the news about some religious fanatics and her," my mom said. As if I didn't know.

"I know, Mom."

"I don't want you getting mixed up in that," she said. She smoothed the front of her worn-out bathrobe as if she was proud of it. As if it was a fine cashmere sweater and not all stained and tattered.

"I'm just bringing her homework."

"Hmm," she said while nibbling toast made from bread that I bought with homework money.

I heard Anne knocking and got up to go, but Mom stepped in front of me and opened the door first.

"I'm Paula Barnes," she said, pulling herself up to her full five feet three inches and sticking out her shaky hand to Anne on the doorstep. I could have died of embarrassment.

Anne shook the hand and introduced herself. In the clear morning light, her smooth hair glowed and her clean face was unapologetic about the sun-damaged skin and wrinkles around her eyes. By contrast my mom looked like a bad makeover, with her plummy eye shadow and caked-on concealer.

"I've been wanting to meet you," Paula said, sounding fake as hell. "Sid talks about you all the time."

Okay, first, that just wasn't true, and second, it was humiliating.

"I really appreciate having Sid's help," Anne said, glancing at me and smiling. "So does Francesca. Today I thought I'd save her the bus fare."

My mom looked unsure. She didn't ask Anne to come in, thank God. I sure wasn't going to. Our place was too disgusting. I just wanted to get away before she said something really stupid.

"Well, is your daughter, uh, okay?" Paula asked. "I mean, I don't want Sidney exposed to the wrong people." She never called me "Sidney." I guess she thought that would impress Anne. She pulled her stained robe together at the neck. She looked exactly like what she was, a hypocrite in a tacky bathrobe.

"God, Mom," I said, wishing she would go inside.

"No, you have every right to be concerned," Anne said. "I'm going to be home with the girls today, and on other days, if I'm working, a responsible adult will always be in the house. In any case, I don't think this is going to go on much longer. There's no real danger; it's just a nuisance."

Paula seemed satisfied. Her face rearranged itself and settled into a half smile. She took a step backward as if to let me go. As if she could really stop me.

"Well, you be good, Sidney," she said, and her shaking hand reached out to touch my arm but fell short and landed at her side.

When Anne and I got to the house, there was a bigger-than-usual crowd in front of the gate, including this TV girl with stiff hair, talking to a camera.

"Can you believe this?" Anne said. She talked to me like we were friends. I shook my head. It was pretty amazing.

"Don't look at them, and don't say anything, okay? Ready?" She opened her door and jumped out. She moved really fast. I had to grab my backpack, so she got ahead of me, and then I was separated from her by people with microphones and cameras. Chester put his big bulk between them and her. I tried to get to him so that he would let me through, but my backpack was caught on something. In the confusion it took me a moment to realize it was a person, holding my pack. She was short and old, with a potbelly and stumpy teeth and stinky breath. She had my backpack strap in one knobby fist; the other clutched my wrist.

"Hey," I said. "Let go."

"Mementos?" she crooned up at me. "Personal items from the saint?"

"No thanks," I said.

"I'll give you twenty-five for a used Kleenex. Fifty for a lock of hair. A hundred for a picture of the saint as a child."

That got my attention. "You're offering *me* money?" I looked around. Chester was keeping a man from climbing over the fence. He didn't even see me. Anne was on the porch, unlocking the door.

The woman nodded eagerly and leaned into me to whisper. Her breath was rank and hot. "People will pay for bodily substances from the Virgin. You supply them to me. I'll pay you."

I could feel my nose wrinkling. "That's disgusting."

She shrugged. "Thirty-five for a used Kleenex. How hard can that be?"

I noticed the increased value. Thirty-five bucks for a snotty Kleenex. How gross! Of course, it wouldn't have to even be Francesca's. It could be mine. No one would know the difference. Thirty-five bucks was thirty-five bucks. I could get thirty-five bucks just for blowing my nose.

"*Any* bodily substance," the woman said coyly.

I had to think about that one. *Any* bodily substance covered a lot of ground. What was I supposed to do, go fishing around in the toilet? Collect spit in a bottle? I shook my head. I had my standards.

"No," I said firmly. "Let me go." I pushed past her, and Chester ushered me through the gate.

"Fifty for a lock of hair," the woman shouted, her voice cracking on the last word.

Francesca was upstairs in her room. It looked like she'd just finished practicing the cello, because she was holding it between her legs, but she wasn't playing. She was talking to Jonah, who was sitting on the bed flipping through Francesca's biology book. He was such a little brain. I mean, the book was almost bigger than he was.

"I saw it on the Discovery Channel," he was saying. "Honest."

Francesca shook her head and twisted her mouth to the side. "I don't think so, Jonah." She put her cello away and got out her fingernail clipper.

"Yes," he said. "It's called parthenogenesis. This zoologist in Scotland was talking about it. He said ewes get babies without having a dad. That's what he said, 'without benefit of the male.'"

"You must have missed something there, buddy," I said, unzipping my backpack and pulling out my algebra.

"Okay, you guys don't have to believe me." He sniffed, closing his book and getting off the bed.

"Fine," I said, catching him under the arms and pitching him back onto the bed, where I tickled him without mercy. He wiggled and shrieked under my fingers. When I finally stopped, I looked up to see Francesca holding her clipper with this totally freaked-out look on her face.

"What's the matter?" I said. Jonah slipped away from me.

"Nothing." She clipped a tiny crescent moon off her pinkie and left it on the bedspread.

"I thought it was cool," Jonah said.

She trimmed a line of nail from her next finger. Her eyes were puffy, as if she was about to cry.

I nudged Jonah. "Shut up."

He made a face and left the room. Francesca kept trimming her nails, making a little pile of clippings on the bed. She didn't look up, and she didn't say anything.

"Are you ready to get started?" I asked. Usually we listened to CDs or had something to eat and hung out for a while before we did schoolwork, but today she was in a terrible mood.

"Come on, F, he's smart, but he's only five. He didn't mean to bug you."

"Just leave the stuff on the desk," she said, still not looking at me.

I stood there amazed. She was waiting for me to leave the homework and get out. She was dismissing me like a servant.

I wasn't going to take that shit. I smacked the algebra book on her desk. She went into the bathroom, closing the door between us. I looked around her room. It was the room of a spoiled brat. CD player, computer, clothes everywhere, shoes to die for, an old-fashioned dressing table and mirror draped with jewelry and hair stuff. She even had her own bathroom to shut herself into, her very own bathroom door to slam in a loyal friend's face.

I felt hot all around my neck. My hands were shaking. I fingered my knife in my pocket. I would indulge later, but now I wanted to smash her and her totally cool stuff into smithereens. Instead I took a deep breath and tried to calm down. Then I tore out a single sheet of notebook paper from my binder and carefully scooped all the fingernail clippings into it, folded it up into a little square and put it deep into my pocket, next to my knife.

ANNE

The clock beside my bed read five-thirty. I knew I wouldn't go back to sleep, but I was too exhausted to get up. I lay in bed, trying to relax. I searched for a memory, a time when I felt light and good. Something I could mine a piece of and cobble onto the present. I called up the dig in Mongolia, two years ago. I tried to find the feeling of vastness I'd had there. I was doing research I loved, I was part of an international dig on a virgin site. The scientists were all highly qualified, and we worked well together. Unearthing specimens of plants that had never been seen by human eyes, it seemed that I had finally arrived at something like happiness.

Of course, it wasn't only the work that was responsible for my euphoria. There was an Australian scientist on the team named Carson Graham. We flirted shamelessly from the first minute we met. What I liked about him was that he was large in every way: his laugh, his body, his generosity, his mind. He was completely ingenuous, exactly the opposite of Peter, and meeting him six months after Peter and I had separated was like falling into a friendly stream on a hot day.

Mongolia was literally the other side of the world. In the area where we were digging, there wasn't any electricity. Automobiles were rare. For six weeks we lived in yurts and cooked game over grass and dung fires. We rode in on horseback and packed our specimens onto a crude wagon pulled by yaks. Our Mongolian guides would disappear without warning for days at a time and then show up again, with game on their saddles. It was a soft and dreamy place, far from the crushing humanity of the Chinese cities. Everywhere I looked, the only things I could see, except for our camp and dig site, were rolling hills of grass under lapis skies. It was paradise.

One day, about three weeks into it, I was two meters down. While tapping open some soft flint, I exposed a fossil of what looked like an ancient ginkgo. In rapid succession I unearthed six more chunks and tapped them open. They each split into nearly perfect halves and revealed fossils so well preserved that the actual leaf was still there.

I carried the original fossil in my pocket, across the site and farther down the butte to where Carson was painstakingly extracting specimens that looked like they might be rodents from beneath the K-T boundary. He worked with tiny chisels and brushes and had two assistants sweeping and chipping with him.

"Are those rodents?" I said, forgetting all about my ginkgo. Rodents didn't evolve until maybe 55 million years ago, and he was digging back to before 64 million years.

"No, just small mammals," he said, jumping out of his hole

to show me one. "See the tooth there? You want to go out to lunch?"

I looked around at the sea of grass and the gouge we were mining.

"Sure," I said.

The Mongolian saddles were made of worn leather, embellished with tassels and woven ropes of bright pinks and greens that stood out in the soft landscape like a hallucination. We saddled up two of the horses, and I packed the leftover noodles from the night before. We rode along the butte until we came to a creek, our water source, where we let the horses drink and graze. We sat on the shady side of the creek bed and began kissing.

At first it was just what I wanted. After fifteen years of marriage to Peter, where there was always too much passion, whether it was love or anger, this was welcome and sweet. I liked that it was warm and safe and friendly and had no urgency to it. But after about thirty minutes of languid making out and no escalation of intensity, it became the slightest bit irritating. Eventually we got around to touching each other, but by then I wanted lunch more than I wanted him. He was determined and slow, but not slow and sexy. Just slow. And the electricity was leaking away.

"Hang on," I said, pulling back. I was bewildered and embarrassed. He smiled into my eyes. Sweet, friendly, safe, and warm.

"Maybe this isn't such a good idea," I stammered.

"It's not a bad idea," he said. And I could see that he meant it. But where was the heat? Now that we were down to the actual act, there really wasn't enough desire in me. Here I was, in a remote and gorgeous part of the world, with a man who I'd been flirting my ass off with for three weeks, and the fire had gone out. I buttoned my shirt.

"Do you think they're putting saltpeter in the food or something?"

He laughed. "Could be."

But I was frustrated and strangely ashamed. "Well, what do you think is happening?"

He shrugged. "I think that I'm not exactly your cup of tea."

I began to protest, and he put his big, reassuring hand on my arm. "Don't worry about it. Let's do something else. Come on. Let's eat those noodles and have a ride."

Since I could see no better alternative, we did just that. We ate the noodles with some dried meat and rode close together, our legs touching sometimes. We let the horses have their heads in the tall grass, and they lengthened their necks and ran side by side. The sky marbled and rearranged itself into a huge tortoise-shell, and I knew that if Carson and I had been lovers, I would have thought that this was a show especially for us. But since we weren't lovers, I could see that it was just sky, an arrangement of water and air and temperature that created an accidental pattern of clouds that I found beautiful. It was not caused by love, or even friendship. In fact, it had nothing to do with us. And the quiet, clean truth of that thought came with a dose of fear: I had nearly fallen into the egocentric thinking of people in love. I would have thrown away reason in favor of interpreting the sky as a personal gift, raising in my own mind the act of sex to something lofty. The sky would have been no more or less beautiful for it.

We reined in our horses, and on an impulse I took out the broken flint with the ginkgo fossil from my pocket and showed it to Carson.

"Look."

He nudged his horse closer to mine and touched the rock with his finger, lifting one edge of the leathery fossil off the rock. His face flooded with amazement.

"Good God, it's actually there. It's not just an impression, it's the plant itself. Look at this, the leaf is still pliable. What is it?"

"It's some kind of ginkgo. I'll have to do an exact identification, but I'm pretty sure it's not like any variety in existence now."

"How old do you reckon it is?"

"About sixty-five million years. There's a lot of them. I dug out about six."

"Ginkgo," he said, examining it closer. "Isn't that the herb people take for poor memory?"

"It's actually a tree," I said, for a second lapsing into botanic precision. "But, yeah, that's the plant. A folk remedy that caught on."

He continued to touch it with his finger. "What would happen if we tried some?"

I smiled. It had never occurred to me to eat a specimen. I was mildly appalled by the idea of eating specimens that the museum and several esteemed universities had financed our finding, and I was alarmed at eating something that was really more rock than plant.

Carson said, "What do you suppose sixty-five million years of time and pressure would do to the potency?"

"Probably nothing," I said. But I was already swirling the idea around in my mind. Time and pressure could have intensified and preserved the herb like freeze-drying. But more likely the ginkgo was merely dust, with no redeeming nutritive quality. It would make an interesting experiment, though, providing you could come up with enough fossilized ginkgo to conduct one in a controlled environment, with placebos and chemical analyses and proper documentation. Of course, I realized that Carson wasn't talking about any controlled experiment. He was talking about eating the fossil then and there. I could feel the corners of my mouth twitch into a smile. This was bad. Bad enough to make me want to do it.

The museum and the universities would never know. To hell with scientific method; there was plenty more where this ginkgo came from. Fuck precaution and safety and common sense; the nearest hospital was hundreds of miles away, and somehow those rules didn't apply here, else we wouldn't be riding horses, and eating everything the Mongolian guides brought us and drinking the water out of the creek.

Carson carefully peeled the ginkgo off the rock. He handed me half of the biggest leaf and kept the other half. We stood there grinning like idiots, holding the ginkgo as if it were a psychedelic mushroom. The sky became brighter and lighter, and it seemed like I could see more than 180 degrees in any given direction. Probably my pupils were dilating already, and I hadn't even tasted the ginkgo yet.

"Cheers," Carson said, putting the entire thing into his mouth and chewing it thoughtfully. I did the same.

"It tastes dusty," he said.

"It ought to," I said. Actually, I thought it was unremarkable. It was leathery and dried out but tasted pretty much like dried ginkgo. As I chewed and swallowed, I thought how strange it was to be ingesting a plant that had been extinct for millions of years. It was almost like time travel. I wondered if my own chemistry would rebel against such old molecules' entering the mix, if the ancient molecules would come to life somehow in the incubator of my body. I tried to remember biochemistry from college and how the ginkgo might affect the brain. I felt myself getting paranoid, almost exactly as I had when I was waiting for magic mushrooms to come on, back in college.

"It seems wrong somehow," I said, full of primitive fear.

We couldn't undo it. I doubted I could vomit up the ginkgo. If it was toxic, a reasonable part of me pointed out, I would know soon. We had committed some sort of taboo, my fear and prissiness said. We had crossed a line in time and disrupted what was buried, almost as excavators of Egyptian tombs in horror movies broke sacred barriers and brought down curses upon themselves.

Carson watched my face as I ran through the increasingly fantastic possibilities.

"You take vitamins and minerals," he said. "Minerals have been around a long time, too. The calcium you took this morning could be older than this ginkgo."

Yes, I knew that. I did. The specter of poisoning faded. I knew that I swallowed traces of dirt from these digs all the time with no problems. That's what dirt is: decomposed plant and mineral mixed together, aged through eons of time just to be breathed in by a scientist on a dig or to nourish a garden or to become a pharmaceutical drug. Molecules were molecules. I shook my head and laughed. That afternoon, as I unearthed a dozen more ginkgo specimens, I noticed that my awareness was slightly heightened, but nothing more.

Now, lying in my bed in the clear dawn of a Colorado morning, worrying about my daughter in the next room, it seemed that my Mongolian memories were so alien to my life that they may as well have been gingko hallucinations.

Something made a soft splat on my window. There was just enough light outside for me to see that it was a raw egg, a snotty mess sliding down the glass. For the most part, the so-called followers were the weak-minded looking for cheap salvation, and they were not much more than an annoyance. But now I was reminded that loonies came in all shades of peaceful and violent, stupid and cunning. I jumped out of bed and pulled on my jeans, suddenly panicked to get out of the glass box my house had become. I would take Francesca and disappear with her instead of letting them lay siege to us. The options circled my thoughts like hawks.

The list of places to go unfolded. Family was out of the question. I hadn't been able to stand more than a few hours with my folks since I'd left home. Peter? We could get on the plane and show up in Italy. But leaving the country seemed extreme, not to mention that Peter would blow a gasket. We could always drive to a motel somewhere in some unremarkable town and hide out. Pretty grim.

After I'd been through it a dozen times, staying home won. As annoying as the hangers-on were, Francesca could still do her schoolwork here and she still had Sid, who came every day.

Ronnie and Rae and Jonah were around, she could still take cello lessons, and even Chester was becoming a familiar, comforting presence. It was common knowledge that home and familiarity and as much normal life as possible were the best remedies for any affliction. Weren't they?

The early-morning light grew brighter. I left my room and padded down the hall to my office, where I flipped through my Rolodex until I found the phone number of Stone School. Francesca's history teacher, Martin, had called several times to see how she was doing and to keep us up to date on things at school. He had always been concerned and offered any assistance we might need. He was a kind, unassuming guy, unambitious in that schoolteachery way. He struck me as completely honest. I needed to bounce my worries off another adult, someone who knew a lot about teenagers. I waited through the Stone School voice-mail menu and then punched in his extension.

We met midmorning in the teachers' lounge at school. He handed me a chipped mug of percolator coffee and arched his eyebrows as I told him my woes.

"How can I help?" he said.

I searched my mind for a response. I had indeed come to him for help, but I didn't have a clear idea what I was asking for. I felt my cheeks go hot, and I gathered my stuff together. Unwelcome tears stung my eyes.

"I'm not sure," I said awkwardly. A rush of isolation and self-pity and fear made me blurt out, "It doesn't seem like anybody can help."

I felt even worse, sounding so needy, whining at a near stranger. I stood up and grabbed my coat.

"I'm sorry," I said. "Thank you for your time."

He watched me put on my coat. "You said you were thinking of going away."

"Yes," I said, looking up.

"If things don't improve, you may need to. I think you should have an escape plan, so to speak. Maybe I *can* help with that. I'm sure Francesca told you about our school trip a few weeks ago? It would be no problem if you wanted to go there. One of the cabins is winterized. The key is inside the old wood cookstove on the porch. You need four-wheel drive to get in, but you could be up there and even I wouldn't have to know about it." He drew a quick map with simple directions on a piece of paper and handed it to me. Gratitude washed through me. It seemed an amazing thing, that someone would hand me an out on a piece of paper.

"Your family doesn't use it? You don't rent it out to skiers?" I asked, taking the paper.

"Nope," he said kindly. "Nobody uses it. It's pretty rough, but there's plenty of firewood. Just keep it in mind, that's all. It's there if you want it."

FRANCESCA

She spends her days shut in the house. Anne treats Francesca like a delinquent who can't be trusted or like Jonah, a five-year-old who can't be left alone. Her mom pays Rae to be in the house with Francesca during the day, so Francesca and Jonah are together all the time now. He's probably a genius; she can see that. At five he can already read, and he's interested in her math homework and watches over her shoulder as she struggles with algebra. But even though he's brainy, he's still a little kid.

She hears him running up the stairs. He knocks on the door but doesn't wait for her to answer. He comes in and flings himself on her bed, not caring that she's in it. Waking up slowly is the one good thing about not going to school, and now she doesn't even get to do that.

"Hi, peanuthead," she says.

"Hi." He grins at her from the foot of the bed, and his clear eyes take in everything. She stretches and realizes that she's not as queasy today. She smiles at Jonah.

"Did you know that earthworms have five hearts?" he asks. His hair sticks up all over his head. His eyes are liquidy dark and sparkling.

"Do they?"

"Yep." He bounces on the bed, and the pressure on her bladder makes her get out of bed. She shuts herself into her bathroom, leaving Jonah chattering on the bed. She pees and then turns on the water in the shower and stands under it so that it pours down, hot and steaming, over her head and face, stretching out her hair past her waist, down to the top of her crack. She manages to keep the thoughts about pregnancy at bay. She concentrates on worrying about the cello lesson she will have later in the day. Her mom, her jailer, has arranged for Keith Jacobson to come to the house for her lesson. She will practice all day to make up for the weeks of slacking off, but even so, she'll never fool Jacobson. The butterflies start up in her stomach.

Out of the shower and into her bathrobe, she sits on the bed next to Jonah and works through the knots in her wet hair. He's still talking about earthworms.

"I might be a paleobotanist, like your mom," he says abruptly. "Or else a trash guy."

"A trash guy?"

He looks at her like she's an idiot. "Because they get to ride on the outside of the trucks."

"Yeah, but you could be a scientist who studies earthworms."

"A helminthologist."

"Is that what they're called?"

"Unless they only study true segmented worms. Then they're called oligochaetologists."

Rae comes in with breakfast on a tray. There is an apple, peeled and sliced and arranged in a circle around a scoop of yogurt that is sprinkled with granola and blueberries. There are marigolds on the tray, and Rae has a big bag slung over her shoulder.

"Get off the bed, Jonah," Rae says.

"What's all this?" Francesca says, while he slips off the bed and stands next to his mother.

"Your breakfast." Rae's face is almost beautiful when she sets down the tray and smiles.

"It's a surprise," Jonah says, hopping from one foot to the other.

"You shouldn't have done it," Francesca says, smiling back at them.

"But I wanted to." Rae's face grows serious. "You must begin to accept devotion. When people want to do things for you, you must let them. When someone does something nice for you, it's really for them. You see, you're not like the rest of us. People receive your blessings that way. I think you'll find it's a good way for you to work with people."

Francesca feels embarrassed, as if she's been scolded for bad manners.

"You should try it," Jonah says. Francesca obediently picks up the spoon and tries the yogurt.

Rae takes clean white towels from the bag, a silver bowl the size of a small sink, and a large blue glass bottle stoppered with a cork. "I learned how to do this in India. It's called foot *puja*. It's for holy people. May I? It's basically a foot massage and a pedicure. My way of showing devotion."

Francesca's face goes hot. The idea of Rae's rubbing her feet
is a little weird, but Jonah is bouncing around her, making faces
and begging for blueberries. She plays with him, popping blueberries into his mouth.

"Just give me your foot," Rae says, putting her towels and
stuff on the floor and getting down on her knees to take
Francesca's right foot in her hands.

Francesca holds her leg stiffly at first, and then Rae begins to
rub the foot, working her thumbs deep into the curve of the
instep and all around the edge of the heel, then spreading and
stretching the ball of her foot and massaging each toe up and
down. Francesca relaxes in spite of herself. She can't help but
close her eyes and surrender her foot to Rae, who handles it as
though it were precious. She pours warm rose water from the
blue bottle, and Francesca opens her eyes to see her foot in the
silver bowl with rose petals floating around it.

"I want to help," says Jonah. His mother shows him how to
pour slowly, so the scented water doesn't splash. She speaks to
him in a hushed voice, but Jonah doesn't follow her lead. He
plays with the water and Francesca's foot and grins up at her like
a young monkey.

"Now you're an actual holy person," he says.

"Shut up," she says, splashing him.

"No, really, all the gurus get their feet anointed," he says.
"Gurudev at the ashram in Tennessee got foot *puja* all the time."

She throws a blueberry at his head, and he ducks, almost
spilling the basin of water.

"That's enough, Jonah," Rae says, and sends him out.

Francesca closes her eyes again and focuses on her feet. She has never given them any attention at all. But now they tingle and glow, and she feels muscles and skin that she has never noticed before. She didn't know feet could feel this good. The right foot soaks while Rae begins to work on the left.

After she pats both feet dry on the clean towel, Rae opens a small bottle of lavender oil and works it into the skin. Then she polishes each toenail with a silver-handled buffing tool that she moves back and forth on the nails to bring out a soft, rosy glow. Finally she takes fresh flowers from her bag, baby pink rosebuds and purple anemones, and, pinching any stem or thorn carefully away, she places the flowers on and around Francesca's feet, which are resting on a folded towel. Francesca keeps her eyes closed. She feels good, from her feet up to the top of her head. She feels relaxed and pleasantly empty. She hears Rae quietly pick up her things and leave the room. Francesca sits on, enjoying the deep quiet. Not even the thought of the cello lesson ruffles her. Indeed, it seems that this is the way she should feel all the time. She can see why gurus in India and Tennessee like this.

After her feet are dry and back in socks and shoes, she meets Keith Jacobson in the living room, where they will have the lesson. Rae and Jonah stay in the kitchen; she can hear Jonah playing with his dinosaurs on the kitchen floor. One look at Keith and her calm is gone. Her palms are sweating. The air around him is a good five to ten degrees colder than the air in the house. His overcoat is worn but of the best quality, as are the rest of his clothes. In winter it's always cashmere sweaters and wool slacks. In summer he wears light wool slacks and a white shirt rolled up from the wrist exactly once. Year in and year out. Being so prissy and inflexible, it seems like Keith is old, but she supposes he's

only thirty-five. Francesca's lessons have always been at his studio, which is one big room of polished hardwood and Turkish
rugs, with a baby grand piano in the center. His own cello waits
in its case, leaning against the wall. Next to the piano there are
two straight chairs, one for him and one for the student. In her
four years of taking lessons from him, this is his first visit to the
house. He looks inconvenienced. His mouth curdles, and his
eyes flit suspiciously around the room, taking in details and
looking personally affronted by all of it. She wonders what he
thinks of the followers outside. She smiles to think of Keith
coming into contact with Chester.

"Nice riffraff," he says, rolling his eyes. "Are you going to be
absolving sins later? God, girl, what have you gotten yourself
into?" He takes his coat off and folds it precisely before he lays
it over the back of a chair. He makes a sweeping gesture with his
hand. "Never mind. I don't want to know. Let's hear the
Brahms."

She begins the measured, steady notes of the sonata, and he
shakes his head before she's finished the third measure. He seems
angrier, more insulted by her playing than ever before. He
makes her work the phrasing, playing the first eight measures
over and over, time and again. He picks apart her fingering and
then reworks the phrasing some more. She can see it in his face;
her playing is painful to him. Her vibrato is weak, her interpretation is tired, her tempo is slow. He taps his hand on her music
stand to pick up the tempo, and she is so startled that she drops
her bow.

He sighs. "This is where you could use a real miracle,
Francesca. Right here in your playing. You haven't been practic-

ing. You're distracted, and no wonder, what with that mess out there. I don't understand what you're doing in a cult, but I have other students who could use the hour. You shouldn't be taking lessons at this level if you don't really want to apply yourself."

He has threatened to drop her before, but nothing ever came of it. He's overwrought and pouty, and he likes to be dramatic. Always before when he's talked like this, she's increased her practice time and tried harder. But today the idea of no more cello lessons, no more Keith, gives her a lift. No more pressure to practice, no more bitchy Keith, no more competitions. It would be a relief. She's always struggled to play; it's never come easy to her. She isn't a prodigy or even gifted, just a hard worker. She's been doing it for four years, prodded along by Keith and her own unwillingness to disappoint her parents. Her mom would be upset if Francesca quit, but she'd get over it. It's her dad who would be furious. He would yell and insist that she stick with it. He would act like she did it to hurt him. But he's in Italy. He wouldn't know. And anyway, it would serve him right.

She carefully puts the instrument back in its case, as Keith has taught her, loosens the bow hairs and slips it in, too. Keith is watching, waiting for her to beg him not to drop her, for her promise to practice more, to try harder. She closes and fastens the cello-case lid. She remembers when she first started lessons with Keith, how tall and scary he seemed. But now she's as tall as he is, and she looks him in the eye.

"I think you're right," she says. "There are talented kids who would love to have this hour with you. So I'll quit." She picks up his jacket off the back of the chair and holds it out to him.

He has no choice but to take it. His face has gone red. His eyes dart around the room.

"Are you sure?" he asks, suddenly sounding not so sure himself. But now she knows it's the right thing. She can feel how right it is. She opens the door. Chester is standing at the front gate, talking with several people who fall quiet when they see her.

"I'm sure," she says to Keith. She smiles the smile of the Virgin at him as he makes his way out of the yard, through the little throng of people who are standing there because they adore her.

She closes the door and walks slowly upstairs to her room, savoring the satisfaction of sending the cello teacher packing. The house is quiet and still. She lies down on the bed. She folds her hands over her stomach; her legs are uncrossed and together, toes up. She lies still, thinking, watching the light play on the textured surface of the ceiling. She feels good. She's free. She laughs out loud thinking how easy it was to quit. She tries to hold on to the relief, but thoughts of her parents, especially her dad, creep in. An edge of guilt curls around the glee, and she can't seem to shake it.

And then she feels the ripple in her stomach. It is almost like the butterflies she had earlier; in fact, she may have mistaken this trilling sensation for common butterflies. But now, lying still, she is sure that this is life, awake in her belly and accompanied by a presence that has been waiting for this moment to let her know: He has arrived.

SID

I had the fingernail clippings in my pocket. I kept them there for three days, feeling the edges of the paper square against the cut on my hip every time I sat down. I didn't bring Francesca her homework. I thought, Let her call me, if she wants it so bad. I went to school and came home. I did my own homework for a change. My mom was working and staying reasonably sober, and I was satisfied to be living my own life for a while. But I knew it wouldn't last. The clippings were in my pocket, and it was only a matter of time before Anne called me to see why I hadn't been coming around. It was only a matter of time, too, until my mom fell off the wagon.

On the third day, I came home from school and my mom was totally bombed, with a bottle of tequila and the salt shaker on the kitchen table in front of her. As a rule my mom wore thick, concealing makeup from the moment she woke up until she fell into bed at night. It was her armor, her mask, and it made her look tough and older than her age, which was only thirty-four, but now the remnants of last night's makeup had been wiped or cried off her face, exposing all her freckles and the puffy, fragile skin around her eyes. Her hair hung straight, instead of styled and sprayed stiff. Nobody other than me ever saw her like this, which I personally thought was too bad, because this was the way she looked best. She looked like a girl, an innocent, pretty young girl. I could see her as she must have been before I was born, before she started being a hard-bitten, hard-drinking "gal."

"Rusty's gone," she said brokenly. By that I assumed she meant the guy who had been coming over this last week, sometimes after two in the morning, and leaving before I got up for school. The total extent of my relationship with "Rusty" was hearing him take a piss each morning, a long, beer drinker's horse piss, with the bathroom door open, which, because of how close it was to my room, put him at about eight feet from my head on the pillow.

"It wasn't exactly like he was part of the family, Mom."

She sat and stared at the shot glass in her hand, filled it again, turning her face away from me, all dramatic and suffering.

"He mattered to me," she said. "You don't know how I feel."

I hated it when she did this. She slobbered all over herself on account of a man she hardly knew and used it as a big excuse to start drinking again. It made me so mad and so ashamed of her that I felt crazy myself. I cursed her, loudly, inside my own head and wished for the thousandth time that she was like Francesca's mom. Anne was organized, and my mom was sloppy. Anne was sophisticated, and my mom was pathetic. Anne had a real job and self-respect. My mom threw herself at cowboys.

I knew the routine. She wanted to wallow and drag me down

in it, too. Lots of times, when she was like this, I would run a bath for her and make her coffee and put her to bed. Lots of times I would listen to the whole sorry mess. Today I just wasn't in the mood.

"I know exactly how you feel, Mom," I said. "You feel the same way you always feel when they take off and you start drinking again. You feel drunk."

She raised her washed-out eyes to me, and I saw shock and a little tightening of her grip on herself. "Don't speak to me like that," she said.

"Oh, I forgot. I should show my respect."

She rose halfway, shaking and furious, with the full shot glass sloshing in her hand, and then sank back into the chair, too drunk to stay upright.

"I picked shit with the chickens to make a life for you, Sid."

"I know," I said. "You've been telling me about it for fourteen years."

I left her there, knowing I had been awful. I went back outside, and since I didn't know where else to go, I started walking. I didn't plan to go to Francesca's house, but that's where I ended up. Like a horse that trots back to the barn, I always trotted back to Anne and Francesca, to Ronnie and Jonah. I missed them. I missed Jonah's little hands on my cheeks and cooking food together and all the stuff we did.

Nothing had changed in three days. A cluster of people waited at Francesca's front gate. Chester stood behind it with his arms crossed. I positioned myself back far enough so that he wouldn't see me right away. I wanted to stay out there and see what it was like, not to be on the inside. The people waiting didn't know her the way I did. They didn't have any real reason to be there. They just wanted to believe in something. People believe a lot of weird stuff.

A gray-haired lady was putting flowers and a small shopping bag on the fence. She smiled at me. "My neighbor down in Littleton says Francesca's really good with migraines," she said. "My daughter gets the worst headaches, every Saturday like clockwork. I figure, it can't hurt. She said to leave flowers and a picture and something that belongs to the person. I brought my daughter's hair clip. Do you think that's all right?"

I shrugged and pushed past her. I wasn't surprised to find the bodily-substance woman materialize at my elbow. I stepped back, and she moved in closer.

"What do you have?" she crooned. I put my hand over my pocket, where I could feel the folded square of paper. The bodily-substance woman's eyes followed my hand.

"How much did you say you'd pay for fingernails?" I said. It was fifty, but I didn't know how else to start the conversation.

"I said thirty-five, darling," said the BS woman.

I realized how dumb I'd just been. "I'm pretty sure you said fifty."

She dipped her head. "So. Forty. Let's see."

I couldn't resist looking around before I pulled out the paper and handed it to her.

"Very good," she said, peering into it. She folded it back up tight and found two twenties from somewhere in her clothing. "Next time bring hair," she said, pressing the money into my hand. "Hair will get you sixty."

And then she was gone, and I had forty dollars in my pocket.

For something that would have gone down the toilet or in the trash anyway. I went over and over it, puzzled about why I felt guilty. I hadn't stolen anything of value. No one would be hurt by what I just did. I put my hands in my pockets and went up to the front of the group, where Chester opened the gate for me. It was easy to take my place, once again, on the inside.

CHESTER

The world was waiting for snow just as it was waiting for salvation. Trees stood naked and ready. Gardens were frozen black. Cristos continued to find flower petals somewhere for his porch poems to the Virgin, but often they would be ruffled by the wind before she saw them. The storm was gathering itself over the mountains, and it was going to be the kind that blankets everything democratically, including the homeless, as we slept along the riverbanks and in the parks. Most likely it would freeze one or two of us dead before morning.

Just as sure as the coming snow, there was a being coming, who would be born to the Virgin and bring on a new world. I still believed that. What I didn't feel so sure about was the part about the flesh. Being around the Virgin the way I was, I couldn't help but touch her now and then, helping her into cars and protecting her from overeager followers. And she didn't seem to fear me anymore, or mind my touch. So I knew she had a real flesh-and-blood body, but I wasn't sure how much the body would enter into the birth of a savior. Just the thought of the Virgin's womb made me shrink inside my own skin. Try as I might, I couldn't reconcile the holiness and purity of her with the thought of "down there."

For that matter, I was having a hard time with the thought of an actual baby. A savior, a messiah, yes. A baby, no. Babies were something I saw from across a street or a crowded parking lot. They were *of* their parents; that is, they didn't have their own smells yet, not until they got to be about six months old. Babies meant diapers and secretions and came with the embarrassing reality of needing to suck on their mothers' breasts all the time. This was something I knew was necessary and even desirable for infants, but I fidgeted just thinking about it. I couldn't believe that the Messiah would be that mortal. The very miracle of His conception seemed to demand a birth unsullied by sexual organs.

The other thing I hadn't counted on was the kindness of Anne and Ronnie and how I felt protective of them, too. I was sorry for what this was doing to them. They couldn't even walk into their own houses without at least one person trying to talk to them, trying to get in to see the Virgin. I knew that people would come. Of course they would. It just never occurred to me that it would be so commercial and that some people would be so greedy.

Rae was such a greedy one. Since she had lived in a half dozen ashrams, she thought she was the expert on holy people and followers. It's true she did know more than I did about how to take care of the Virgin. She knew how to attend her. But I couldn't help noticing that a lot of the people who came from out of town were friends of Rae's. And she encouraged the followers to write letters to the Virgin. She talked to the reporters. She fanned the flames, talking all the time about the healings and miracles.

But I couldn't do what Rae did. I couldn't attend the Virgin's body or be in the house with her. Anne had offered me a bed inside; so did Ronnie, but I couldn't accept. I knew if I tried sleeping under a roof, the terror would come. It was always the same. When I lay down to sleep, the ceiling above me would start to drop like the underside of an elevator, until I either had to run out of the house or be pinned beneath the weight of it. So I slept outside. I knew the warmest spots in town: under certain bridges, the eastern wall of the public library, the steam vents from university buildings, the underground walkways on the Hill. There was even a large doghouse I knew of whose inhabitant was extremely hospitable. For some reason, that doghouse roof never dropped on me.

Since I couldn't stay inside for long, I couldn't stop Rae from calling people and publicizing Francesca. She did what she wanted without asking me. She was very close to the Virgin and used her status to intimidate. She began organizing ways for people to meet the Virgin, and I didn't have the nerve to object.

As Francesca's protector, I didn't roam anymore. I was pretty much stuck in Ronnie's yard or Anne's. As long as it wasn't wet, I was fine in my bag, but I knew that on the first snowy, cold night, I would be in trouble, and it was coming soon.

I was sitting on the back-deck steps, drinking a cup of coffee from a thermos that Anne had left for me, appreciating the rich aroma that temporarily blocked out all others. I was contemplating how to solve my winter camp problem when Francesca herself came out of the house.

I rarely saw her in those days, since she stayed mostly inside in Rae's care, so I was surprised when she stepped from the twilight of the house, blinking, into the noonday sun. A beach bag hung on her shoulder. She sat down next to me, her shoulder almost touching mine, and mirrored my position: knees up, arms wrapped around them. Her bare feet emerged from under frayed denim, and I studied each rounded nail and toe, alarmed at how pink and vulnerable they were, like two litters of albino mice. I shifted my gaze and moved an inch away, so as not to touch her or see the disturbing toes.

"I'm going nuts in there," she said.

I nodded. I understood it all too well.

"I need to go somewhere," she said.

I looked at her. "Where?"

"How about down to the drugstore? Can you drive?" She peered into my eyes, seeming to ask my permission.

I shook my head. "I don't drive." Not since long ago, when I was an undergraduate. When I drank several beers and ran my car, with four friends in it, into a brick wall. Of the five of us, one died right away; one died after twelve hours in ICU; two had broken noses, collarbones and internal injuries; and I had a concussion that put me in a coma for three days.

"We can walk, then. It's not far. I mean, it's just to the store and back. I've been walking there since I was eight." I thought of Anne, who would certainly say no. I thought of Ronnie, who wouldn't approve. But ultimately I didn't take my instructions from either of them. I always put the Virgin first. If she wanted to go somewhere, I would make sure she was safe. I would do anything she required. I didn't question her requests; I simply did what she asked. She took sunglasses and shoes out of her bag and tied her hair up under a bandanna as a sort of disguise.

We set off, climbing over the back fence. We made our way along the ditch as far as we could and then cut through the yards over to Ninth Street, walking the three blocks from there to Broadway without anyone's recognizing us.

Inside the store she immediately went to the aisle that had women's private things. I stood by the door looking out, so that I couldn't see what she was buying. She paid for her item, and we were out the door when a guy in a chair wheeled up so close to us that his chair almost touched our legs. I knew this old guy, name of Little John. He'd been a paraplegic as long as I knew him, but his years on the street were getting harder with age. Last winter he took to parking his chair under the streetlights in front of the hospital at night, choosing to sleep in the open, next to the busy street, rather than take the risk of being tipped out of his chair in a less public place. People driving down Broadway were disturbed by having to look at him, and dozens of calls came in to the police department to take him away. But sidewalks are public, and unless he was actually lying down on one, Little John had a right to be there. Letters appeared in the paper, and a debate ensued, and finally, last I heard, concerned citizens were trying to arrange for an institution to take him. I guess the sight of him slumped in a chair held together with duct tape and covered in a filthy acrylic blue blanket put them off.

"Hey, you're that girl," Little John said, looking up at Francesca out of webby red eyes.

She stiffened. I took in the stench of him. He smelled like rotten meat with a sharp undercurrent of axle grease and something else I couldn't identify. He pulled the knit hat off his head and into his lap, an old-fashioned gesture of respect that touched me.

"Heal me," he said piteously, closing his eyes and holding out the injured hand to her.

Francesca and I both looked at an oozing sore about three inches across. The stink of fungus and putrid flesh assaulted my nostrils.

The Virgin tightened her grip on her beach bag and took a step backward. "I can't do it," she whispered, nearly gagging. "I can't touch him."

Little John opened his eyes, and bitterness settled with the saliva in the corners of his mouth.

"I knew you was a fake," he said, showing his few brown teeth and wheeling forward until his chair nearly rammed her. He thrust the infected hand at her again, but this time it was a taunt, a threat.

"Hey," I said, stepping between them and with my foot sending his chair back to where it had been. "Why don't you go across the street to the hospital? They'll clean that up and give you medicine for it." I guessed they would find a bed for him, too.

"And let them take my kidneys and give them to some rich fucker? No, sir. I ain't a fool. I won't be no science experiment." The loose skin on his face flapped when he shook his head.

Many people on the street believed they were valued by the medical community only as living junkers for spare parts. I had heard that if you were one of us and had to go to the hospital these days, they wouldn't treat you unless you signed a paper saying that if you died, you would donate your organs to science.

He reversed the chair, using the wounded hand with difficulty, and turned around so that his back reproached us. Then he stretched his hat onto his head, farted loudly and malodorously, and wheeled away.

I was shaken. If anyone needed the Virgin's touch, it was Little John. He represented all that was painful and undignified and sad in humanity. Yet she had refused him. I assumed there were reasons far beyond what I could see, but it bothered me.

Later, after I got her home, I walked to the mental-health center and stood at the door. People came and went through it, but I stayed where I was, thinking. There had been a doctor there a few years back who'd tried to get me to take some new pills.

"These drugs are different from what you had before, Chester," he'd said. "You won't have as many side effects. I think you'd find yourself feeling a lot better."

I had been almost ready to try it, but the caseworker, a woman who smelled like asparagus piss, got pushy, so I declined. Now I wasn't so sure. If there was a pill that could weaken the smells a little, if a pill would allow me to sleep under a roof so that I could take care of the Virgin better, then maybe I should take it.

Eventually the people who worked there filed past me on their way home for the day. I hoped I would see the doctor I had talked to before, but no one familiar came out.

"Are you waiting for someone?" a woman asked. She reeked of the bitter brown smell of disillusionment. I shook my head.

"I work here," she said, on the verge of irritation. "Do you need something?" She reminded me of all the social workers I'd ever known. Stressed out and limited in scope. The last thing I needed was another social worker trying to fix me. The last thing I needed was to be off my game when the Virgin might need me.

I turned around and walked off. I realized I didn't want anything from the mental-health center, with its do-gooder stink. Little John was right. Only a fool would take such medicine.

FRANCESCA

The days stretch into a week. Each morning a new flower-petal painting appears on the porch. Twice more Rae washes and oils Francesca's feet. Every day she brings flowers and notes from the people outside. She talks to them. She learns their stories and tells them to Francesca. It becomes part of Rae's job, to bring news from the devotees, as Rae calls them. Francesca finds that she is interested in these people who come and wait for her. They stand down there, outside the fence, and she can feel them wanting and needing her. She can feel their pain and their despair. And their love. She begins to think about them a lot. She begins to send them, via Rae, a word or two of encouragement and thanks for their gifts.

On the next Monday morning, she wakes from a dream in which she was playing the Bach Prelude in G Major that she used to play, before she got Uncle Randolph's cello. There was a sweetness to the dream, as she played the familiar piece. It reminds her of the years before her parents' divorce, and its hopeful, strong notes make her ache until she wants to cry.

Rae is standing at the foot of the bed with an armful of white roses.

"Remember last week when I brought you the note from Stephen, the man whose wife has the terrible shingles?" Rae says. She is smiling and smug. "Well, he came back today to say that after she touched the note you had blessed, her pain began to fade, and within twenty-four hours she was free of the shingles."

Francesca says nothing. She doesn't know what to say. She can't really think about the few who get healed. She can only think about the ones who haven't. She worries about them. Rae puts the roses in a vase and goes to the bathroom to fill it with water. Francesca closes her eyes again, wishing she could reenter the dream, wishing she could play the Bach prelude in actuality, but she hasn't been able to take her cello out of the case for days.

That night she can't sleep, with a weight of worry on her chest, thinking about a man named Joe who has been sending notes through Rae almost every day for the past week. In the morning, when Rae and Jonah awaken her with a tray of fruit and yogurt, she asks about him.

"How's Joe?"

"He's out there every night after he gets off work," Rae says, placing the tray next to Francesca. Jonah hops onto the foot of the bed, and automatically Francesca lifts the tray so that he doesn't dump it with his bouncing.

"Who else?" Francesca asks. Jonah settles down, and she puts the tray aside again. "Who else comes a lot?"

"Oh, lots of folks. There's a woman and her little boy every morning, and those three sisters come almost every night. There are probably fifteen or twenty regulars."

"Why do they keep coming?" she asks. She needs to make sure she understands.

"Well, they all hope they'll be the next one to get a healing."

Francesca goes to the window and looks down on the front yard. She sees Chester standing before the gate and three or four people on the sidewalk.

"You're kind of famous," Jonah says.

"I know you've been going out," Rae says quietly. "Your mom wouldn't like it if she knew."

It's true. Anne would pitch a fit. She would probably stop going to work in Denver. The house would become even more like a prison. Francesca watches Rae's face to see if she is going to tell.

Rae goes on. "Meeting the devotees is good, don't you think? I think it's good. I mean, they need to see you, and you need to see them. So maybe we should think of a way to do that without you crawling out of the window all the time."

"I don't do it all the time. I did it once. The other time I just walked out the back door. Chester was with me both times."

Rae smiles. "You don't have to explain. What I'm telling you is that maybe you should consider having a couple of really special cases come in to see you. Maybe just on Tuesdays."

Francesca spoons the yogurt into her mouth. Today is Tuesday. She knows that Rae said Tuesday because that's her mom's long day in Denver. Anne leaves in the morning and works in her office at the museum all day and then teaches an evening class at the university. She's never home before ten.

Rae waits with her hands clasped in front of her as if she were a singer in a choir.

"What have you cooked up, Rae?"

Rae's smile remains calm. "Shall I see if Joe is outside? Shall I invite him in for a few minutes?"

Francesca closes her eyes. There's a bar of tension across her forehead. She must make the decision. There isn't anybody else. It's not like quitting cello; it doesn't feel exhilarating, it feels more like she must do it and she must take the consequences, whatever they may be.

She tells herself to lighten up. It's really no different from sneaking out. It won't hurt anything to let this one guy come in. Rae and Chester will be there to make sure everything is all right. She nods, tickling Jonah in the ribs until he gets off the bed. "Give me ten minutes, and I'll be downstairs to see him."

She puts on a loose dress, for comfort around her belly. The ripples she has been feeling seem somehow fragile, and she can't bear the thought of a waistband pressing against her. She braids her hair at the back, and when it gets too long for her arms to reach, she pulls it over her shoulder and braids it down to the end.

The man Rae brings into the living room a few minutes later is portly and balding and pink in the cheeks. He looks like a science teacher or someone who would work behind the counter of an automotive dealership. Chester hovers near the door. Jonah has moved his toys to this room, and he is playing on the rug. Francesca sticks out her hand and feels her shyness slip away. Once again, when she's with a devotee, everything she does is golden. All awkwardness disappears.

"You're Joe."

Joe hesitates a second and then takes her hand. He seems about to bow or kneel, so she sits down on the couch before he can do it.

"I've been concerned about you," she says.

He looks up, startled.

"You wrote me a note about how you want to die, and you're surprised that I'm concerned?"

He blushes. The top of his head goes pink.

"What do you want?" she asks gently. She doesn't know why she says this. It's just the thing she must say.

His face is blank with shock.

"What do you want?" she asks again.

His mouth wobbles violently, and tears slick his cheeks. "I don't know," he says.

She waits a minute to see if there is more. He continues to weep, sitting on the edge of her mother's chair. She looks up at Rae, over at Chester. For a moment, she doesn't know what to do. Rae brings the man a glass of water and nods at Francesca.

Francesca closes her eyes. This man has been dreaming of his own death. He said in his letter that he was working up the nerve to kill himself. He's come to her for help. It seems too big a task, to take on this man's sadness.

She can feel them all waiting for her to speak. Her own sweat is hot around her temples, and at the same time, the peculiar trilling motion begins in her belly, like a muscle in spasm or a moth beating its wings against the inside of her womb. The wonder and amazement of something living inside her, someone sharing her body, fills her until she has to smile at the man sniffling before her.

"There is so much happening that we don't get to know about," she hears herself say. "And sometimes you are just touched by grace. All I can tell you is this: You are more than this wish to die. That's all I know. Stay and see how it plays out."

Joe is hustled out of the house. Francesca goes back to her room and lies on the bed, curiously elated. Telling the man those things was unexpected. She didn't think she had any advice or important things to say. But she had opened her mouth, and the right words seemed to come out. And the words weren't only for Joe. It was as if somebody else was speaking to both Joe and her.

The thrill of the morning begins to wear down as the day goes on. She and Jonah read. Rae performs another foot ritual. She wonders if her words to Joe were as powerful as she thought. Maybe they meant nothing to him. Maybe she'd confused him, causing more harm than good. Perhaps it was her own pride that made her think her words were the right ones. She may never know. She settles into a foggy grumpiness.

The silent cello reproaches her from its corner of the room. Doesn't it know she's quit playing? She goes to the instrument and begins to unsnap the case. She sees the gleaming wood inside. When she first started working with Keith, she was ten and still had a chance to be exceptional. She learned quickly, and when it came time to perform, she had imitated the passionate way others moved their bodies when they played. Eventually she forgot that she was imitating. There had been, in those days, a rarefied calm when she played. She could move through the music, and it would move through her. But she hasn't had that feeling for more than two years. It is lost. She snaps up the case again and turns the cello face in to the corner.

At the end of the day, Sid is standing in the doorway to her room, holding Francesca's homework.

"Where have you been?" Francesca asks.

Sid blinks. "You don't remember our fight the last time I was here?"

Francesca thinks hard, but she can't remember being angry at Sid.

"I remember being kind of mad at Jonah, but not at you."

"I guess it wasn't that important."

Francesca clears a place on the bed for Sid to sit. "I missed you."

Sid plops onto the bed, and they open the books. And now Francesca can see them as if she is outside the house looking in through the window. They are two teenage girls with their heads together, working and laughing as if everything were perfectly ordinary.

SID

The bodily-substance woman and I worked out an arrangement. If I had something for her, I would nod as I passed, and she would meet me at the bus stop ten minutes later. I brought hair from Francesca's brush, washcloths she'd left scrunched in a ball on the edge of the bathtub, a pair of socks she'd worn and then thrown out because of a hole in the heel, and yes, I even brought used Kleenex: hers, not mine. All of these things I handed over in Ziploc bags, just the way the bodily-substance woman liked them, and in return I got money. I could have done more, but I drew the line at getting anything out of the toilet and actual stealing.

The money in my pockets made me proud and ashamed at the same time. I told my mom that the Dunns were paying me to help around the house, and in a sense they were; they just didn't know it. She didn't ask me how much I was making per hour or why I had hundreds in my pockets; she just took it and paid the rent and bought tequila. I bought her a nice outfit for the next dry season's job interviews. Francesca and I were nearly as tight as before, but not quite. Things had changed. With Rae as her secretary and Chester as her bouncer, she was holding court in her living room on Tuesdays. Notes asking for an audience now numbered between twenty and forty a day. Rae did her best to keep the Tuesday audiences secret, even leading the lucky petitioners around to the back door one by one, so that any reporters that might be out front didn't see them go inside.

"There are so many," Rae said. "We need to find a place where you can see a lot of them at once."

I had to snicker to myself. I'd seen Rae out there taking payola from anyone who wanted to get in to see Francesca. But I couldn't even think about busting Rae because of what *I* was doing.

"You want to make some real money?" the bodily-substance woman asked me one evening while I was waiting for the bus in a dirty swirl of sleety rain that would turn to snow by morning. "Get pictures. Baby pictures, school pictures, family pictures, but the most valuable are recent ones, especially close-ups."

A few days later, when Francesca and Jonah were napping like drunken sailors and Rae was in a chat room on Anne's computer, I closed Francesca's bedroom door and tiptoed down the hall to Anne's room.

The door was always open, and whenever I had passed, I'd seen an enticing corner of a dresser with silver frames on it. I entered as if it were a shrine. I touched the silver frames, which held snapshots of Francesca through the years and a picture of Anne holding up a huge dinosaur bone and grinning from ear to ear. Those I wouldn't take.

Gingerly I pulled open the dresser drawers. They were full of T-shirts and cotton underpants and socks, hardworking stuff, not the slimy, lacy gear my mom had in her top drawer. I looked around the room. The old iron bed was large and stacked with striped pillows on a worn quilt of small pastel squares. I made up my mind right then that I would have such a bed someday, right down to the sheer bedskirt and the cedar chest at the foot.

I found the pictures under the bed in some hatboxes, in yellow envelopes marked with the month and the year. I silently thanked Anne for being so well organized. I took a sampling of older shots, but I knew I had hit the jackpot when I found a close-up of Francesca taken last summer at the beach. She was smiling into the camera, dark eyes shining, wrapped in a sweater with her hair blowing all around her. This would be the one the bodily-substance woman would shell out for.

We went through the afternoon, doing French vocabulary, American history, and algebra. The photos generated their own heat from their place in my pocket. By the end of the afternoon, I couldn't wait to find the BS woman and unload them. She wasn't there that day or the next, but on the third day, she materialized at the bus stop.

"Let's see," she said, holding out her yellow palm into which I placed the plastic bag with the photos, the one from the beach on top.

"This is good," she breathed. "I'll give you five hundred for the bunch."

I smiled. I was learning how to do this. If she had offered three hundred, I would have known I would end up with five or six hundred. But she had started at five hundred.

"A thousand," I said.

She squinted up at me and counted out eight one-hundred-dollar bills into my hand.

"That's the best I can do," she said, curling my fingers over the bills.

I stared at my hand. I had never held so much money at one time. I stuffed the bills deep into my pocket.

"Now I want something really special," she said.

I wanted her to go away. The money in my pocket already felt dirty enough. Suddenly her gummy smile and potbelly made me sick. I looked around at the empty street and saw my bus coming from several blocks away.

She stepped closer. I had to force myself not to push her away.

"Hey, back off," I said as she clutched my arm.

"A key," she said in a stage whisper, so that her warm, beery breath rose into my face.

"What?" My bus was a block away now, stopping at the light.

"Get a key," she whispered. "Three thousand dollars for a key to the house."

I did push her away then, roughly, so that she stumbled as she stepped back. I stood on the curb and held up my arm so that the bus wouldn't miss me. I didn't look at the BS woman, and I closed my ears to her entreaty, but I could still feel the heat of her hand on my arm. The bus seemed to take a lifetime to rumble over the sewer drain, shift gears, and make its way to me.

As I stood in the gutter, I could feel the half-formed scab on my hip, under the seam of my jeans. It was sore and itchy at the same time. I placed all my attention on that spot. The secret to making a good scar was not allowing the scab to heal. When I could, I would lift off the thin membrane and expose the under-layers of skin and flesh again. There would be a deep trough where the scab had been, where the tissue around it had begun to regenerate. Each time the scab was torn away, the scar would be better. It would be deep purple at first, and then it would fade to a slick, rubbery white that would stay with me forever.

The bus wheezed up to the corner, and its doors gasped open. I got on and sat on the other side, where I couldn't see her and she couldn't see me. Even so, as the bus pulled away and I ducked down in the seat, I could feel her eyes following me.

ANNE

I was raised in a tough family. We didn't piss and moan. We got busy. You played basketball when you were blue; you ran a couple of miles when you felt like you were coming down with something. You got up off your ass and didn't take it, whatever "it" was, sitting down. So keeping Francesca in the house went against my grain. It didn't seem to be doing her any good either; she had dark circles under her eyes and pasty skin. And instead of fading away, the crowd outside grew.

I came home after class late one Tuesday night, and to get to my front door, I had to walk through the clot of people who were always on my sidewalk. The front fence was littered with flowers and junk. Chester was not in his usual place. I hoped he was asleep somewhere. The strangers who had made themselves comfortable in front of my gate didn't see any need to move themselves to let me into my own home.

"I've been here every day for the last week," a small woman

with blond dreadlocks sitting with her back against the gate said to a large woman next to her.

"Maybe next week," said the large woman.

"Excuse me," I said, putting my hand on the gate. The woman who sat with her back against it looked through me.

"It's worth waiting for," the large woman said.

"Please move," I said, making my voice louder.

The woman with dreadlocks looked at me from under her heavy eyelids. She scooted forward a foot so that I could get the gate open, but not wide enough to get through. I was about to grab her under her scrawny arms and lift her away from the gate when Chester showed up.

"You know you can't hang out on the sidewalk," he said to them. "Go into the park."

The two women slowly climbed to their feet and moved off like cats caught with their paws in the fishbowl. From over her shoulder, the blonde with dreadlocks shot me a feral grin.

When I was at last in the house and had sent Rae home, I checked all the locks on the doors and windows. Then I paced the floors for hours, agitated and edgy. I peered out my windows from behind the curtains, afraid to be seen. It infuriated me that we were trapped in our own house, on display for the public like zoo animals.

I passed Francesca's room, where soft snoring sounds came through the door. Above me was the attic, where we kept suitcases and camping equipment among the boxes of old clothing and discarded toys from Francesca's childhood. The cord to the pull-down stairway hung in front of me. Everything we needed to survive in the wild was up there. I had freeze-dried food, down bags good enough for polar expeditions, compass, maps, water purifier, tent. Hell, it was my business, it was my work, to know how to stay alive far from civilization. It would be no problem for me to take her away.

I yanked the cord, and the stairs swung down. I climbed into the cold attic darkness, found the light, and began rummaging around. I tossed the sleeping bags and tent down into the hall-way. My camp stove, backpack, and all the rest went through the hole, too. I scrambled back down the stairs and folded them up into the ceiling, then moved all the gear downstairs to the front door. From the hall closet, I pulled out waterproof shells, hiking boots, snow boots, down coats and mittens, hats, and wool socks. October was a good time to camp, I reminded myself. It would be cold and clear and not crowded with tourists. Francesca needed to get out in the air and walk under the weight of a pack, sleep out under the stars. I had enough freeze-dried food for about ten days, if we ate lightly.

When I opened the front door, it was dead quiet outside. A melon-rind dawn was showing itself in the east. I stepped over a triangular design made of chrysanthemums and coneflowers. On my first trip to load the truck, Chester materialized.

"I'm getting her out of here," I said, tossing stuff into the truck and going back for more. Chester didn't say anything. But he stood by the unlocked truck and waited.

Upstairs, I went into Francesca's room. She was breathing slowly and deeply, the way she had when she was a baby. In her first few years, she sometimes slept so soundly that I had to wake her to reassure myself that she was still alive. Now I sat on the bed and stroked the hair off her forehead. Her face was like polished marble. She had the wise and sad expression that children wear when they sleep.

"Wake up, Francesca," I whispered.

The sullen teenager slowly returned to her face.

"No," she said into her pillow.

"Yes, come on," I said, and pulled back the blankets. "We're getting out of here."

She opened one eye. "You're crazy."

"Yep."

She opened the other eye and sat up, pulling at the Boston University T-shirt she slept in. I rifled through her drawers for jeans and sweaters and underwear. She sat on the bed and stared into space.

"What time is it?" she asked in a thin voice.

I looked at my watch. "Almost six. Let's drive a few hours and then have breakfast."

She made a face and fell back on her pillows.

"Francesca, get up," I said, exasperated.

She rolled out of bed and made it into her bathroom, all in one fluid movement, which I first took for sudden enthusiasm. She only half closed the bathroom door before she vomited loudly and copiously into the toilet.

I sat on the bed with her clothes on my lap. If I didn't know better, I would think this was morning sickness. I told myself to stop being paranoid. She'd never even had a real boyfriend. There had been those flowers left on the porch, but the boy never made an appearance. She hadn't ever had a date or, as far as I knew, even a first kiss. This couldn't be pregnancy. Not my Francesca.

"I don't feel good," she said in the strained voice that comes after violent retching. She got back into bed and pulled the blankets up to her chin. I put my lips against her forehead. She was a little warm. Her face was flushed.

"Sid says everybody at school has stomach flu," she said weakly.

I was sure my face showed my disappointment. "I don't suppose you want to spend the day in the truck and then backpack in about ten miles?"

I knew I was defeated. She ran into the bathroom and vomited again. I walked back out to the truck and unloaded our things.

CHESTER

Cristos and Briggs were there every day, along with Mary Lein and Lou and the others, telling anyone who would listen about the healings. I couldn't begrudge them the free meals and donations coming their way because of it. Joe, the three sisters, and a host of strangers came, too. And while they waited, they talked. They took every bit of grace that came and embroidered and exaggerated it, adding their own interpretation. I was growing sick of them.

It was early in the day, the quiet time. Most of the devotees didn't show up until later. There came a Canadian Jesuit, a young priest with the smell of bitter chocolate about him, named Greg Gervais. He didn't ask to see the Virgin; he just talked to me. At first I was suspicious: a priest who didn't wear priest clothes, who looked more like a rock climber, with two days' beard and expensive hiking shoes. I eyed him in a way that I hoped would let him know he didn't fool me.

"The church sent you to see if she's the real thing, didn't it?"

He scratched the side of his face and smiled into my eyes. Very cool, he was, and young. He looked about thirty-five, not one of the roly-poly fathers of my youth.

"The local bishop asked me to investigate. Right now I don't get to have an official opinion about whether this reporting is legitimate," he said. "That comes much later, and if things get to that point, a team is dispatched to determine authenticity. For now my job is simply to document what's occurring."

I liked that. His attitude was academic. He was neutral about the Virgin and everything surrounding her. He was smart and wasn't after her for anything. He was there because it was his job to go all around the world, wherever healings and visions of divine beings were reported. His detachment was a cool breeze through the clutter. I found myself wanting to know him, to be friends, a desire I hadn't had in years. He looked at the CNN truck parked across the street, blocking our view of the park.

"How long has that been there?" he asked.

"Three days now."

"And it's just you out here keeping things together?"

I nodded, glad for his sympathy. I had gone from elation at serving the Virgin to wariness of all the parasites that were attaching themselves to her. I wasn't tired of *her,* I was just tired. And things were escalating. It was getting colder, the media were getting edgy, and Rae was becoming a serious problem. Anne still didn't know the full extent of Francesca's involvement with the people outside, but I knew she couldn't be kept out of the loop much longer. I was uneasy about my part in the deception. I still felt my first loyalty was to the Virgin, but Anne was fair and kind to me, and I didn't want to mislead her. I felt it in my marrow that something was about to shift. A change was coming.

"Can you take a break?" Gervais asked. "Can I buy you breakfast?"

I considered. No one was on the street. Anne was in the house with the Virgin, and I was hungry. So we went to Ronnie's Café, a rarity for me on a weekday. We sat in a booth by the window and ordered huevos rancheros and coffee. My hips ached from standing at the gate, from sleeping on the ground. To sit in a warm place with food coming was good, and the ceiling seemed to be staying where it belonged.

He cut into the layers of tortilla and beans and egg with his knife and fork. I did the same. "You've been involved with Francesca Dunn since the beginning, haven't you?"

I stiffened and stuffed my mouth full of food. I liked this guy, but I didn't give interviews. I applied myself to the food.

"I'm sorry," Gervais said. I nodded and broke the egg yolks with the corner of my tortilla. Ronnie came out of the kitchen, drying her hands on her apron.

"Chester, Little John was found dead early this morning," she said, putting her hand on my shoulder. "I just heard. They said it was natural causes."

It caught me off guard. Nothing had seemed different on the street that morning. But then I'd been sleeping in Anne's yard. I didn't know what was going on downtown.

Natural causes. Little John died of natural causes. Was it *natural* for a man to be living in a wheelchair without roof or food or family? Was it *natural* for somebody who lived on the sidewalk in front of a hospital to have an untreated infection? And then I thought of the Virgin, and how she had refused to touch him.

Now the broken egg yolk turned my stomach. I scooted out of the booth, afraid I would be sick right there. I left the priest and Ronnie and the huevos rancheros and went out the back door into the alley. Sure that Ronnie would come after me, I forced myself to walk, trying to keep my stomach down. I didn't go back to my post at the Virgin's. I walked the alleys where people left their discards. The stench of their lives assaulted me. I caught whiffs of bad marriages, despair, and illness wafting out of the houses like dissonant notes. I tried to concentrate. I needed to think about Little John and what had happened. But all I could do was smell the hidden wreckage of lives I didn't care about and circulate three thoughts. One: He had asked for her blessing. Two: She had refused. And three: He had died. I didn't know what to make of it.

For the second time in recent weeks, I found myself at the mental-health center. This time I was able to find the doctor I had seen before.

"I want to clear my mind," I said. "I need to stop smelling everything." He nodded, perfectly happy to give me the drugs. But I wanted to argue with him, to make him listen.

"I can't protect her very well if I can't live in the world, can I? If I can't take care of myself? If I don't understand why one person dies on the street and another gets a healing? What good are my smells if they can't help me in this?"

He looked professionally concerned, but his eyes wandered to the door behind me, to a room full of people who were waiting to see him.

"Why don't you make an appointment to talk to a counselor?" he said. He handed me a small bottle with specific instructions to take a pill every day. He made me swear to take them regularly and to come back when I was down to the last five pills. I accepted the bottle and held it in my hand until I was outside again. Then I put it into the deepest pocket of my pack, knowing that I didn't yet have enough courage to open the bottle and swallow one down.

ANNE

I had started toying with the idea of getting on a plane with Francesca and going somewhere far away. But I was frozen, stuck in the headlights of what was running us down. Her stomach flu, if that's what it was, seemed better, but she said she didn't want to travel. Maybe it was the flu and maybe not. But I did wonder, when I let myself, about the possibility that she was pregnant. I couldn't imagine how or with whom, but stranger things had happened in this world. I knew that it was far more likely she was simply knocked up than that she was, as the tabloids said, a holy virgin about to give birth to a messiah. That was a hysterical fantasy concocted by ignorant fools. But I was afraid to talk to her about either notion.

We were putting in long hours at work. The entire Hell Creek exhibit was spread out on every available surface in the collection room, to enable us to fit the new findings into the previous classifications. London's job was to unwrap the new specimens, assign a museum number, and record it in the field notebook. Seth was using a rock trimmer clamped to a table to slice larger rocks into smaller sections. Rocks of all sizes, in all stages of processing, sat around the room next to half-eaten hamburgers and stale fries. Since falling for Hayden, London, who had been an adamant vegetarian, couldn't get enough burgers.

"Hey, why don't you have some of the 'dee-vo-*tees*' come in and help us get this stuff organized?" Hayden said. He was using the air scribe, a pen-size, carbide-tipped jackhammer, to clean the rock away from a fossil he held in his hand. London laughed a little too quickly. Since Hell Creek, she laughed at all his jokes.

"Give it a rest, Hayden," Seth said, breaking open a large chunk of shale and examining the contents closely. "Wow. This is different," he said.

"What have you got there?" I said, going over to take a look.

"I don't know. Looks kind of like magnolia."

"Probably liriodendron," I said, looking at the double lobes of the fossil leaf. "Only it's not quite like the living plant."

Hayden couldn't resist a possible new species. He put down the air scribe, and the air compressor sighed as he came to peer over my shoulder.

"Look, there's an attachment." Hayden pointed to an unmistakable section of stem and a tiny scrap of what may have been flower. Probably half of what we found at Hell Creek were undescribed or new species, but rarely did we find more than a leaf form. To find leaf, stem, and flower in one fossil was a real discovery. If we could prove that it was unknown, and that was far easier with flower and stem attached, we could describe, name, and publish it. As a doctoral candidate, Hayden wanted to publish as much as possible under his own name, and he had become pushy about it. As a master's candidate, Seth could publish, too, but he didn't have Hayden's drive to put his mark on every new species we found. Being an undergraduate intern, London didn't have any claim at all.

"I saw the attachment," Hayden said. "So it's mine."

I shook my head. "It will 'belong' to whoever does the research," I reminded him. "If you spend the next several months reading all the literature to make sure it isn't already described and then correctly place it in the nomenclature, you can publish it. If Seth does the work, he will."

"Take a Polaroid of it," I said to Seth. "Then look for more from the same location."

Hayden pulled his goggles over his eyes and went grumbling back to his air scribe. "Then put the '*dee*-sciples' on the grunt work to classify it," he said. "We can set them up in the library. What do you say, Anne?"

He and London laughed. I tried to laugh with them. It wouldn't do to get stiff and self-righteous. He was just kidding around.

"At the very least, you should get them to clean your truck for you. That truck of yours is a disgrace."

"I could use a few disciples myself," London said, looking coy.

"I'll be your disciple," Hayden said, kneeling before her and mugging through the safety goggles. "I'll be your love slave."

"That's enough, you two," I said. "Get back to work."

Hayden shuffled across the floor on his knees and prayed up to me. "Have I displeased you, O Guru?"

"Back off, Hayden," Seth said. Hayden quietly gave Seth the finger, something he did several times a day, and Seth didn't seem to take it personally. But a few hours later, when we were locking up to go, Hayden found me in my office.

"Sorry," he mumbled.

I nodded. Hayden had been on my team for almost a year. He was an asshole, but he was a good research assistant. I knew he didn't mean any harm; he just liked to tease. I put on my coat.

"If you don't mind my saying so, you're stressed out," he said. "Look how tight your shoulders are."

"You don't have to tell me," I said, rolling my head on my sore neck.

"If you need anything, let me know." He fixed me with a meaningful stare, and I realized he was making an offer.

I snorted. "What, do you mean, drugs or something?"

He shrugged. "You can't tell me you're sleeping, Anne. No offense, but you've got some serious bags under your eyes."

He pulled a small, unmarked bottle out of his jeans pocket and handed it to me. There were five or six yellow pills in it.

"I don't think so," I said, holding it out for him to take back.

"Look, I'm not giving you ecstasy or acid or anything. Just good old Valium. It's exactly what the doctor would give you."

I gazed at the pills. I'd smoked pot. I'd eaten psilocybin mushrooms and prehistoric ginkgo, but I'd never taken pharmaceuticals. Valium conjured images of 1950s housewives popping "mother's little helper" to make it through their dishwater days. Still, I hadn't slept a full night in weeks. I pocketed the pills.

"Thanks. I'll keep them just in case," I said on my way out the door.

*A*t home later, at about ten o'clock, restless and worried, I wrapped myself in an afghan and went outside to smoke my daily cigarette. My best times of the day were out there in the dark, in the fresh air, where I could think. Chester was perched on the edge of the deck, rocking back and forth. He had caught on to my smoking habits and was often there when I went out. As usual, he didn't look at me directly. The sound of people singing in the park across the street came to us on the breeze.

"What do they think they're going to get out of this?" I said grumpily. It was really a rhetorical question, but his lips moved as he prepared to speak.

"They want enlightenment."

I snorted. "And what's that, Chester? Some sort of watered-down Buddhism? Next you're going to tell me it's karma."

"It's what they want. It's what we all want. We all want to become gods."

It was an interesting point. We human beings had evolved our monkey bodies about as far as they would go. In the last several millennia, the real action had been in the brain. We were evolving chemically, neurologically, with each generation. But I was hard-pressed to say whether we were going forward or backward. It was like the Galápagos finches: Darwin first saw natural selection in that isolated population, but in recent years scientists had discovered that it wasn't entirely a forward-moving process. The finches would select for drought in one generation, causing the longer-beaked animals with the smaller, lighter bodies to survive, reproduce, and pass on their genes. A year or two later, they would select for an extremely rainy year, and the larger, shorter-beaked animals would survive, reproduce, and pass on *their* genes. Human evolution had the same kind of swing. The ability to survive might require physical prowess and courage during wartime. Then, a generation later, it needed the ability to maneuver and survive in an economically controlled environment where mental dexterity and intimidation ruled.

"But people don't become gods," I said.

"No? We create. We manipulate our world to suit ourselves and enjoy the fruits of it."

I inhaled the harsh smoke. It felt good to feel my lungs from the inside, even though I knew that my body didn't like the assault. "Is that what you think God does?"

"Yes, I do. A few of us have achieved divinity, but the rest of us are watching, and if we're smart, we'll learn how."

"Divinity?" I said. "What is that?"

He dipped his head to the right, and his eyes squinted in that particular way that meant he was going to explain something. Not for the first time, I wondered if Chester had been a teacher of some sort before he started living on the street.

"You know, there is a tradition. Holy ones are discovered before they know they are holy. Lamas in Tibet. Hindu and Christian saints. The story of Jesus. In each case someone finds them as children; there are signs, like a virgin birth. Did you know that Pythagoras and Plato were both believed to have been born of a woman but fathered by spirit? Mary didn't think of herself as holy. The angel had to come to her and tell her she was with child."

"But that's just it. Francesca isn't 'with child.'"

He looked at me as if I were demented.

"She isn't," I said, but inside I was already crumbling.

He ducked his head to the left as if to say, If you say so, but you're wrong.

I tried to seem sure. "She's not. I know she's not."

He held his silence for another minute. When he spoke, the words were suspended in the cold air along with his breath.

"Do you?"

Now I had nothing to say. A metallic ache took hold. Abruptly I got up and went inside, shutting the door behind me, reestablishing a barrier of civilization between Chester and me. I told myself he was wrong, but the dread was there, and it wouldn't go away. This had nothing to do with holiness or evolution or any of our heady talk. It was a normal, everyday mother's dread, the dread that my daughter might be pregnant. I had all the usual thoughts: How can you know what they're doing every minute? How can you be sure they have taken your warnings seriously? And even: How could she do this to me? All the strange happenings of the last few weeks aside, it was possible that Francesca could be very humanly pregnant.

I ran up the stairs and knocked on her door.

She was on her bed, surrounded by notebooks and papers, leaning on her elbows so that her hair made dark pools on her work. The face she turned up to me was distinctly guilty. I knew that face; it was the same one she wore when she got caught faking a sore throat in the third grade.

"Francesca, do you think you're pregnant?"

She didn't protest, didn't answer, didn't move. I sat down next to her.

"For God's sake, how far along are you?"

She shook her head and looked as though she might cry, but I was too furious with her to feel any pity.

"I don't know," she said.

I felt like hitting her, something I'd never done, something neither Peter nor I believed in. We'd actually talked about this moment once or twice when Francesca was little and how we would be sane and supportive if our daughter made such a mistake, at the same time reassuring ourselves that our excellent parenting would insulate her from it. And now I was behaving like an ignorant, shotgun-wedding sort of person, and I couldn't stop.

"I didn't even know you had a boyfriend. Was it the boy who left the flowers on the porch? Why didn't you bring him home? When did it happen? You must have some idea."

She looked as if I'd called her a whore. "It might have been this summer at the beach," she said finally.

Well. I sat back and wrapped my arms around myself. It made sense. Peter wouldn't have been paying enough attention to know anything about it. It could have happened as easily as wishing.

"So there was a boy?" I asked stupidly.

She nodded, staring down at her hands.

"Are you in love with him? Are you communicating with him?"

She shook her head no.

"Is there someone you're seeing here? Someone else?"

"No." Her lips trembled, and tears began to run down her face.

I couldn't think of anything else to ask. I closed my eyes and quickly added up the months. She had been in California with Peter and Stacey in July. August, September, and this was October. About three months. Maybe not too late to get an abortion. From outside, the police searchlight passed over the window shade, which glowed white and went dark again.

"I didn't know how to tell you," Francesca said. "Everything's been so strange."

The jagged corners of my heart softened, and I wanted to rock her in my arms. A pregnancy at fourteen was something we could take care of. It was in the category of unfortunate, but certainly not bizarre or unusual, events. I reached out to touch her hand, expecting rejection, but she let me hold it. So I gathered her to me and whispered into her hair.

"It's okay," I said. I was suddenly willing to do anything to help her through this. *This* I could handle. "I'll take care of it. Don't worry." I stroked her hair and thought of all the women of the last century, fighting so that my daughter could have an abortion without ruining her life.

"I'm tired," Francesca said, her head on my shoulder.

I kissed her. "It's late. Go to bed. We'll talk about it tomorrow."

I got up and helped her put her books away. She wiped her tears with the back of her hand and went into her bathroom. I realized, looking at the door between us, that she wasn't my little girl any longer. She was a woman, in the fullest sense of the word. Knowing it made me feel hollow inside.

I went to my own room. My mind raced over the problem of arranging an abortion. My gynecologist, Cecilia Barrett, was pro-choice. We'd been friends for fifteen years. In spite of the late hour, I called her at home.

"Could you see her tomorrow?" I asked.

"No problem," she said. "Come in at noon."

"And Cecilia, can you make sure that this doesn't get out?"

"Her name won't be on the schedule, and no one but my nurse will know. How's that?"

I hung up and wandered around the house, doing my ritual door and window check. Not feeling sleepy, I climbed into bed anyway and turned out the light. My mind chewed at the thought of Francesca's pregnancy. I couldn't imagine it. She hadn't even started dating. She didn't talk about boys at school. I had no warning that this would happen. Light flooded the window shade for a moment. I was wide awake and once again aware that we were under siege. I sat up and rummaged in my bag for Hayden's bottle of Valium. I was desperate for sleep, so I swallowed one. I needed to be rested for tomorrow, because tomorrow Cecilia Barrett would root out the cause of our troubles. I put my head on the pillow, and while I waited for the pill to take effect, I thought of Chester, saying that people really want to become gods. I shook my head. Being a mortal mother had brought more responsibility than I'd ever thought possible. How much more would there be for a god?

FRANCESCA

In her room Francesca prepares for the hour when, for the first time, she will go out to meet her assembled following. She washes her face with cold water to rinse away any evidence of crying. She tries to breathe deeply. It has finally happened. Her mother has confronted her about the baby. Anne still doesn't get who the baby is. She doesn't grasp the connection between the baby and all the strange events that have been taking place. But she has figured out that Francesca is pregnant, and tomorrow she will press her to get an abortion.

Francesca knows she must shut the conversation with her mother out of her mind. She knows that there will be no abortion. Of that she is absolutely sure. The contents of her womb will be protected. She doesn't know *how* the baby will be protected, but somehow it will be all right. Tonight is the meeting that Rae has arranged in a church outside of town, and Francesca must be ready. She has been simultaneously aware of the preparations and also not aware, the way a pampered bride knows of

the machinery behind the upcoming wedding but remains bliss-
fully ignorant of the details. Word of her public appearance has
been spreading quietly through the network of people who seek.
She knows that followers are coming from as far away as
England. The only one who doesn't have a clue about tonight's
gathering is her mother. Rae says that Anne has been indulging
in her own denial, avoiding the knowledge that her daughter is
"who she is." Rae says it's better not to tell Anne more than she's
ready to hear.

Francesca waits and fidgets. She walks over to the cello that
has been facing the wall and takes it out of the case. She sits with
the instrument between her knees, but she doesn't play. An
itchy, irritated feeling travels through her, and she knows she
wouldn't be able to play if she tried. Her concentration goes to
her hard, slightly distended belly. She listens to her womb from
the inside, still holding the cello between her knees, straining to
hear the child whisper through her bones and blood. She understands that the cello is one of the things that has been denied her
in exchange for the power she now carries. She has come to
accept the trade-off, to embrace it even.

At the designated time, she gets up and opens the window.
The cold wind on her face invigorates her; it feels welcome after
the oppressive heat of the house. The first kernels of snow hit the
roof as she pulls on a thick sweater and eases out through the
window. In the western sky, an eyelash moon hangs in a silver
cocoon. The snow spits at her now, as she crawls along the splin-
tery incline. When she reaches the edge, where the fence and the
house meet below, she lets herself down, using the gutter pipe,
until her feet find the top rail. She jumps, landing in the front

yard. The cold, which had been bracing at first, now bites through her sweater. She wraps her arms around her chest.

It seems a long time that she stands in the falling snow. Her hair and shoulders grow thick with it, and she can see it on her lashes when she blinks. She wonders for a minute if she will be found here in the morning, frozen and covered with snow. Then Chester's bulk emerges from around the side of the house and Rae's old beater of a car comes around the corner and a door opens for them. Sid slides over to the middle of the front seat, making room. Rae turns up the rattling heater and reaches around Sid to brush the snow off Francesca. Chester takes his place in back. The car moves down the snowy street. Francesca glances back at Ronnie's house, where Jonah and Ronnie are sleeping, and at her own darkened house, too.

The drive out north of town is quiet, as if their very thoughts are muffled by the snow that begins to hurl itself into the windshield. The wipers brush away the accumulation over and over again. The headlights illuminate only far enough ahead for her to see the hood of the car, but Rae drives as if she can see a mile down the road.

Eventually they turn off into a field where cars and trucks and media vans are parked. In the distance, fuzzed by the snow, she can make out the bright lights of the press, the clapboard church, and two glowing white tents, hovering next to it like spaceships.

Rae throws a blanket from the backseat around Francesca's shoulders and the four of them, bent against the snow, which is falling faster now, make their way to the church. Francesca is aware of people lined up on either side, watching her as she passes by. There are lights and microphones and cameras. Rae leads her, speaking for her, telling them to give her room. Rae seems to know several members of the press as well as the devotees, and she greets them softly as she keeps one arm around Francesca and guides her through. Francesca holds the blanket together with one hand under her chin, and with the other she touches hands that reach out to her. The press and the devotees and the simply curious murmur collectively as she walks by. Ahead, the church doors open in a swirl of snow, and she is led into a warm, steaming room packed with people. A small platform has been erected in front of the altar, and a large pillow waits. Her hair is soaked, and so is her sweater. Rae places a dry, soft cloak around her and helps her sit on the pillow.

She observes her devotees through incense smoke and candle heat, over vases of flowers and other offerings. They sit, respectful and rapt. Their faces, like a field of flowers in the sun, are turned toward her. There are no pews in this church; instead the people sit on cushions and blankets on the floor. A few have brought folding chairs. Some pray, and some are meditating. Some have pictures of Jesus or Mary or of various Hindu saints. And then she sees that several have *her* picture, the one that the boy took on the beach last summer. For a second it is warm, and she can taste the salt on her lips and see him holding her camera. Then it's as if the sound has been turned off. Her ears seem to shut down. The photo absorbs all the sound in the room. In it she is blushing and smiling, wanting him to like her, and the light is in her eyes, and her hair is whipping around her face in snaky ropes. It doesn't belong here. She can't imagine how they got it. She looks at Rae, who is talking with some people to the side. Chester is watching her from his place by the door with an attentive, worried expression. She looks for Sid and can't find her. She thinks of her mother, oblivious, sleeping at home in her bed.

A cold dread comes over her. She can't for a moment remember why she is sitting here, facing these people. Why do they have pictures of her, and what do they want?

And then they begin to sing. Their mouths open simultaneously, and the sound pops back on. They sing "Amazing Grace," and a hundred harmonies weave in and out of the melody. Male and female voices sing. And Rae is next to her, holding her hand and patting her back.

Rae says, "This is what you were born to do."

She sees families, some with small children, couples holding on to each other, people with shaved heads and pierced body parts, people in expensive clothing and some in rags. She recognizes several familiar faces from Ronnie's Café. She feels herself come into focus in their eyes. She is surprised at the gratitude that wells up in her and pushes tears out of her eyes. She watches them, and they watch her, and it is incomparably beautiful.

"Mother, bless us," a woman in front says. And time becomes a strange new substance that she negotiates with ease.

CHESTER

The temperature had to be close to zero, because the hairs in my nose were frozen. The prairie around the church was flooded with media light, and snakes of diesel exhaust and sulfur fumes writhed on the ground. The hot lights plus scores of feet had churned the frozen dirt into a slick ooze. Rae had said that this was going to be a small, intimate group, but the press was everywhere. The one or two cameras and reporters from the house had grown into this snarl of equipment and bodies, and the scene had a new, pushy edge to it. When the sheriff approached us, I distinctly heard Rae say she was Francesca's mother.

My first thought, after security for the Virgin, was for Anne. She would see this tomorrow on TV, and she would know. She would blame me. And why shouldn't she? I was the Virgin's self-appointed protector, yet here I was, letting her be the center of this debacle. I could already see the look of betrayal on Anne's face.

It was all wrong. It was supposed to be a private meeting for the people who had been keeping vigil for the Virgin. It was supposed to be a chance for them to see her and talk with her. But somehow it had been whipped into this mud-slick news event. And I knew who had done the whipping, too. It was Rae. No one else would do it. There she was, standing next to the platform, talking urgently to a stranger and keeping her eye on her prize, the Virgin. From the beginning I had mistrusted Rae. Her rank smell told me all about her dishonesty, but the Virgin and Ronnie and even Anne seemed to trust her. Against my better judgment, I had let Rae take control.

This wasn't what I had envisioned that night when the Virgin first came to me. This wasn't what was called for. I had seen a quiet and reverent greeting for the new savior. I had thought her presence among us would soothe the modern heart, but I was wrong. Rae left the platform and made her way over to me. I averted my face from her cloying, pruny smell.

"I think things are okay in here, Chester, so maybe you should stay outside and keep too many from coming in at once."

I was relieved to get away from her and out of the church, out from under that roof. Outside, there were many more who wanted in. With the press and Rae's publicity, the church wasn't big enough. Journalists stood around, cold and bitching. It was a mess. It made my heart sick.

I listened to the singing inside. It sounded gentle enough. Half of my attention was inside the church with the Virgin, and the other half was on a reporter who kept trying to get past me, when I saw a group of five men in combat fatigues and military gear come into the light from the west. They carried a wooden cross as tall as a man, wrapped like a young fruit tree.

"We are now in the end times," announced their leader, a serious redheaded man with huge forearms, who spoke angrily and loudly.

The crowd shifted uneasily, and those nearest these men moved off, but the same cell-phone conversations and complaints about the weather continued a few feet away.

"Behold, the Antichrist will soon be loosed upon the world," the redhead shouted at no one in particular. He directed his men to plant the cross in the mud. The police were paying attention, but I knew they couldn't do anything. Here were five people, presumably exercising their rights of assembly and association just like everybody else. They carried no weapons that I could see. The cross wasn't burning. I supposed they weren't breaking any law, but they had a threatening air, there was no denying it.

"The Aryan peoples will prevail, and all others shall perish," yelled the leader. He was answered by a few hisses and boos from the crowd, which was now paying attention.

The soldiers assumed the military "at ease" stance with their hands clasped behind their backs, eyes straight ahead, and legs apart. They were the picture of lidded aggression. TV cameras moved in closer, and crews trained their lights on the line of men.

The leader stepped forward and gestured to a young female TV reporter to come closer. In front of the cross, he began to recite from the Bible. The reporter held the microphone for him.

The leader's forehead furrowed into deep lines of concentration as he delivered his message at the top of his lungs.

"Behold, the Lord will lay waste the earth and make it desolate, and He will twist its surface and scatter its inhabitants. The earth lies polluted under its inhabitants. Therefore, a curse devours the earth, and its inhabitants suffer for their guilt; therefore the inhabitants of the earth are scorched, and few men are left."

Abruptly, before anyone could stop them, one of the other men pulled out a lighter and lit the cloth on the cross. It must have been soaked in chemicals, because the thing went up in a near explosion. Everybody jumped back, tangling in the equipment. In the chaos the five men stepped out of the bright lights and disappeared into the swirling snow, leaving the burning cross where it was.

The sheriff and policemen knocked the cross to the ground and stamped it out, but the damage had been done. Those hoping to get inside the church began to look panicky. Talk turned to suspicion and fear. Many decided to go home.

I didn't know what to do. I had done my best to protect her, but I must have been doing something wrong for it to go like this. I scanned the faces, some cynical, some greedy, some in genuine need. One face stopped me, the familiar, calm face of Greg Gervais, the Jesuit. He made his way through the crowd and took my arm.

"Things are heating up, aren't they?" he said. "Is Francesca all right?"

I winced. "It shouldn't be like this," I said. I felt weak,

unable to stand between her and all that waited out here. I could feel the whirl and roar of danger, growing and gathering force.

I pulled Gervais to me, gripping his hand. I was desperate. I had to stop what I had begun.

"Get the mother. Her name is Anne. Go wake her up and bring her here."

He took in what I was saying. Without another word he moved quickly toward the parked cars.

SID

I didn't see the BS woman at Grace Lutheran, so I worked the crowd myself. The stupid people freezing their asses to get a glimpse of Francesca were ready to buy anything. And I just happened to have a shitload of stuff they wanted. So I raked it in. Being careful to stay out of Chester's sight, I sold four T-shirts for thirty bucks a pop, a dozen locks of hair and fifteen prints of the beach picture for twenty-five each, and a bunch of handwriting samples, which were actually cut from the first draft of her term paper on *Lord of the Flies,* for fifteen each. I accepted only cash, and soon my pockets were full. I worked quietly, keeping an eye out for old BS, because she was going to show up eventually, and I knew she'd be pissed that I was selling directly.

By the time I caught sight of her, I had pretty much sold out anyway. She moved through the crowd, hawking her stuff for more than I had, and still people bought. She didn't see me. To be on the safe side, I moseyed up to Chester all innocent, and he let me into the church. I stood just inside the door, stamping my frozen feet to get the feeling back into my toes.

The place reeked of incense and wet bodies. I saw a lot of copies of the beach picture. Francesca must have seen them, too. I had a moment of guilt thinking she would figure out that I had taken the picture from her mom's box. But then I had to laugh. My little scam was nothing compared to Rae's. And there was Francesca herself, pretending to be the Mother of God. I mean, who was doing who? Watching her being the "purest of the pure" took away any bad feelings I had for selling a few pictures. I fidgeted and fingered the bills in my pockets, mentally trying to add them up, while she sat there entertaining the suckers. My toes started to thaw and burn.

She was talking to a girl maybe five years old and her mother. The kid looked like a dried apricot, all yellow and wrinkled, with no hair except some wispy fuzz on her head. Francesca patted her lap, and the girl climbed into it and settled among the flowers. She stroked the girl's cheek and bent her head to whisper something. The kid smiled and closed her lashless eyes. The mother stood back and watched, her face twitching into a sad smile. The little girl climbed back out of Francesca's lap and gave her a single rose. It was a rosebud, really, wrapped so tight that it looked as if it was hugging itself from the cold. I'd seen those in the grocery store, going cheap because none of them ever opened. Those roses were a scam, too, as long as we're talking about scams.

Francesca held the rose and twirled it. She brushed its tight little head against her lips. She motioned the next case to come closer. An older woman with silver hair stepped up. She and Francesca spoke for a few minutes, Francesca twirling the rose the entire time. When the old lady was done, Francesca beckoned to the sick girl again. She held out the flower. I almost didn't pay any attention to it, because the next person in line was this dude with the fattest ass I'd ever seen, and I couldn't wait to see him sit down on the platform. But I looked from the fat guy back to Francesca just in time to see the girl take the rose with her skinny yellow hand.

I blinked and looked again.

No way would I have believed it except that I saw it with my own eyes. That nasty supermarket rose, dried up, never to bloom, forever a bud, was now lush and pink and firm on its stem. And somehow perfectly full-blown.

ANNE

Someone was pounding on the door at 2:00 A.M. I opened it, still deranged by the rare sleep I had been enjoying, thanks to Hayden's Valium, and stared dumbly at the stranger on my front porch.

"I'm Greg Gervais. Chester sent me. He's with your daughter, and he wants you to come immediately." He handed me his card, which I couldn't make out with my Valium-hazed eyes.

I took in the man's lean, unfamiliar face, his SUV running at the curb, the fine, tight snow pelting through the high beams, and slowly realized that he wanted me to go with him. Something about Francesca.

"But she's upstairs asleep," I said, trying to clear my brain.

Gervais cast his eyes down the way I'd always imagined people did when they were going to tell you that your child was dead or that she'd been in a terrible accident and wouldn't walk again.

"I'm afraid not."

Panic bit through the drug, and I was at last fully awake. I left him standing at the door and took the stairs two at a time. I saw for myself that her bed was empty, the window stood open. My knees went weak. She had purposely deceived me. She had climbed out her window after admitting to me that she was pregnant. And now anything might have happened, and this man Gervais had been sent by Chester to fetch me. I raced to my room and pulled on a pair of jeans over my pajamas, shoving the man's card in my front pocket. Downstairs I stepped into my boots and threw on a parka.

"Is she all right?" I said, running past him. I was in the passenger side of his vehicle before he could close my front door.

"She's not hurt," he said, getting into the driver's side. "Though I believe she may be in danger. She's at Grace Lutheran church outside of town. There's a large gathering there."

I put my head in my hands. "I don't believe this," I said.

He put the SUV in gear and drove, not bothering to stop at the stop sign at the corner. The road north was icy and the visibility poor, but Gervais was a good driver, and he didn't waste time.

"Why did Chester send you?"

"I suppose because he trusts me. I'm here as a representative of the Catholic Church. I'm a priest. But I don't want anything from your daughter."

I stared. His face was smooth, and his jaw was strong. Even in my panic and confusion I saw that he was handsome by most standards. I could almost hear Peter writing him off, saying, "Cheap good looks."

Gervais kept his eyes on the road. "You see, the church doesn't ever simply endorse a reported miracle or a sighting. Our position is to exhaust all other explanations before we consider anything miraculous. We usually find rational reasons for these things."

I marveled that, for the first time in my life, I was on the same side as the Catholic Church, and the irony of having such an ally wasn't lost on me. I wondered what Greg Gervais would think if he knew that I had Francesca scheduled for an abortion the next day.

"While I was making my report, I became worried about your daughter. Does she have anyone she can talk to? I don't mean a priest, necessarily. But maybe a doctor or a school counselor?"

He was disarming. In spite of his cheap good looks, he seemed kind and straightforward and open-minded.

I said, "I'm taking her to the doctor tomorrow. And I've been thinking about a shrink."

"That's good," he said. "Don't underestimate the damage that's possible."

"But that's just it. Until tonight I thought that this was going on *around* us and that keeping her away from them was enough. That's what I was told to do. I didn't think she was going along with them. I didn't think she was having any contact with them. I had no idea."

He nodded and turned the windshield wipers on high. Even so, the snow built up on the glass between each swipe.

My mouth went dry before I asked, "How involved is she?"

He brushed his nose with the thumb of his glove, hesitating.

"Just say it."

He glanced across the width of the car at me, sizing me up. "It's bad," he said gently. "It seems to me that she believes what they're saying about her. She's trying to be what they want her to be."

I could feel my panic rising. Breathing in and out was becoming terribly difficult. "Thanks for telling me," I finally said, and I meant it. Out of all the people involved with this crazy mess, I knew that he alone was telling me the truth.

We pulled into a field next to the old Grace Lutheran, a church that had closed its doors in the eighties and remained vacant ever since. Light poured from the windows of the small building, and floodlights crisscrossed the area outside. The crowd was several times bigger than anything we'd seen at the house. Gervais broke a path for me through the throng at the door, where I found myself face-to-face with Chester. I was furious.

"I didn't know it would be like this," he said, his eyes imploring me to forgive him.

"Let me in, Chester." I didn't want to talk to him. I didn't even want to see him. Obviously he'd known about this farce in advance, but as mad as I was, I knew that he wasn't capable of planning this. I clenched my teeth and pushed past him, ready to yank Francesca out of there and take down anyone who got in my way.

The place was packed with steaming heaps of people, sitting on the floor in their coats or wrapped in blankets. It was slightly warmer inside, but their collective breath was still visible in the air. The focus of their rapt attention, at the far end of the room on a makeshift dais, was my daughter, wreathed in flowers. The sight of her stopped me in my tracks. She had something dark and velvety draped over her shoulders. Her hair rippled down the soft folds of it, giving her the look of a medieval queen. Her face was stark white, her eyes were black and glittering. It reminded me of the way she had looked with scarlet fever when she was five years old. She had the same feverish stare. Rae stood behind her, directing the stream of supplicants and casting a watchful eye over the crowd. I knew I had found my organizer. Rae had engineered all of this.

Francesca's eyes passed over me as I tried to make my way toward her. Calmly, eerily, she acknowledged me with a nod and then returned to the woman kneeling at her feet. The woman could have been anybody, a clerk in a bank or a bookstore. She was middle-class, middle-aged, and kneeling awkwardly in a straight skirt and nylons. Francesca had her hand on the woman's head and leaned over to whisper something in her ear.

I moved forward, as if in a bad dream. The bodies in front of me didn't yield when I tried to push past them. My legs felt hobbled. A sweat broke out on my forehead and palms. I was still having trouble breathing. I saw, in the hands of some of the people, a picture of Francesca from last summer. The negative and print were at home in the box under my bed. Or so I'd thought.

"Excuse me," I said to a man in front of me. "Where did you get that picture?"

He jutted his chin in the direction of the door. "She's selling them outside." I followed his gaze and saw a familiar coat, familiar dirty-blond hair. My heart sank to see Sid, and then my anger flared again. She had gone through my things and taken this picture, made copies of it, and now she was making money off it. And there was Rae, standing behind Francesca. Of course, she could have stolen the photo just as easily as Sid. It didn't really matter which one had taken it. They'd both lied to me. Both of them had hurt Francesca. I stared at Rae until her eyes found me. I saw the shock of seeing me go through her. I held her gaze, refusing to look away first. I wanted her to see that I knew everything. I wanted her to see that I despised her.

I thought I would have to drag Francesca off her little throne, make a scene to get her out, but when I had finally battled my way to her, she stood up, stepped down from the platform, and brushed past me. Rae hurried in her wake. Francesca moved steadily and quickly through the outstretched hands, working the room like a politician. My shy, awkward, teenage daughter was behaving as if she'd been raised to be a queen, accepting their adulation as though it were her due. I was left to follow the procession. Chester and Gervais closed in behind me.

"You're coming with us," I said to Sid, who seemed to pale at the sight of me. I was angry at her but determined to take her home. Outside, I pulled Francesca away from Rae. "Get lost," I hissed into her face.

Rae flinched and stepped back as if I'd hit her. Her hair was thick with white snow, which, by contrast, made her skin and teeth a sallow yellow. She stood there and gaped. When she saw that I wasn't going to back down and Francesca wasn't going to speak, she turned on her heel in the mud, and a pack of TV journalists swarmed around her. With Chester and Gervais pressing back the mob, I opened the door to Gervais's car, and Francesca climbed in. She didn't resist me at all but went strangely placid and pliable. My confidence wobbled. She was beyond me, and I had lost any way to approach her. Nothing I knew about my child and nothing I knew about being her mother applied here. Francesca offered me no explanation. I could see she believed the illusion they were spinning. It wasn't a farce to her anymore. And that's what scared me the most.

Sid ran around to the other side and got in. I sat in back with them, my arm around Francesca, holding on to my child as if she might bolt out of the speeding car. Chester sat in the front passenger seat, and I watched the snow melt in his matted hair. Gervais drove, talking softly to him all the way. I couldn't make out the words, but his voice calmed me, and somehow we got Sid home, and then we were home ourselves.

Later I sat by Francesca as she slept through what was left of the night. She slept the way she had as a small child, mouth open, face wide and innocent. The color had come back into her cheeks. I watched the smooth transfer of air, in and out of her body. I pressed my hands to my eyes and forced myself to think. I reminded myself that I was a capable person with a brain that routinely sorted out difficult problems and dispatched them. I was a scientist, which meant that I was supposed to possess more reasoning skills than most. One thing was sure: I needed to get her some help. And I needed some help for myself. This collective obsession was caving in on us, and I had to dig us out, but I didn't know how.

I crept back to my own room and dragged the box of photos from under the bed. I knew the beach photo wouldn't be there, but I had to go through the motions of looking for it. When I was sure it was gone, I picked up the phone and punched in the long combination to Rome. It was time to tell Peter. I couldn't handle this alone. He was her father; he should know about it and help me.

I heard the foreign rings echo all the way from Italy. I would simply tell him he had to come home. Francesca listened to him more than she did to me. Maybe he could get through to her. With luck he could be here in a day. But the deep buzzing rings kept sounding in my ear, and I realized that he wasn't home. There wasn't even an answering machine. I could E-mail, but, knowing Peter, he might not look at it for days. I tried to remember how people contacted each other in emergencies aside from the telephone. It came to me that people still sent telegrams. No one would ignore a telegram. I got a pad of paper and pencil and attempted to compose a message that would sound relatively sane. I tried, "Daughter is leader of religious cult. Come home now." Or "Francesca in huge mess, Pls come." I finally settled on, "Dire situation Francesca. You must come home. A."

He would be frantic at the word "dire," imagining her in a hospital bed or lost in the wilderness somewhere. But nothing he could imagine would come close to this. Pregnant and insane was plenty dire.

Francesca slept on. Daylight broke, and still she slept. Good. She would need her strength for what this day would bring. In the fragile light of dawn, I went downstairs and tried to spend my rage. I scoured the sink and mopped the floor. I wiped old dust from the grate on the front of the refrigerator. I took the stove apart and soaked the parts in sudsy water. I vacuumed, sucking crumbs and hair and fuzz from the cracks in the uphol-stery, and my anger narrowed itself into a fine point aimed directly at Rae. I had trusted her with my daughter's safety while I was at work. She had come into my house all those weeks and accepted the pay I gave her, and the whole time she'd been misleading me and fanning the flames of some undetected emotional weakness in Francesca.

And I was furious with Ronnie. She must have known that her sister was one of "them." For the second time, Ronnie had withheld the truth from me, thereby exacerbating the situation. I thought about the two sisters as children in New Jersey. Ronnie had told me that she and Rae had been everything to each other. Their mother had died of polio when Ronnie was ten, and their father had run off, so they were raised by a grandmother. Ronnie didn't talk about it much, but she let me know that their childhoods were bad. Still, there was no excuse for what they had caused, one by design, the other by trying to please.

I worked as the light climbed the walls. Francesca slept. At ten o'clock I opened the back door to shake out a rug, and there was Chester, sitting in twelve inches of snow, humped over in his place on the edge of the deck. The snow had soaked dark stains on his coat and hat. I realized with a start that I hadn't thought about Chester since Gervais had dropped us off. As always, my feelings about him were jumbled. He was part of the madness. He had started this thing, and now it had grown too big and scary for him. I felt a mix of protectiveness and irritation toward him. He was smart. He and I had managed to have some real conversations on this back porch. Homeless and crazy as he was, he had always shown a kind of integrity. He was absolutely true to his belief. And he was intelligent enough to alter that belief according to new data. I had seen him growing concerned about Francesca's predicament. Ultimately he had seen the wrong at the church and sent for me, and for that I was grateful.

The face he turned to me that morning was as tortured as any I had ever seen. He looked much worse for the night out in freezing temperatures and the punishment of his own thoughts. If ever a person seemed eaten by guilt, it was Chester. I felt ashamed that he was outside, on the thin edge of survival, and I hadn't offered anything to him.

"Come in for a meal, Chester," I said, fully expecting his usual refusal. But to my surprise, he clambered to his feet and followed me through the door.

Four

FRANCESCA

She knows that her mother has sent Rae away. From her window she sees Rae's things come out of Ronnie's house and get packed into Rae's car. She sees Jonah put into the front seat and the angry faces on Rae and Ronnie as they say good-bye.

She goes to the clinic without a word, without resistance or argument. There is no need. The life, the fluttering deep in her pelvis, will come to no harm. And she will be taken care of, too, she knows it, but not by her mother. Her mother doesn't see what has happened. She can't see that Francesca is no longer hers, that Francesca is now above the restrictions of flesh.

"First things first," Anne says, helping Francesca into the truck as if she were a small child or a cripple. Or maybe she's afraid that Francesca will bolt. If she ran, Francesca knows her devotees would take care of her. Rae and Chester would take care of her. She is under the highest protection; whatever she does is going to be all right. So she climbs into the truck, docile and submissive.

Her mother chatters as she drives, keeping up a conversation with herself. She talks about the town, the doctor, about "getting it taken care of." She glances over at Francesca. Francesca stares out the windshield. Without focusing her eyes, she can see in four directions at once, the cars behind, the cars in front, and several blocks on either side. She sees a man shoveling snow to her right, and simultaneously she watches a dog on her left. She notices with amusement that the yellow light in front of the grade school flashes in time with her heartbeat and the red light at the intersection turns green when she glances at it.

She knows that this is grace. She is passing through the crude physical world, and yet she's not of it. All the things she has done, the healings and helping people, have been because of the grace that is with her now.

It has taken some getting used to. In the first days, she was drained and exhausted whenever she worked with people. Gradually she has become more resilient, has learned how to do it, or rather to let the power do it, without tapping her own personal reserves of energy. She smiles through the windshield, and another light turns green.

Dr. Barrett's office is in a women's clinic. Her mother stays in the waiting room while Francesca is taken to an examining room and instructed to put on a paper gown with the opening in the front. The nurse, whose name badge says GRETCHEN, takes her blood pressure. Francesca understands without needing to be told that Gretchen is unhappy. At the same time, she sees a poster on the opposite wall where peach and green diagrams show how to perform breast self-examination. It's as if she has two sets of eyes and two brains concentrating on different things at the same time. She finds that with small adjustments of her concentration, she can focus on the nurse and the band around her arm, and the poster on the wall will stay in the background.

Dr. Cecilia Barrett is a small, athletic-looking woman with cropped gray-blond hair. She wears half-glasses on the end of her nose, which she looks over as she speaks.

"Your mom told me a bit of why you're here," Dr. Barrett says. "Do you want to tell me what's going on?"

"She wants me to have an abortion," Francesca says bluntly, looking for a reaction. Cecilia Barrett raises her eyebrows and nods, unimpressed, but holds Francesca's stare.

"First we have to see if you're pregnant." She hands over a plastic cup. "Why don't you give us a urine sample and then come back in here. Gretchen will test it while I examine you."

Francesca pads to the bathroom in her bare feet, pees in the cup, pads back to the examining room, and hands the cup to the nurse, who is writing something on a clipboard, her mouth drawn down so that the skin around it folds into dark creases.

"Gretchen, you could use a change in your life," Francesca says softly. The nurse looks up, startled. Francesca smiles at her. "Step away," she says. "Just get up and go."

Dr. Barrett comes back in the room, and Gretchen leaves, her face shaken and disarranged. Francesca lies back as directed and puts her feet in the stirrups. The doctor sits on a stool that puts her at face level with the stirrups. She adjusts a lamp. Francesca can feel the warmth of it on her genitals. She bites her lip and closes her eyes from embarrassment as she feels the latex fingers spread her outer labia.

"Well, your hymen is partially intact," the doctor says from between Francesca's knees. She pulls the paper gown back over

Francesca's crotch, takes off the latex gloves, and comes around to stand next to her. She places both hands on Francesca's belly and presses deeply but gently, turning her head in concentration, as if she is listening. There is an answering flutter from Francesca's womb, but the doctor doesn't let on that she feels it. She changes her hand position and pushes again. The pressure on her womb is uncomfortable, and Francesca holds her breath until the doctor lets up. Gretchen comes back in and whispers to the doctor. Cecilia Barrett stands up straight and clasps her hands in front of her. She fixes her gaze on Francesca over her glasses.

"When you're dressed, you and your mom can meet me in my office."

Francesca nods. She gets up and begins to dress. She pulls on her underpants and her loose dress, holding her hand to her belly, which feels a little sick and shaky from the prodding. Her cheeks are still hot from embarrassment.

When the three of them are in the office with the door closed, Dr. Barrett perches on the edge of the desk and waits for Francesca and her mom to sit in the chairs. This would be the room where the doctor gives patients bad news, Francesca thinks. Soft lighting and polished wood to ease the blow. There are family photos arranged on the desk: Dr. Barrett on a boat with a couple of kids, school pictures, and a family portrait from several years ago, she can tell, because Cecilia's hair is longer and blonder and her face is sweeter, less tired. On the wall behind the desk chair, in plain view, lest the patient have any lingering doubt about who is in charge here, are the diplomas. Two of them.

"Francesca, you're not pregnant. In fact, technically, you're still a virgin."

"But she said she's had sex," Anne sputters. "She's missed several periods."

The doctor frowns, picks up the clipboard, and looks over the form that Francesca filled out. "Your last period was in July?"

Francesca nods happily. This is perfect. Urine tests and doctors' examinations are small obstacles for this power. She wishes she could tell Rae.

Dr. Barrett turns to Anne. "In that case let's get a blood test, just so there's no doubt. Even if it's negative, it might show something to explain why she's missed some periods. But no matter what, I'd like you to make an appointment with a psychiatrist who specializes in adolescents with body-image problems."

Anne wrinkles her forehead. "Body image? You mean anorexia?"

Cecilia addresses both of them, though Francesca knows she's really talking to her mother. "Not exactly. After we rule out hormone imbalance and a few other things, I'd be thinking of pseudocyesis. False pregnancy. It's rare, but it mimics real pregnancy to the point of periods stopping and distended bellies. It's like anorexia and bulimia in that it's a conversion reaction, a kind of defense against depression or possibly bipolar disorder. Together with the other things that are happening to Francesca right now, I'd say it would be a definite possibility."

She scribbles something on a piece of paper and hands it to Anne. Francesca is taken to another small room, where Gretchen waits to draw the blood. It's a waste of time. Francesca knows that the tests will show nothing, but she willingly gives up the vial of blood anyway.

"How did you know?" Gretchen whispers as she tightens the rubber tourniquet on Francesca's arm.

"Know what?"

"That I was thinking of leaving my husband."

Francesca smiles and shrugs. "I just knew, that's all." The nurse slips the needle into her arm. Francesca focuses on Gretchen's amazed face and finds that it doesn't hurt at all.

*T*hey step out of the clinic into clear autumn sunshine. A group of people wait at the bottom of the steps. Of course, word got out that she was here, the same way word always gets out about where she is. She is tired, but not too tired to be among them for a moment. She goes to them, shaking off Anne's restraining hand on her arm, and then she realizes that something is different. Some of the people are devotees, but some are not. Some are full of the ecstatic love she's come to expect. Some are not ecstatic at all. A woman with black hair and thick black glasses is holding a sign with a picture of a dead baby.

"Christ killer," she sneers, her face an ugly threat. Immediately the woman is absorbed back into the crowd. Devotees press forward to touch Francesca and tell her their stories, the usual desire for recognition. But there is more urgency and something new in their faces. They don't look trusting and loving now; there is an edge of suspicion.

Her mother's grip is strong. She pulls Francesca away from the clutching hands and into the car. As they drive off, Francesca can see there are several antiabortion signs bobbing above the crowd. She counts five before the car turns the corner. And then she knows that hate and love are following her hand in hand.

ANNE

Getting Francesca to safety was my first priority. I drove her home, got her inside, and then dug out Gervais's card and dialed his local number. He was the only person I completely trusted.

"Will you come and stay in the house with Francesca while I go back to the clinic?"

"Of course," he said. No questions asked. He was there in ten minutes. Francesca had gone up to her room.

"I just need to go back there and try to talk to that group," I said at the door. "If I can just explain to them how wrong they are, then maybe this can stop."

His face was grave and careful. "It's worth a try," he said. "But sometimes they don't want to hear an explanation. They want to believe what they've worked themselves up to believe."

I knew he might be right, but I had to try. I drove back to the clinic thinking, This is what I should have done the first day. I shouldn't have stayed quiet and let it pass. I should have been making public statements contradicting all the rumors and claims.

When I arrived, the protest was escalating. The press was there along with the police. The peaceful "devotees" had been eclipsed by the right-to-lifers and some others whose signs read BEWARE THE ANTICHRIST and FALSE PROPHET. The protesters had lined the clinic's front walkway and were making a show of chanting slogans. The police stood by uneasily, watching for transgressions. I walked steadily and resolutely between the lines of angry protesters, avoiding eye contact with any of them. People with faces distorted by rage pushed against the police to get at me, yelling about the devil and dead babies. By the time I was in Cecilia's office, I was shaking.

"They're getting really worked up out there," I said. "They seem to think you performed an abortion on Francesca."

Cecilia took off her glasses and rubbed her forehead. "We get protesters all the time. It probably doesn't have anything to do with Francesca."

"I recognize some of them from the house. And a number of them have signs that say something about the Antichrist."

Cecilia went to the window and looked down on the angry mob.

"Listen, Cecilia," I said, "I've always despised people who air their personal lives on TV, but I think it's the only thing I can do. I'm going to make a statement to those cameras out there. Will you say something to them, too? Something official? We have to tell them that they're wrong about Francesca. This needs to stop now."

Cecilia and I went out and stood together at the top of the clinic steps, which hushed the crowd enough so that we could speak.

"I'm Francesca Dunn's doctor," Cecilia said loudly and firmly. "I examined her today. I have permission from her mother to tell you that she is not pregnant now and she was not pregnant when she came into my clinic."

Then it was my turn. "Please stop following my daughter and harassing us. You're wrong about her. She isn't a demon *or* a saint. She's just an ordinary girl, and I'm asking you to please back off."

I was drowned out by renewed shouting and sign shaking. "Murderers!" a woman in an awful black wig and thick glasses shouted.

"You don't understand," I shouted back. "She didn't have an abortion."

The woman shook her sign again and started up the steps. The others swarmed behind her. The police closed ranks to keep them back. They pushed the crowd off the clinic walkway, their faces expressionless compared to the distorted faces of the protesters. A police van appeared with lights flashing and siren howling. Two officers escorted Cecilia and me back into the clinic, and from the window upstairs, we watched them disperse the crowd. The woman in the wig and glasses ditched her sign and slipped away. Cecilia put her arm around my shoulders, and I was grateful to have her there, fighting alongside me.

Is Francesca okay?" I asked Gervais when I got home.

"She's sleeping," he said. "How did it go?"

I took off my coat. "I think I might have made things worse. You'll be able to see for yourself on the news. Cecilia was good. I was a total ass."

He handed me a glass of wine.

"Mind if I stay for dinner? I'll cook."

"There's hardly any food," I said. I hadn't been to the store for days. But the idea of his staying sounded better to me than anything else I could think of.

"You have eggs and cheese. I checked."

So he made omelets from the last eggs in the house, and I brought one to Francesca. Gervais and I ate in front of the TV.

"Here it comes," I said when the anchor read the introduction to the story. The piece proceeded like a train wreck. They showed the now ubiquitous picture of Francesca on the beach and a few seconds of the burning cross at Grace Lutheran. Then they cut right to me screaming at the woman with the sign.

"It's even worse than I thought," I groaned.

Gervais winced. "These things can backfire."

"So I see."

He went to the window and looked through a gap in the curtain.

"Well, there are exactly two of them out there now, so it's probably okay." He came to the chair where his coat was folded. "Are you all right? Do you want me to sleep here?" It was a polite offer, but he had his hand on his coat. I shook my head. I had never asked a man to stay over for protection. It was a point of pride. Plus, Chester was outside keeping an eye on things. And anyway, it would be awkward. I could see the tabloid headlines already: VIRGIN'S MOTHER HAS AFFAIR WITH PRIEST AFTER ABORTION OF SAVIOR!

"No, I'm fine," I said. "Thanks."

He gave me a chaste peck on the cheek and was gone. But he was wrong about the danger's being over.

The mob showed up later, loaded with malice. I watched from the window of Francesca's darkened room, where she lay on her bed and wouldn't talk to me. There were more of them than ever, and they massed silently in the park. This new quiet scared me more than the earlier shouting. They filled the street in front of the house and stood facing us with their signs raised, each one angry and mean. I called the police, and then before I could think about it, I dialed Peter's number in Italy. To my surprise he picked up. I took the phone out of Francesca's room and into my own, where I sat on the bed and told him everything, without stopping to breathe or hear his responses. I unloaded it all, relieved to have finally reached him.

"And so," I said, "maybe Francesca and I should come there? To Italy. We could get an apartment. She needs you, Peter."

The connection was bad, and everything he said came with a two-second delay. "You're overreacting," he said. "You're making no sense. Francesca, some kind of guru? Come on, Anne." I tried to speak again, and so did he, but we were cutting off each other's sentences even more than usual, and the timing of the conversation became stilted and awkward.

"Peter, it isn't just the press or the followers, it's *Francesca*." I got up and shut the door so she couldn't hear me. "Peter, she thinks she's divine or something. She thinks she's healing people. She thinks she's pregnant. The doctor says it's some sort of 'conversion reaction.' This is serious."

He said something that cut me off again. "I didn't get all that, Anne." His voice was tight and irritated.

This time I yelled. I couldn't control it anymore. I had to make him see. "She thinks she's the fucking Virgin Mary, Peter!" The line blipped and crackled, but he didn't say anything.

"Did you hear me that time?" I said, nearly crying and still shouting into the phone. After a minute he spoke again.

"First you say I should come home. It's an emergency. You send a telegram that scared the shit out of me. Then, before I can even make arrangements to come home, you call and say you're coming here. What do you expect me to think? You sound pretty mixed up yourself, Anne."

"You know what, Peter? Fuck you."

"Now, wait. Just hold on. I think you should bring her here. That's what we're doing now, isn't it? You're bringing her to me. But as for this idea of me finding you an apartment, that's going a little too far, isn't it? Bring her here and stay in the *pensione* around the corner for a week or two. Then you can go back."

He still didn't get it. He thought I was talking about a vacation. He could not grasp the idea that Francesca was flirting with a major mental illness and that she needed a safe haven *and* both of her parents *and* a good shrink. I still hadn't worked out how we would find a shrink in Italy, but I was sure the university would have a list of English-speaking doctors. These things could be done. But that I should leave her there was the most ludicrous thing I could imagine. I took a deep, shaky breath.

"We'll have to talk about that when we get there, when you see her. Peter, she's sick. You need to understand that she's very, very sick."

Again I could hear him saying something on the other end that cut off my words before they reached him.

"Let me know when you're coming, and I'll be there to pick you up," came through at the end of it, and then he hung up.

I went back into Francesca's room and looked out the window at the milling people below. Still no sign of the police. This was a real mob, and it was beginning to move, pulsing and stirring and edging closer to the house. They were standing four deep against the fence. The rest filled the street. I felt trapped. Up against it all alone with my child to protect. I was afraid, but I also knew that I would tear out their throats with my teeth if they got inside.

"He doesn't want us to come, does he?" Francesca said softly from her bed.

"What? No, that's not it." I tried to think which part she might have overheard.

"Mom, I heard you screaming at him."

"Yeah, well, he can be really irritating."

"No wonder he doesn't want us to come," she said.

I watched Chester in front of the gate, trying to hold them back, trying to calm them down all by himself. "Christ, where are the police?" I asked out loud.

Francesca spoke. "This is because of you. You and Dr. Barrett. They're confused now. They think the wrong thing about me." She sounded genuinely hurt that she could be so misunderstood. A stiff snort of laughter burst from my mouth.

"Meaning they all knew the truth about you before?" I couldn't keep down the sarcasm. I was worried sick about her. I knew she was ill, somehow, and that she needed help. But it was hard not to get pissed at her amazing narcissism.

Chester was pressed up against the fence, and they were pushing him. I threw open the window and stuck out my head to hear what they were saying.

"Please," Chester shouted. "Calm down. She didn't hurt anybody."

The woman in the wig and glasses who had called Francesca a Christ killer at the clinic was jabbing her antiabortion sign into Chester's gut. I heard the faint sound of sirens coming.

"Get back," he cried. His face was pale and strained. "Go away before the police get here."

And with that the woman thrust her sign into his face, knocking him off balance. He went down, and the fence went down with him, proving itself to be flimsier than I'd thought. They swarmed into the yard and onto the porch, and I lost sight of the woman with the wig. The sirens became unbearably loud, and several police cars and vans skidded to a stop in front of the house. Officers in riot gear spilled out.

The mob writhed in chaos. This time most of them threw themselves on the ground and refused to move, clutching their dead-baby signs in their hands as they were dragged into vans. I looked for a black wig and glasses, wanting to see the woman locked in the police van. But I couldn't see her. Knowing she might be somewhere on the dark streets didn't make me feel any safer.

In the next minute, two officers pulled Chester off the ruined fence and handcuffed him. I ran down the stairs and unbolted the door.

"Stop," I shouted from the porch. The officers who were holding him turned to me. "Not him," I said. "He's a friend. He was trying to help. Come in here, Chester." I opened the door wider.

The officers let him go. Breathing heavily, his face a bloody mess, Chester stepped into my house for the second time.

CHESTER

Anne's smell had improved over time. When I first met her, back when the scene around the Virgin was still new, she smelled dusty and bitter, like trapped moths. But now she smelled more like pencils, the fresh smell of pencils being sharpened. Not an unpleasant smell at all.

She stopped the bleeding on my forehead and made me drink a cup of hot, sweet, milky tea at the kitchen table.

"I'm sorry this happened to you. I should have known, after I was on TV, that this might happen."

"You were on TV?" I asked.

She nodded and pulled open cupboard doors. "I'm sorry there's not more to eat. I haven't been to the store in a while," she said. She moved to the refrigerator and took out cheese. Then she opened the freezer door and searched through all the frozen stuff. It looked to me like there was a lot of food in there.

"That's okay," I said. "I don't need anything."

She found a bag and pulled it out. "Here are some English

muffins." She cut open two of them and put them in the toaster. Then she handed me the cheese and a knife and a plate.

"You can do this while I talk to the police in the living room," she said. But she stopped at the door and looked back at me.

"Just so you know," she said, "I took her to the doctor, and she's not pregnant. The doctor says it's a mental illness. She only *thinks* she's pregnant." She disappeared into the living room and spoke to the police.

I cut some cheese and put it on the English muffin when it popped up. My empty stomach welcomed the food, though chewing hurt my temple, near the cut on my head. I thought about what Anne had just said. Doctors' opinions didn't mean all that much to me. But I turned the information over and over in my mind just the same.

I ate and made myself a second cup of tea, carefully repeating Anne's motions and being sure to wipe up drips and crumbs. I'd rinsed the plate and put the cheese in the refrigerator when Anne came back, led me into a bathroom, and turned on the shower.

"Take off those clothes and get in there," she ordered, then left me alone with hot water and a stack of soft towels.

So I peeled off my layers. After much debate with myself, I left them in a pile on the pristine white tile floor: boots first, then socks, pants next, folded small to fit on top, shirt and sweater, and then finally the old, heavy coat, wadded into as tight a ball as possible. My entire wardrobe, 50 percent of my belongings, made a miserable little pile in a room that smelled of soap and clothes dryer and bleach.

It was a long time since I had been naked in a well-lit room.

The shelter showers were timed, five minutes in a cement stall with somebody always waiting. I took a quick look down the length of my body, saw the reptile-white skin hanging loose on my belly, the wrinkled and shrunken penis and sac below. The legs were still strong enough, I supposed. The feet were a disgrace. I stepped around an alarmingly white rug placed in front of the shower door.

Hot water beat on my face, stinging the cut in my forehead until the pain gave over to itching and the water felt good running through it. I chose the bar of simple white soap over the assortment of perfumy shampoos and washed the bloodlust of the crowd out of my hair and beard. I scrubbed my hands and arms and legs and then soaped my head again. The water poured over me, warming and softening my skin. I breathed the steam, smelling only water and chlorine and soap. I lathered my feet and scrubbed them all over, especially between the toes. The bathroom door opened again.

"Here are some clean clothes," she said. I swiped at the steam on the glass to see her taking my clothes away and putting others in their place. I turned off the water and stepped over the white rug. Even after the shower, I was sure I would dirty such a thing. I preferred to drip on the floor, which I could clean up. After I was dry, I wiped down the tile with my towel and cleaned the hair from the drain. Not knowing what to do with the wet towel, I folded it up as small as I could and placed it on the toilet lid.

The clothes she left for me were old. They smelled of attic and disuse, but nothing worse. My guess was that they had belonged to Francesca's father. The khaki pants fit well at the waist but were several inches too short. I pulled on the socks and stretched them up as far as possible, to narrow the gap. The shirt was made of heavy wool and roomy enough through the shoulders, though the sleeves left a wide stretch of wrist exposed. As there weren't any shoes, I left the bathroom in stockinged feet.

Anne was waiting in the kitchen with a pair of scissors and a comb. She pulled out a chair and said, "May I?"

I would have avoided it, but she seemed determined and I didn't care enough to argue. I found I trusted her. So she cut my hair. Long mats of it fell around my feet.

"Well, Chester," she said from behind me and down through the top of my head, "what do we do about Francesca now?"

I thought about it. Because of me, she was hunted and misunderstood and in danger. I had failed to do my job. I didn't know how I could have protected her better, but now her mother was asking me what to do, and I found I had an answer.

"Take her somewhere. Get her away from here. Hide her."

Anne sighed. "I think so, too."

With my hair gone, I felt lighter. I ran my hand over my head. I liked the feel of the short, clean hairs against my palm. She trimmed my beard with the scissors, too, and then produced an electric shaver and proceeded to expose my tender white chin.

"That's better," she said, finishing up.

She took the chair opposite and held out a hand mirror, but I refused it. I didn't want to see. Feeling was enough.

"I want you to sleep in here tonight," she said carefully. Just the mention of it made the ceiling drop a few feet. "You can't sleep out in the open anymore, Chester. It's too cold. And the police will be watching outside, so you don't need to worry about that."

I ran my palm over the newly vulnerable skin of my cheeks and chin. I felt the sharp ledge of my cheekbones and the right angle of my jaw, the tender, soft dip beneath the lower lip. She hadn't given me my boots. It was close to zero outside; I wouldn't last long without them.

She kept talking. "The guest bedroom has clean sheets. You can keep the window open if that helps, or sleep in your bag if you want. Or sleep next to the back door, if you won't take the guest bedroom. That way if you need to go out during the night, you can." She watched me from far behind her eyes, and I understood that she was trying to see it from my point of view, trying to work out what might be bothering me. It was new for me, someone's wanting to see things from my perspective. Or at least it had been a very long time since anyone had cared enough to try. All at once my eyes were stinging and watering.

"Your boots are by the door," she said finally. "So is your pack. I'm just saying I think you should stay."

"Where will you take Francesca?" The Virgin's name sounded awkward coming out of my mouth, but somehow I knew I should use it.

Anne's lips pressed together. "Her father is in Italy. But you know, she needs to see a doctor, a psychiatrist. I'm not sure that taking her to another country is a smart idea at all."

I thought of the pills in my backpack, which I had yet to take. Perhaps Francesca would be given a similar drug. Perhaps it would take away her ability to heal people and the presence of

God in her, the same way the drug in my pack would take away my smells. I didn't know exactly what kind of power Francesca possessed. I was confused about her. I knew that I had seen her change people's lives. At least for a while, she'd held the mystery of life in her hand. Maybe she still did; I couldn't be sure. I'd been wrong about some things, that was certain, but not wrong about everything.

I thought of all the holy people throughout history, all the mystics and martyrs, artists and visionaries, and what the world would have been like if they'd all been given medication to make them ordinary. There would have been less suffering, no doubt about it, but I couldn't imagine a world without saints and madmen. Someone had to walk the outer edges. Someone had to stir things up. We were important.

And yet later, when I lay down on clean sheets for the first time in many years and the ceiling dropped, I broke into a trembling sweat. Terror made my eyes stick open, my body become a dead weight, but I wanted to stay in this safe white bed in a house where people cared for me. I couldn't go outside again, all shorn and shaved. I had been stripped of the tough crust it takes to live on the street. Out there I would die of exposure. Of my own tender skin.

The ceiling dropped to my chest. It toyed with me, enjoying my fear. I had no right to this soft bed, it let me know. I deserved to live like an animal on the street. I sweated and strained to take a breath, to get control of my fear. I could smell Francesca and Anne, roses and pencils, each distinct from the other, upstairs in their rooms. I could smell the food in the refrigerator, a cacophony of flavors wafting from the cupboards, the synthetic fibers in the carpet, the paste used in the drywall and the paint over top of it.

I crawled to my pack and took out the bottle of pills. My great gift of knowing all and smelling all was of no use to me if I couldn't survive it. Being a person who smelled the inner lives of everybody who walked by was no better than being an average dog who sniffs the ass of every other passing dog. I was tired of it.

I looked at the pills in my hand and realized that I would give up the drops of God in my blood in order to be able to stay in this house, to be able to sleep like other people for one night. I was ashamed that I had succumbed. I huddled there, shaking in terror of the ceiling and the drug both.

But as soon as I could make my hands open the medicine bottle, I didn't hesitate. I didn't sniff it or taste it. I just swallowed the potent little pill and prayed that it, too, was part of the plan.

SID

The story on TV about Francesca at the abortion clinic didn't faze me. I knew she wasn't pregnant. That part was bullshit. It was the rose that bothered me. I couldn't stop thinking about Francesca twirling a tight, dried-out bud until it bloomed in her hand. It was rocking my world.

I took the bus to her house after school, armed with assignments and vowing to be different than I had been. I told myself that I wouldn't have anything to do with the BS woman from now on, and I wasn't going to take anything from the house. But as the bus rattled closer to her neighborhood on the nice side of town, I began to worry. I didn't know if Anne knew about my selling. She hadn't said anything about it at the church, but she must have seen the picture. In spite of how careful I was, Chester could have seen me and ratted me out.

I could always blame it on Rae, now that she was gone. I never liked her. She was such a suck-up, and there was something just plain bad about her. She hid it under all that New

Age bullshit, but she was downright dishonest, I could tell. On
top of everything she did to Francesca, she didn't give her own
kid enough attention, and she was mean to Ronnie. And the difference between me making a profit from Francesca and her
making one was that she made the Grace Lutheran thing happen.
Rae set stuff up.

So good. She was gone. I had made a lot of money, and now
I was getting out of it, no harm done. But it ate at me. I couldn't
get straight with it. As a result I now had several places on my
legs and feet that I opened with my knife at night, but even that
wasn't helping.

The house looked different. The fence was flattened. For the
first time in weeks, there wasn't anybody around except for this
one guy, sitting on the porch step. At first I thought he was
maybe a plainclothes policeman, but he didn't have the face of
a cop. It was the bad haircut and the way his face hung off
his cheekbones. He looked sort of foreign, as if he hadn't been in
the country for long. But there was also something proud and
quiet about him. I studied him as I walked up the path, and
when I stepped onto the porch, his eyes slid sideways to me,
and all at once, I knew. It was Chester, cleaned up and made
presentable.

"Wonders never cease," I said.

He nodded to me. "She'll be glad to see you."

Anne opened the door before I could knock.

"Good," she said. "You're here. I need to ask you something."

This is it, I thought as I went inside. Now she would tell me
I was a sneaky little shit, a liar, and a criminal. A policeman
would step out from behind a curtain and arrest me.

"Sid, what were you doing at Grace Lutheran church the other night?"

I shuffled and cleared my throat, trying to think up what to say. "I don't know. Everybody was going."

She nailed me with her blue eyes. "What do you know about the photograph of Francesca that I saw out there?"

I stuck my fingers in my pockets so that the cuts on my hips hurt against the seams. "Nothing," I said, breaking my vow to be honest. Anne stared at me hard, and I made my eyes stay on hers.

"We're going away for a few weeks, so you don't have to bring the homework anymore. Do I owe you any money?"

She owed me twenty dollars, but I let it go.

"No, you don't owe me anything," I said. A phone began ringing in the kitchen.

"How's Francesca?" I asked, following Anne into the kitchen, where she picked up the phone. "Where are you guys going?"

She listened to whoever it was for a long minute. I could hear a voice buzzing excitedly, but I couldn't make out any of the words. Anne hung up the phone and turned to me. Her upper lip trembled when she spoke.

"Dr. Barrett has been shot," she said. I assumed she meant the same doctor who'd been on TV. I didn't know what to say. It was hard to believe that anyone could be so whacked. Anne leaned against the countertop as if her body was too heavy to move. I wanted to touch her or say something, but I didn't know what to do. She pulled herself away with an effort and was gone, leaving a damp palm print on the Formica.

A yellow pad lay on the countertop where Anne had been making a list. I pulled it toward me and read it. It had all the kinds of things that anyone would write down before they went on a trip, but three things caught my attention. She'd written "Gervais" and a local phone number, then "Alitalia," and finally "Call Martin." It didn't take a genius to know that Alitalia was an Italian airline. So I knew they were going to Italy. Gervais was the guy who drove us home from Grace Lutheran. But Martin? Why would Anne want to call the history teacher? Next to the list was a single unmarked key. It wasn't a car key or a key to a padlock. It was a house key I'd seen before. Francesca had one just like it. It had a Y cut into the top. It was the key to their house.

I could have reached for it. It would have been easier than breathing. It would have been easier than standing there not knowing what to do, feeling invisible and useless. I thought about the BS woman's offer of three thousand dollars for the key. Three thousand would buy us a car. My mom could drive to work instead of taking the bus. And when I turned sixteen, in a year and four months, it would be mine. And here it was, practically handed to me. And no one would know the difference, all the way in Italy.

I could have pocketed the key. But I didn't.

FRANCESCA

The mattress and sheets have formed a mold of her curled-up form. The weight of Cecilia Barrett's shooting lies on her heart, inside a membrane of silence. She hasn't been able to move, to get out of bed for a whole day and night. She feels over and over again, in her own flesh, the cold, heavy bullet enter Cecilia's body. She feels the blood run, the rush to surgery, the tickle of death. She feels Cecilia's daughter, home from college, waiting, finger-nails gouging palms, for her mother to take up life again.

From time to time, Anne sits on the edge of the bed and spoons soup into Francesca's mouth. The glass in the window goes leaden and then dark. Her mother doesn't turn on a light, and Francesca doesn't ask for one. By unspoken agreement they both feel safer in the dark. Her mother whispers the news of the day.

"Dr. Barrett is out of intensive care. It looks like she's going to be all right."

Francesca allows herself a moment of relief. She turns her

head to look at her cello. Its reproach has become a soft murmur that is absorbed into the whiteness of the walls and hardly disturbs her anymore. She finds that when she is quiet, as she is now, she can almost hear the music again.

From here she can see her mother pack their dressy clothes, as if every night in Italy will be a party, as if the changes in Francesca can be undone by a simple trip abroad. Even the thought of seeing her father, which two months ago would have sent her into a frenzy of happiness, doesn't elicit anything more than a dull sense of loyalty. The fact is, she has changed in these last two months. She has been altered in some fundamental way. It's as though her very cells have been exposed to a potent force, a quintessential energy that has determined her new course. She can't go back to being the old Francesca Dunn any more than she can reverse the bullet's direction in Cecilia Barrett's chest. When her mother finishes packing the suitcase, she lies down on the floor next to Francesca's bed. Francesca can hear from her breathing that she's not asleep, but listening.

She knows that a police car sits outside in front of the house. Another cruises the perimeter of the park. Because of Dr. Barrett, the police are guarding Francesca and the house, having decided that now she could be in real danger. But the black-and-white cars and their elliptical lights don't give Francesca a feeling of safety. They remind her of sharks, circling, waiting for blood to be let. She is sure they would feed off her if given the chance, as readily as would the devotees or the protesters or the press.

It has dawned on her that the people who first came to her for healing and comfort and encouragement now come for blame. She is the repository of all their desires. She is their object. She misses Rae, who taught her that divinity is not necessarily bliss. Rae said that the work would be painful and exhausting, which it is proving to be.

"Mom?"

There is a stirring from the floor. Francesca doesn't know if her mom is there because of her own fear or Francesca's, but it doesn't matter. It's good to know she's not alone.

"Yes?"

"Where's Chester?"

Anne gets up, goes to the window, and looks down into the front yard.

"I don't see him, but I know he's out there."

"You didn't make him go away, then?"

"No. He's been sleeping in the guest room. He took a shower, and I cut his hair. You should see him. He looks good."

The thought of Chester without hair or dirt is strangely troubling to Francesca. "But what's happened? Why has he changed?"

Her mother is quiet, intent on something beyond the window. Francesca can hear the squad car pass in front of the house. At the same time, she hears glass breaking in the kitchen. She realizes, as her mother's eyes widen with alarm, that people are in the backyard. While the police cars cruise out front, someone has broken a window in the kitchen.

"Stay here," her mother says. But Francesca smells gasoline and something burning, and she jumps out of bed. She follows Anne downstairs to the kitchen. Because the lights are on, she can see that the window over the sink is broken and a wrapped stick is burning on the floor. It smokes and sputters, and the flame doesn't look like much. Her mother starts toward it, then hesitates and returns to Francesca, pushing her back to the stairs.

"Stay on the steps, where it's dark," she says. "They can't see you there." Francesca does as she is told. She huddles on the third step and watches through the balusters. The hole in the glass above the kitchen sink is black and dense compared to the shattered, glittering glass around it. It is a rupture, a violation. Francesca stares at it, terrified of what might come through it next. She hears her mother open the front door. The stick is left smoking on the kitchen tile.

"What happened?" Chester's voice says.

Two police officers, a woman and a man, cautiously come through the house. Chester and Anne follow. Chester is strangely pale without his hair, like a creature that never sees the sun, and the back of his exposed neck looks vulnerable. The police go into the kitchen and pick up the smoking stick.

"Do you have any lights in the backyard?" the woman cop says, dropping the stick into the sink. Anne shakes her head. Francesca's mother hates what she calls "light pollution" and has never had them installed.

The man cop opens the back door and goes outside as if it's nothing. "Whoever it was, they're long gone," he says.

The woman cop unsnaps her holster and puts her hand on her gun before she steps out behind him. "They probably never intended to come inside," she says. "They're just trying to scare you."

Other police cars wail to a stop in front, and four more officers come through the house. In the kitchen Anne kneels on the floor and sweeps the shards of glass into the dustpan. The woman cop comes through the back door, holding a plastic bag full of black hair and a pair of thick glasses.

Francesca goes dead quiet in her place on the stairs and watches her mother gesture frantically at the wig. She realizes that the wig woman, and perhaps a lot of people, want to hurt her. They are out there, and even with police all around, she is no longer safe. She puts her hand over her belly to quiet the twitching movement there. She watches Chester bring down a piece of plywood from the attic and nail it over the broken window while the police shine flashlights around the outside of the house and yard. It goes on a long time, and she's tired, but she won't go upstairs.

Chester shuffles toward her, twitching and nervous, and sits on the step below her. She realizes that she is crying.

"Where did the *good* people go?" she asks. "Where are the ones who love me?"

He tilts his head, and his eyes search frantically for an answer.

She waits, but he has nothing to say.

ANNE

In the morning Chester worked in the front yard, reconstructing the fence while I waited for the glazier to come and fix the window. Ronnie had brought over a pot of coffee and a bag of bagels, and I accepted it awkwardly.

"We're leaving tonight," I said stiffly. "I can't tell you where, but we might be gone for a long time."

"Anne, I'm sorry," she said. I held up my hand to stop her. I didn't want to hear her apology. I was sitting there with Ronnie because I needed something from her, and that was all.

"Never mind," I said. "Can Chester stay with you?"

She put down her cup. "Chester doesn't stay anywhere. I've offered before, but he won't do it."

"He might now. He's been staying in our guest room for the last two nights."

"Chester?"

"The new, clean-shaven, hair-cut Chester. Haven't you seen him?"

Ronnie shrugged her shoulders. "Well, yes, but I thought he was, you know, still the same on the inside."

She watched him from the window. He was holding a section of fence and nailing it to a post. His face was raw-looking, but he was calm and concentrated. He moved slowly, but with a new confidence.

"He looks younger, doesn't he?" she said softly.

"He does," I said, noting the interest in her voice. It was hard to stay mad at Ronnie; she was so easy to read. She hadn't meant to cause any trouble, but her passive nature had contributed to our problems just the same. I couldn't afford to forget that.

"I always thought he had beautiful eyes," she said.

I cleared my throat to get back to the business at hand. "So go ask him," I said.

She opened the front door and went out. I watched them talking by the fence. Ronnie looked up at him when she spoke, shading her eyes with her hand. He listened attentively. They were easy and familiar with each other. A passing stranger might assume they were a married couple discussing yard work. In Peter's old down vest, new Levi's, and boots that I'd bought him, Chester looked like any middle-aged guy in town. I shut the door quietly, so I wouldn't disturb them.

The glazier came in mid-morning. While he repaired the glass in the kitchen, I stripped the beds and brought the sheets down to the laundry room. Our suitcases were sitting by the front door, packed with city clothes for Rome. I was determined to be full of good intentions. I told myself that when Peter realized the seriousness of the situation, the three of us, including Stacey, would concentrate on getting Francesca well. And for now the question of how long Francesca and I would stay there was open-ended. I was writing the check for the new window when Gervais showed up.

"Are you all right? I just heard about the last two nights." His forehead was creased, and his eyes were worried. "I wish you had called me. I should have stayed here."

"Please. There was nothing you could have done."

He cleared his throat. "I'm afraid I have some bad news. It's been leaked that you're going to Italy. An ambitious journalist tracked down your husband in Rome."

"*Ex*-husband," I said, trying to stay calm, but the thought of our bags next to the front door suddenly made me furious.

"Shit!" I yelled, and kicked the cabinet beneath the sink. The phone rang, and I picked it up.

"Anne, don't get on the plane tonight," Peter said, from half a world away. "Reporters are all over the place here."

"I heard," I said. "So do you still think I'm exaggerating?"

"God, there's this one guy camped out on my stoop. He's been there since last night."

"Inconvenient, isn't it?"

Gervais leaned over the sink to check out the new glass above it.

Peter's voice was tinny in my ear. "It's not safe. For Francesca. Let's give it a few more days." I couldn't help thinking that Peter sounded awfully eager to postpone the trip, but with Gervais standing there, I wasn't going to start an argument.

"She's going to be disappointed, Peter."

"I know."

"And you realize it isn't exactly safe here either? They threw a burning torch through the window last night."

"God, Anne. Where can you go?" Good old Peter, always happy to have it be my problem, not his.

I thought of Martin's cabin. My last-ditch resort. It was remote, but I knew how to live in the rough. And no one had any reason to think we would go there. Francesca had been there before, which might be a good thing. But most important, we'd be close enough that I could take her to doctors in the city.

"I'll call you tomorrow and let you know," I said. I put down the phone and watched Gervais run his fingers over the new caulking. I didn't want to tell anyone about Martin's cabin, but I needed help.

"There is another place we can go," I said out loud, and he turned around. "But with them watching us, I don't know how we would get there unnoticed. They certainly know me and my truck."

"I could help," Gervais said.

I watched his face, looking for signs of deception beneath the open gaze and finding none.

"It's in the mountains. If you could somehow spread the word that we're going to Italy as planned, we'd actually go the other way. And if you could rent a vehicle for me, that's all I would need. Oh, and you'd have to lie to the press."

He smiled a mischievous, bad-boy smile. "I'm not worried," he said. "If you like, I'll keep your truck key, and in a week or so I can drive it up to you and take back the rental."

Suddenly the new plan seemed far better than the original. I gave Gervais the directions to Martin's cabin and found that it felt good to have him know where we were going. I wouldn't tell anyone else. Not Ronnie. Not Chester. I would call Peter from a pay phone in the mountains tomorrow. I was going to be alone with Francesca. We would settle into the business of getting her well.

Gervais rented an anonymous-looking SUV with tinted windows, not unlike his own. He parked it around the corner and brought me the keys. I gave him the spare key to my truck. I packed the down bags and camping gear into backpacks and readied it all by the kitchen door. There were six hours to go before we were supposed to be leaving for the airport. So, with Gervais staying in the house, I went to the hospital to see Cecilia.

$\mathcal{A}$ plastic tube jutted awkwardly and, it seemed, painfully out of her chest. An IV ran into her arm, and a slender green oxygen hose was fastened under her nose. Still, she looked better than someone who'd been shot in the chest had a right to look. Her face was pale and slack, but her eyes were bright.

"Jesus, Cecilia, I'm so sorry," I said.

She shrugged, moving only her eyebrows and mouth. "I'm going to be fine. How's Francesca?"

I sighed. "We're leaving tonight. I haven't taken her to a psychiatrist yet, but as soon as I get her away from here, I will."

Cecilia nodded. Her eyelids fluttered slightly. She looked tired. "And how are *you* doing?" she asked me.

I stared at the speckled hospital floor, working to keep my

face composed, hoping the tears wouldn't fall. "I'm just worried about her. And about you."

She nodded slightly. "We'll both come through this. She's a smart girl with great sensibility. You have to be careful, though. The guy who shot me may come after her, too."

"Who was he?"

She shook her head, more a shudder around her eyes than a shake. "The cops don't know. No group has claimed the shooting, but they're pretty sure it was political, not random. The guy was waiting for me in the parking garage. He knew who he was after."

"Did you see him?"

"Just enough to know he was a white male in a knit cap pointing a big gun straight at me."

I took the hand without the IV and squeezed it gently. I wanted to tell her about Gervais and going to the cabin, but Cecilia had suffered too much by her association with us, and I couldn't involve her anymore. I let her believe that we were getting on an airplane that night, bound for Italy.

"Hey," she said, as I was turning to go, "take Francesca to the Vatican and show her *The Annunciation* by Raffaello Sanzio. I spent an entire morning with it once, a long time ago. It made a big impression on me."

When I got back from the hospital, Gervais was outside with Chester. Francesca was up and dressed for the first time in two days. She was waiting for me by the front door, edgy and tense.

"Did you notice?" she said, pouncing on me.

"Notice what?"

She whipped her hair out of her face and stared at me. Her eyes were dilated and wild.

"No flowers." She pointed at the front porch. I was blank for a moment, and then I knew what she was talking about. For the first time since the beginning of all this, there was no flower-petal design on the porch floor.

She blinked rapidly. "That's one thing. The other thing is that I can't go to Italy without my cello."

"Slow down," I said. I had never seen her so hyper and over-wrought. It was scaring me.

I considered the cello. I couldn't put it with the decoy luggage because then it wouldn't go to the mountains with us. But I had to keep up the pretense that we were going to Italy.

"We really can't take it," I said. "It can't go with the luggage, and there isn't anyplace to put it inside the plane with us. It's too big."

She twisted her hands. "I can't go without it," she said. Her brows worked together and she began to pace. This agitation was the exact opposite of the lethargy she'd been showing ever since Cecilia was shot. I wished I knew what to do. I was beginning to wonder how I was going to take her into the mountains in this condition. I didn't realize until now that I had been counting on her staying dull and sleepy for the switch. Given her mood, it was possible that she would refuse to go.

I went into the kitchen and fished in my purse for Hayden's Valium. I stared at the four remaining pills. One would calm her down. But I didn't think she would take it willingly. I weighed the need to get her to safety against the guilt I'd feel if I drugged her to do it. Safety won out. I pulled a hammer from my junk drawer, crushed one of the yellow pills, and scraped the powder into a strawberry yogurt I found in the back of the fridge.

"It's going to be a long flight. You should eat something," I said, and handed it to her along with a spoon. She took the yogurt without breaking stride.

"How am I supposed to practice without my cello?" she asked, putting the first spoonful of yogurt into her mouth.

"Well, I'm sure we can rent you a cello in Rome," I said, watching her take another bite.

She flopped down on the couch and took two more bites. "I'll talk the airline into letting me hold the cello on my lap," she said.

I argued with her so that she wouldn't get suspicious. "Francesca, you haven't played in weeks. You quit lessons, remember?"

Keith had been so outraged that he'd called me the night she quit. "You're letting her make this decision?" he'd sputtered.

"I guess so," I'd said. Right then the cello was pretty far down on my list of priorities. It still was.

Francesca got up and put her cello with the luggage by the door. "I quit because I couldn't stand Keith anymore. I'm going to take it," she said.

I didn't say anything further. I sat with her while she finished the yogurt, and in a few minutes she started slowing down until she was yawning.

At the designated time, Gervais loaded all of our Italy luggage into his car, in plain view of the waiting group, including Chester and Ronnie. I moved the cello to a spot near the backpacks. Francesca never even noticed. She lay on the couch, stoned on the Valium. Gervais came back into the house, ostensibly to bring us out to his car, but instead we got ready to go out the kitchen door. I grabbed my pack, took Francesca by the hand, and led her out.

"Where are we going?" she asked in a slurred voice.

"We're going another way, to ditch the press," I said. Gervais followed with Francesca's pack. "Bring the cello," I whispered to him, and he went back for it.

At the fence I stopped and waited for Gervais. He came across the dark yard holding the cello with care. It made me smile to see him so reverent of the instrument. All at once I was awkward, as though we were saying good night after a first date. He smiled and gave me a hug, and then he took Francesca's hand.

"You must try to get well now," he said gently.

Francesca was sleepy and confused by the drug. I put a stepladder against the fence and went over first. Gervais handed over the packs and the cello. Francesca climbed the stepladder and lost her balance as she threw one leg over the wood. She sat down hard on top of the fence and wobbled there. It should have hurt, but because of the Valium her face registered no pain.

"Give me your hand," I said, but she ignored me. She swayed and then fell in a heap at my feet.

"We're taking the backpacks?" she mumbled as I helped her up and buckled her into her pack. I could feel Gervais waiting on the other side of the fence.

"Is she okay?" he said softly.

"She's fine. We're going now," I said through the wood, and somehow it was almost soft and intimate.

"God bless you," he said.

I shouldered my pack along with the cello and steered Francesca to the passenger door of the rented SUV. How ironic, I thought, that this vehicle, an Armaggeddon tank, as Hayden and Seth would call it, was going to save us. I had been known to launch into tirades about the rich housewives who drove these monsters to soccer practice, talking on their cell phones all the while. I had always been proud of my late-eighties, no-frills pickup.

I helped Francesca out of her pack and into the passenger seat, where I buckled her in. The packs lay flat in the back, and I placed the cello carefully on top. I started the engine, and we rolled through town at a crawl, hidden by the tinted glass. Once the car began moving, Francesca nodded off. It reminded me of when she was a baby and the only way we could get her to sleep was to put her in her car seat and drive around the neighborhood with her.

I drove slowly, so as not to attract attention. We passed the intersection to our street. I could see the crowd and the cameras facing our front door, still waiting for us to appear. Gervais was there, speaking to them, stalling for time. I figured he could keep them distracted for maybe another fifteen minutes. But by then we would be well into traffic and headed west.

FRANCESCA

They have stripped her dry. She is so tired there isn't a bottom to it. She understands that Anne is driving them in a rented car and by a circuitous route, in order to lose the cameras and the reaching hands and the greedy open mouths.

The rhythm and noise of the tires on the pavement and the soft sky sifting into dark lull her until her head rolls on the leather neckrest and she is dozing. She is aware of herself, even in sleep. She is viewing herself from above, watching her own head resting against the car seat, her long, ratty braid coiled around her neck. From far away in a tunnel of sleep, she comes back to herself, the car, her mother. The packs and her cello wait in the back. She opens her eyes, her attention momentarily focused.

"Where are our suitcases?"

Her mom doesn't take her eyes off the road. "They're in Gervais's car."

She closes her eyes and tries to think about why the suitcases are in Gervais's car. And every time she thinks of it, her mind skids away. There's something wrong with Gervais's having the luggage for Italy while they've got the backpacks and sleeping bags. She scans her body, relaxed and melting into the nice leather seats of the SUV. The life in the pit of her womb is ticking, soft as a whisper, sweet as a kiss, making Himself known to her, reminding her that He is still there.

She is unable to ask the question that's on her lips. She must sleep. Opening her eyes is more than she can do. Her body insists that she give in to the comfortable lulling of the road. The SUV takes a curve, and then another. Her mother downshifts and she can feel that they are going uphill. She is dimly aware that they are in the mountains and not going to the airport far out on the plains. But it doesn't matter. Her body, and His, must rest. Not until the last second before she falls asleep does she have the realization, like a stone falling into place, that she has been tricked.

ANNE

Once we got off the main road at the abandoned schoolhouse, Martin's map directed me along the river on my right. Then I followed the road left at the fork, past the split pine with the *R* carved into the trunk, and onto a Jeep trail covered in unbroken snow. It wound farther up the mountain than I would have thought possible. With the high beams and moonlight, Martin's landmarks were easy to find. The snow-covered track passed right through a creek bed, and if his map hadn't clearly shown that a road existed on the other side, I would have turned around, figuring it to be a dead end. This was no tourist cabin, no skier's chalet or mountain development. This was a lot of land. Fifty acres backed up to the national forest, Martin said, without sewer, water, or electricity. If there was anywhere on the Front Range that was off the grid, this was it. I bumped the SUV into some ruts that would have taken off a lower vehicle's muffler, then hugged the curve of the creek, hoping I was still on the road. Francesca nodded and stirred but didn't wake up even on the roughest part of it. I came upon a row of dilapidated structures with no windows that looked more like stables than cabins. Finally there appeared a larger cabin with glass windows and a front porch. By moonlight it looked romantic, like Heidi's grandfather's hut. The logs shone, and the chinking gleamed white. I wished there were a friendly grandfather inside, and a fire and a warm meal waiting. But even in the dark and cold, it was better than I had imagined.

I shut down the motor and lights and sat a moment listening to the singing quiet of the snow-weighted trees. Francesca slept on. Her face was turned to the seat, and she was breathing deeply. The car was warm and would stay warm for a few minutes, so I let myself out and waded through the knee-high snow to the porch.

The key was inside the old woodstove, just as Martin had said it would be. The lock turned easily. Inside, there were a few kerosene lanterns; one of them had a few inches of fuel, and the others were empty. I lit the one and could see that the cabin had a wood-burning cookstove, a pile of old newspapers, and a fireplace, but there was no kindling or firewood in sight. The cabin was a single large room with one big bed and a bunk bed, a rough table with a few chairs, and one shabby, overstuffed rocking chair. Requisite elk and deer heads hung on the log walls over a river-rock fireplace and a rough wood floor. Simple, but I had slept in much worse.

I shouldered the ax and went outside in search of wood. The box on the porch had a few sticks of kindling, but nothing more. I stepped into the snow and headed in the direction of the outhouse. If I lived in this cabin, I'd put my woodpile on the way to the shitter, knowing that I would want to bring back wood with me and save a trip. Sure enough, halfway to it, I found aspen and pine stacked in neat piles. I knocked the snow off the top layer and filled my arms with the drier wood from underneath. I dumped my load into the kindling box on the porch and split one log into kindling as fine as I could manage. Then I took it inside and piled it on top of newspapers in the fireplace. I arranged some smaller logs over the kindling and lit it, praying that raccoons or squirrels weren't living in the chimney. The smoke pulled straight up the flue, the kindling caught, and after wavering between snuffing out and catching, the wood caught, too, and I fed it until the fire looked cheery.

Francesca was awake when I opened the car door, though she was dull and slow from the Valium.

"We're here," I said, holding out my hand. The temperature was dropping. My ears and fingers were frozen. I knew she must be cold, too. Her hands were tucked inside her sleeves.

"Come in. There's a fire."

She gave me a dirty look, though she could hardly keep her eyes open. "You tricked me."

My head dropped in acknowledgment. "Yes."

She blinked, sleepy and suspicious.

"Do you remember this place?" I said. In spite of herself, she left off hating me long enough to squint at the cabin. I saw recognition cross her face before it went slack again.

"What about Italy? What about Dad?" Her voice rose at the end of each question.

"It wasn't safe to go. Reporters found Peter. They figured out that we were going there and have been hounding him. It was his idea to wait. So we're kind of hiding out here, until we can get away without anyone knowing. Maybe we'll go into town tomorrow and call him."

Her head fell back against the seat. Her eyes closed, and she struggled to open them.

I held out my hand again. "Come in now. We'll talk about it inside." She stumbled out of the SUV, and I walked her in, putting her in the big rocker by the fireplace. Then I went back out and grabbed both packs and the cello and brought them all inside.

The fire was crackling now, but it didn't give off much heat. Most of it was going up the flue. I was too tired to fiddle with the cookstove tonight. Tomorrow would be soon enough for that. For now I dug the camp stove out of my pack and set it up on the table. I filled the pan with clean snow and lit a flame beneath it.

Francesca watched the fire, barely awake. I found sheets in a wooden chest and made up the big bed quickly, spreading our down bags on top. The water boiled on the camp stove, and I dumped instant soup into it, stirred it, and poured it into a mug from the cupboard. When I put it in Francesca's hands, she held it, peering through the steam at the fire.

I pulled out the long underwear I had packed for both of us and held hers in front of the fire to take the chill out of it. It reminded me of the countless times when she was little and just out of a bath on a winter night. Peter would be drying her in a big towel, and they would be singing Beatles songs, and I would run downstairs with her pj's and put them in the dryer for a few minutes and then run them back up so that she could put them on, all toasty warm. Her face would emerge from the warm flannel, rosy-cheeked and clean, and we would bundle her off to bed in a shower of kisses. It seemed like another lifetime, feeling so warm and safe and happy.

The kerosene lantern began to gutter out, so I gave her the longjohns, thinking she would put them on while I worked on pushing the iron bed closer to the fire. We wouldn't be able to feel any heat unless we were right next to it, but at least there would be light when the lantern quit, and anyway, the fire nearby made the bed seem cozier.

When I finished tugging the bed around, feeling much warmer for the exertion, Francesca still hadn't put on the long underwear. She sat with the mug untouched in her hand. I took it away and began to undress her. She was limp and didn't resist. I panicked quietly inside. She seemed completely gone. I worried that I'd done the wrong thing, giving her the Valium and bringing her here.

I lifted her heavy arms and put them in the sleeves and then pulled the top over her head. I unlaced her boots and pulled off her socks and pants, then struggled to put on the longjohns while she sat as unresponsive as a rag doll.

"Please help," I said, sounding exasperated. But I was scared. I wanted to get her dressed and into the bed, but she wouldn't even lift her foot to let me slide her legs in, so I did one and then the other.

"You have to stand up, Francesca," I said. The leggings were pulled up to her knees, but I couldn't move them over her thighs and hips unless she stood up. She didn't move. She was nodding off, staring at the fire. She didn't seem to know she was sitting there with her pants around her knees.

I finally stepped on her feet and pulled up on her arms, using my body like a lever to get her to stand. Then I walked her the few steps to the bed and dropped her down into it, pulling up her longjohns when she was lying down. I put on my own and sat next to her and fed her some of the soup. When she wouldn't swallow any more, I drank the rest myself, put another log on the fire, blew out the lamp, and got into bed, arranging both of the bags on top of us.

She lay on her side, facing the fire. I snuggled in close to her back, putting my arms around her, bending my knees into hers. It had been a long time since I'd slept in the same bed with my daughter. I couldn't remember exactly when the last time was. Tears, far warmer than my skin, ran sideways across my nose and into our mixed hair on the pillow. I should have grieved her passage into adulthood before this, but truthfully, I hadn't noticed until now.

FRANCESCA

They drive a long time, all the way to Denver, to another world, where there is a doctor's office above a street of shops. She sits in the chair provided and watches out the windows as a man in a mechanized pulpit strings Christmas lights through the bare trees lining the street. The daylight hurts her eyes. She tries to reclaim the feeling of divinity and the holy being in her womb, the power she had at Grace Lutheran. How many days ago? All of it seems muddy and lost. She can't feel the spirit the same way, and it shows. The people she passed on the way to this office didn't give her a second glance.

The doctor is a heavy woman with dark eyes and blunt black hair to her shoulders. She sits with her forearms on the armrests of her chair and observes Francesca. Her expression is kind and professional. Of course Anne would choose her. She will not see divinity; she sees only illness.

Francesca gets nothing from this woman. She doesn't know the doctor's weaknesses or hopes. She can't read her heart. They sit face-to-face, stubbornness to stubbornness, and the seconds tick away.

"I'd like to know what you think about your situation," the doctor says, crossing her legs.

Francesca takes her time. There's no need to rush to answer. Let the doctor wait. "I didn't choose to come here," she says at last. "I don't want anything from you."

The woman nods. "So everything is fine?"

Francesca nods.

"You're on the run with your mom, and Dr. Barrett got shot by the people you're running from. You're stuck in a cabin in the mountains, and you haven't been to school in months, and you'll probably have to repeat the year, but everything is just fine?"

Francesca shrugs. She doesn't have to answer. The shrink is arrogant, and she doesn't know what she's talking about. And that bit about repeating the year is just wrong. Francesca's been doing her schoolwork. Nobody has said anything about repeating eighth grade. She struggles to think ahead to next year, to her first year of high school. It's difficult to think about being in school at all, much less staying in middle school. She's been on TV and in papers and magazines. She's famous. She has healed people, and people have come to her to receive blessings. Being left back is not part of that. It is not an option. She looks hard at the shrink, feeling very angry with her, wanting to put her back in her place.

"Excuse me, but you don't seem fine," the shrink says.

Francesca stares out the window. She considers standing up and walking out.

"You still believe you're pregnant?" the shrink asks.

Francesca nods, almost imperceptibly.

"You went to Dr. Barrett and had all the tests, and she said you weren't pregnant. What do you make of that?"

Francesca shrugs. It's the chasm between what she knows and what they say. But the shrink is the first one to ask the question. It's a question she hasn't quite asked herself. She just knows that she is still carrying the Savior. The doctor uncrosses her legs and shifts her weight in her chair.

"Your mom says you're sleeping a lot. Do you think you might be depressed?"

Francesca doesn't answer.

"Feeling sad or overwhelmed? Hopeless?"

Francesca rolls her eyes. "I'm not feeling hopeless."

"Okay." The doctor makes a note on her pad. "But I imagine being pregnant, with the Savior no less, and healing people and being hounded by the press, has got to be a little overwhelming? Or maybe not."

Francesca doesn't like this shrink. She's sarcastic. She doesn't see how fragile Francesca is right now, how much she's responsible for: Dr. Barrett and the baby and all those people who believe in her, and now all those people who think she's a murderer. It's a lot. It's a whole lot. And this shrink has got a lot of nerve mocking her.

"Of course it's overwhelming," she says sharply, to shut the woman up. What she doesn't count on are the tears pushing from behind her eyes.

The doctor's voice comes softer now. More gently.

"There's a lot on your shoulders, Francesca. More stress than one girl should have."

Francesca looks down so that the shrink can't see her eyes.

"I want you to know that it's my job to listen to you. It's my job to help you with the stress. You can call me any time of the day or night, and I'll listen, okay?"

Francesca has to look at the doctor then. She nods, and tears slip over the rims of her eyes.

"We'll be talking every day for a while, okay?"

Francesca stands. She realizes that the time is up. She is embarrassed. She didn't mean to cry. She leaves the room without looking at the shrink again.

On the way back, Anne stops at a grocery store and comes out with bags of food and a phone card. They drive to a pay phone outside a gas station, and her mom gets out and punches in the numbers.

Anne hands Francesca the phone. Her dad's voice is small and far away.

"How are you doing?" he asks. "How's the cabin?"

She answers each question with "fine" or "yes" or "okay," and he seems satisfied. He doesn't seem to notice that they aren't really talking.

"I'm worried about you," he says at the end. "Do you want me to come home?"

She thinks about the little cabin and how it would be with all of them in it. His presence would be too big there. He would take up too much air.

"I don't think it would be such a great idea," she says. He is so surprised that he doesn't say anything for a moment.

"Well, you hang in there," he says finally, sounding fake and relieved and guilty. "Call me anytime, day or night." She rolls her eyes, waiting for him to stop saying things he doesn't mean. Then her mom talks to him, and after she hangs up, they get back in the car and drive again. Francesca closes her eyes, letting the motor's vibration lull her into another sleep.

CHESTER

I chopped vegetables, washed dishes, worked the meat slicer, made plate setups. Since we only served breakfast and lunch, I prepped for lunch at breakfast and for breakfast after lunch. And at the end of the day, I cleaned the place from top to bottom. In exchange I got room and board at Ronnie's house and one hundred dollars a week.

We walked together down the hill to the restaurant every morning and back again at night. We worked alongside each other every day. We ate breakfast and dinner at Ronnie's table. We slept under the same roof, a roof that, increasingly, stayed where it belonged. We talked some but we were quiet together most of the time.

According to the doctor at the mental-health center, I was responding to treatment. His pills had worked, and I should keep taking them for the rest of my life.

"It's rare to find such a good fit between medicine and patient," he gloated. He wasn't concerned about the side effects.

That my short-term memory was iffy, that my hands trembled, that I felt a lead weight in my head didn't concern him at all. That my dreams were drab and that I couldn't smell anything anymore was irrelevant to him. That I felt guilty when I served food to my street friends was not an issue. The apparent productivity in my life impressed him. I could work. I could earn money and contribute to society. I had a place to live. So his drugs were a success.

"I miss the smells," I told Ronnie one night. She put down her book and looked at me over her reading glasses. "It's as if someone died." I ran my hand over my doughy chin, concentrating on the gritty feel of the stubble there.

"Do you miss Francesca?" she asked.

My heart contracted. All that had been divine was gone to me now. I couldn't say anything.

She looked sad. "I do. And Anne, and Jonah. And Rae."

That stopped my misty mood. "Not Rae," I said. "I don't miss Rae."

She got her back up. "She's my sister, and I miss her," she said. "You don't understand. I raised her. She looks up to me. I didn't do a very good job, and that's why she's such a mess."

Everybody on the street had a story about how they were abused, how they didn't get what they needed. But that didn't make character. Character was something people made for themselves, in spite of the rest.

"It's not your fault she's how she is," I said. "She doesn't have a clue what she's looking for."

But I did. Or rather I used to. The smells were my way to get in deep. They were a gift, a blessing. And I hadn't used them well. A place to live and no fears of ceilings didn't make up for losing them. It didn't replace being an occasional participant in the mystery. It was grief I was feeling, even with the drug's opaque drape over it. I was grieving the loss of my smells.

The Virgin's following had begun to fall apart. Those who hated her were finding other targets. Those who worshipped her were moving on, now that she was gone. Gervais was doing a wonderful job of convincing the press and devotees and cranks that nothing extraordinary had occurred. He smiled to the cameras in his white collar and made people remember that there was a large, well-organized institution whose business it was to declare, document, and officiate over saints and divine manifestations.

"The church has looked into the matter of Francesca Dunn, and we see no reason to investigate further. We see no evidence of either miracles or miraculous circumstances." He was smooth and good-looking and reasonable and ordained, and everybody believed him. Nobody, not even me, really, remembered the ratty homeless man who had brought the Virgin forward.

FRANCESCA

The days are relentlessly bright. The white world cocooning the cabin reflects everything and conceals nothing. She wears sunglasses her mother has bought, but still her eyes water and squint. Even inside, she can't seem to get away from the glare.

Her mom makes her work. She doesn't want to. She feels weak and shaky, and she doesn't want to move, but her mom pulls her out of the warm bed and makes her crunch through the snow, back and forth, transferring wood from the pile by the outhouse to the porch.

She is also expected to do the dishes. She has to collect clean snow in a big pot and put it on the woodstove until it is hot for washing. Same routine for a bath, only then they use all the big pots and kettles in the cabin until they can fill the largest tub, the size of a wheelbarrow. Then they squat shivering in front of the stove to take a sort of bath. Just existing is work. Going to the outhouse is like punishment.

"What is this, some kind of concentration camp?" she complains while Anne splits wood with an ax.

"Stop your bellyaching. It's good for you to get outside and do things," Anne says, handing her another load of wood to carry to the already full porch.

Francesca works and sleeps and goes to the shrink. The feeling of holiness becomes vague and tentative. The longer she is away from her devotees, the harder it is for her to feel it. She misses their adoration and making miracles for them. But most of all she misses Rae and Jonah, Chester, Ronnie, and Sid.

There is only one visitor to the cabin. Greg Gervais arrives in her mom's pickup on a blinding afternoon. He brings bags of groceries, newspapers, drinking water, and kerosene. He helps her mom put the stuff in the cabin, and the whole time they're working Anne is wearing a silly smile that Francesca has never seen before. She looks like a girl waiting to be asked to dance, like someone with a crush. And the Jesuit smiles his wolfish grin and kids around with her mom. When Anne excuses herself to go to the outhouse, he comes over to Francesca, by her place on the bed, next to the fire. She should offer him the chair, but she doesn't.

"How's it going for you up here?" he asks pleasantly.

"Fine."

He nods. "You know, things have settled down a lot back in town. I drive by your house now, and there isn't anybody in the park anymore. I haven't seen anything about you in the papers for a while. I think it's going to be all right for you and your mom to come home in a few weeks." He smiles at her as if he's given her a gift, as if she should thank him. She stares back at him, hoping to intimidate him, but he just smiles at her.

"You don't look like a priest," she says, eyeing his jeans and down vest and the longish hair that keeps falling into his eyes.

"No?"

"What made you decide to become one?"

He raises his eyebrows and squats with his elbows on his knees. "Well, becoming a Jesuit isn't an overnight decision. And some Jesuits get ordained and some don't. I studied for about ten years before I was ordained."

He looks as though he would like to launch into a long story about becoming a priest, so she changes the subject. One thing she has learned, as the Virgin, is how to probe for soft spots, how to put a person off guard.

"You didn't believe what they were saying about me," she says. "You didn't believe that there were any miraculous things happening around me."

He doesn't answer. He looks down, and the hank of hair falls over his forehead. She begins to enjoy "working" with the priest. She feels her divinity more than she has since they came to this frozen place.

"Do you think virgin birth is possible?" she presses. "Do you think a miracle could ever happen?"

He purses his lips. "I take it on faith that it happened once."

"Once but never again."

"That's right."

"But how can you be sure?"

He looks down at his hands, which are playing with a piece

of kindling. He doesn't seem so sure of himself now. "That's what faith is."

"I want to know," she asks, leaning forward, sensing she might have found a place in him that is susceptible. "Have you ever seen a real miracle?"

He answers slowly, "No."

She sits back, gazing at him out of her best goddess eyes. "Then would you know one if it was right in front of you? How can you be sure God isn't inside of me?"

He coughs and looks up as Anne comes back into the house, bearing an armful of wood that she dumps into the woodstove through the top burner.

"Greg, would you like to stay for dinner?" she asks.

He stands up and sticks his hands in his pockets. His face is calm and mild. Francesca wants to fluster him, but she can't. "I'd better be getting back," he says.

Francesca tries again. "You didn't answer my question, Greg. Or am I supposed to call you 'Father'?"

He swings his head around to look at her again. She smiles.

"What was your question?" Anne asks. Her forehead is furrowed as she looks back and forth between Gervais and Francesca.

"My question was, how can he be so sure how God works?"

Anne clears her throat. "That's quite a question, Francesca."

Francesca refuses to let her mother defuse the power in the room. She waits for the priest to respond. He closes his eyes for a moment, seeming to search for the answer. When he finds it, he opens them and addresses her directly. His eyes register discomfort and perhaps some pain, but they are still calm. "I'm not always sure how God works, but He is always the God of surprises." He takes the truck key out of his pocket and hands it to Anne, clearly indicating that he has nothing more to say. She gives him the rental-car key.

"I'll walk you out," Anne says, shooting a perplexed look at Francesca.

Francesca watches them through the window. The glare of the day is extinguished when the sun slips behind the hill. She feels dull and heavy again. All the power she felt when Gervais was here seems to have seeped through the cracks between the logs. She sits on the bed. The cabin is smaller than her room at home. No TV, no computer, no phone. There is always a fire in the cook-stove, but it doesn't entirely heat the place, so bed is the warmest, best place to be. She crawls under the covers and closes her eyes.

She is almost asleep when she first hears the music. She cocks her head as if to catch every wave of the beautiful low notes. The rich sweetness of the sound pours into her ears, and she almost doesn't dare breathe for fear of missing some of it. She follows the melody, the mournful, dark sweep of it, and realizes that it is the Brahms, the sonata she wasn't able to play for Keith. It is there, fully present, so much so that she can feel her bow touching the strings and her fingers moving on the neck of the instrument. The vibration of the lowest notes enters through her pelvis and goes up into her chest.

When she opens her eyes, she reaches under the bed and feels for her cello case to make sure it's still there. It hasn't been touched or moved. And yet when Francesca looks at her smooth fingertips, where there haven't been any calluses for weeks, she sees dents in the tender skin, as if she has actually been playing.

SID

I kept working weekends at Ronnie's. No way could I make as much money there as I had from scamming, but that was fine with me. And anyway, I liked Ronnie. I liked her café. I wasn't hanging around because I missed Francesca. I just felt like being there, that's all.

Francesca and Anne had been gone for two weeks, and I still thought about that rose every day. I told myself a lot of things: that it had been another rose and I hadn't seen the switch, that those hothouse rosebuds often burst into bloom, that the light was playing tricks, that the heat from her hands opened it up. I was pretty sure that one of those explanations was the right one. And yet when I woke up in the dark, before the clock went off, I saw it open again and again.

The other thing on my mind was Chester. Every time I came to work, there he was, looking like a regular person. I mean, he was clean, he did his work washing the dishes and helping out. You could see his face, and it wasn't that weird without the hair.

In fact, I bet that when he was young, the girls probably thought he was pretty hot.

I watched him over the weeks that Francesca was away, and I was more and more amazed as time went on. He stood up straighter and stopped moving like he might break. He didn't lurch anymore. Lots of the bums talked to him. You could see him out in the alley with them. He had gotten out somehow, and they wanted to know how he did it. It was like that damn rose. Here was Chester, the lurchiest-looking bum of all, and after hanging around Francesca, he suddenly comes in out of the cold and gets a life.

A lot of stuff had happened since that first day he'd grabbed on to Francesca and started the whole thing. Lots of people, including Cristos and Briggs, still said they'd been healed. And when I thought about it, because of Francesca I had made enough money to take care of my mom. And there were all the strangers who had seemed to get something from her, even if it was only hope.

But nobody talked about her anymore. Even the bums went back to their usual weekend-breakfast routine. They stopped asking where she was or how she was doing. With them, the here and now was all that mattered. If Francesca wasn't with them, she didn't exist.

Still, the rose nagged at me. It was bugging me so much that I asked Ronnie about it one Sunday before breakfast. The snow had been falling all night, and it was piling up around town. We would have more people for breakfast than usual.

"Did you ever see anything strange happen around Francesca?" I asked.

She stopped slicing onions and stared at me like, uh, hello? "Honey, everything around Francesca has been strange for a while."

"No, I mean miracles or anything. Did you ever really *see* anything *happen?*"

She opened and closed the door to the cooler. "I saw what you saw. I saw a couple of guys claim that their heart pain and ear infection went away."

I told Ronnie about the rose. She gazed at me, unimpressed. "You know what I think?" she said. "I think you miss her. She's your friend, and you miss her."

I served scrambled eggs to the bums that day, and to stop obsessing about the damn rose, I thought about my car. I was planning to buy a car for my mom for Christmas. I had it all picked out from the used-car place. It was a blue Audi, 1981, 150,000 miles on it. All I had to do was wait for a day when she was sober, and we'd go buy it.

I was right about the storm bringing in more customers than usual. The bums came in with frozen hands and faces. Everybody sat over extra coffee. Around noon we started shooing them out, and the place was empty by twelve-thirty. The bell on the front door jingled, and I turned around to tell whoever it was that we were closed. But instead of a customer, it was Rae, wearing some kind of nasty fake-fur thing and sunglasses. She looked like a dead mouse gone Hollywood. And she was carrying Jonah. Rae brought a sour taste to my mouth, but I was glad to see Jonah. I was happy to take the little guy from her.

"Hey, kid," I said to Jonah. He was all bundled into his coat, and his face was pale, but he gave me a big hug.

"Where's Ronnie?" Rae asked me, as pushy as ever.

Now, there are only a few places where Ronnie can be in the café: the dining room, the kitchen, the walk-in refrigerator, or the bathroom. Anyone who knows Ronnie knows that you just come in and find her. You don't have to stand at the door and announce yourself. That's what I was about to tell Rae when Ronnie came walking out of the kitchen and saw her.

"Ronnie, Jonah's sick," Rae said, before Ronnie had a chance to speak. "I need to stay at your place tonight. We'll go in the morning."

Ronnie didn't seem surprised to see her. She came over and held her lips to Jonah's forehead.

"He's hot. Has he seen a doctor?"

"Yeah, he's seen a doctor But that's not what he needs."

"What did the doctor say, Rae?"

Rae shrugged. "They said it was a bug and to give him fluids and Tylenol and rest."

Ronnie frowned. "Well, Chester's got your old room, but you can have the fold-out couch." Rae actually managed to look grateful and took off with little Jonah sleeping on her shoulder.

After we'd refilled the ketchup bottles and rolled the napkins and silverware, I walked up the hill with Ronnie. Chester was still at the café prepping for tomorrow and cleaning the kitchen. The snow was up to our boot tops already, and it was coming down steadily. Rae was on the couch in the living room with Jonah. Now he was whiter than Ronnie's wall. His eyes were like big glassy marbles. He was awake, but he wasn't jabbering and being his usual chatty self. That's what really scared me. Usually you couldn't shut the kid up.

"I know you know," Rae said slyly, while Ronnie hung up her coat.

"Know what?"

"Where Francesca is."

Ronnie closed the closet door. "I don't. Look, Rae. Nobody is interested. They don't believe in her anymore."

Rae set her jaw. "Well, I do. What harm would it do to just tell me where she is? Look at him. She could make this fever go away."

Ronnie shook her head. "I told you, I don't know where she is."

"Sure you do."

Ronnie rolled her eyes. "No. Really, I don't. Nobody does. Call your doctor again. Or let's take him to the hospital. Come on, I'll drive."

Rae said, "Take me to Francesca."

I looked at Jonah, wondering if his mom was so whacked that she would use her sick kid to get to Francesca. He was breathing hard and staring dully out of his overbright eyes. He looked awful, but no worse than somebody with a bad cold. And yet, I thought, if Francesca could make a dead rose bloom and if people had gotten better from her, then Rae might be right. Jonah had already been to the doctor. He just had a fever. No big deal, kids got fevers all the time. If Francesca could fix it, why not?

I hadn't forgotten Anne's list. It said "Alitalia" and "call Martin," and it had Gervais's phone number on it. Alitalia:

Forget that. Everybody knew they didn't go to Italy. Gervais's number was no mystery either. He and Anne were pretty tight before she left. Maybe he even knew where they were. But why call Martin? It hit me all at once. They were at Martin's cabin, where we went for the Stone School bonding trip in September.

I hated it that they didn't tell me. They should have known I would figure it out. They could have brought me along, kept me on the inside. I could have helped Francesca catch up on schoolwork. Obviously I didn't matter to them.

"I think I know where she is," I said softly. Rae turned to face me. Her full attention was suddenly trained on me. I felt a pinch of guilt, but then I looked at Jonah again. He didn't look so good.

"Is she close?" she asked.

"Not that far. Our history teacher has a cabin in the mountains. We went there last fall. I'm pretty sure I can find it."

"Let's take him to the hospital, Rae," Ronnie pleaded. "Just to check him out."

Rae stood up and started bundling Jonah in his snowsuit.

"Rae, please don't do this," Ronnie said. Rae ignored her. For a minute I saw why Francesca had liked Rae's attention so much. She was obnoxious, but when she focused on you, the intensity made you feel like a star.

"Sid, don't," Ronnie said. But now I was totally into it. We would take Jonah to Francesca and find out if the rose thing was for real. It was going to be an adventure, and I was at the center of it.

"Look outside," Ronnie said. "Your car will never make it in the mountains, Rae." She followed while Rae collected Jonah's boots, put them on his feet, found blankets and his little stuffed puppy.

Chester came home and stooped to untie his boots at the door. His eyes went to Rae, slid over Jonah, and then landed on Ronnie. "Jonah's got a fever," she explained. "Rae wants to take him to Francesca."

Chester shook his head. "Don't do that," he said.

"Too late," Rae said, scooping up Jonah and pushing past Chester.

"Maybe we should go with them," Ronnie said to Chester, eyes all imploring. Jesus. It was like they were married or something. He shook his head.

With the snow coming down almost as fast as we could scrape it away, Rae and I dug out her big old boat of a car. I worked on shoveling snow from under the rear tires. When I got enough of it cleared, I could see that the tires were bald. Rae started it, and the car was spewing smoke from the tailpipe when Ronnie came running out of the house in her boots and coat.

"I can't let you go in that thing," she said. "My Bug has chains on it. It can get through anything."

So we dug out the other car, but it didn't take as long as Rae's boat. Chester watched us from the front porch, looking like a beached whale.

"Please don't do this," he kept saying.

But we all piled into the car, Rae and Jonah in back. I rode shotgun, and sure enough, Ronnie's old Bug plowed right through the snow, no problem.

CHESTER

I paced the house, looking out the windows at the storm. Snow pelted down through the streetlight's beam across the way. Ronnie had made a mistake. It was stupid to go with Rae. She shouldn't have done it. Now all of them could come to some harm.

I didn't like having people to worry about. I wasn't comfortable being inside, warm and safe, while others were out in the storm. But it would have been wrong to go with them. I couldn't have faced Anne. I had caused enough pain for them already. I wasn't going to be part of it anymore. And there was another thing, which I didn't like to think about, but which haunted me. I was afraid to see Francesca. I didn't want to know what psychiatrists and drugs had done to her. I didn't want to see her stripped of her power, and I didn't want to see her without being able to savor the intoxicating rosy smell she emitted. It was by far the most wonderful smell that had ever blessed my nose. In a bed underneath Ronnie's roof, I dreamed of the smell of the Virgin. I was entitled to my memory. Even though something had gone terribly wrong, my initial vision of her, and the early healings, had been real, true signs of something divine, and I intended to believe in them as long as I could.

ANNE

"For Francesca's type of disorder, there are many medications," the shrink had said. "And more are being approved every month. People react to them in different ways. Sometimes the side effects are too extreme. Sometimes the drug doesn't do enough good to justify itself. Usually we try several drugs or combinations of drugs before we find the right one, and, to complicate matters, some of these medications, like the one I'm starting her on, take weeks or even months to achieve their full effect."

Francesca never said she liked Dr. Hadley, and I wasn't allowed in their sessions, but she didn't complain about going there either. In fact, I was amazed that when Dr. Hadley told her to take the pills, she did it without question.

Other than the start of medication, we'd had a typical day: the long drive to Denver in a light snow, Francesca's hour with the psychiatrist, then the drive back to the cabin in a storm that made me grateful to be driving my own familiar truck. At the cabin I made a one-pot meal on the woodstove. I couldn't care less about cooking at home, and out in the field I ate whatever was quick and easy. But here my main occupation was to keep the ancient stove going and try to make something nourishing on it. I chopped kindling. I chopped logs into smaller logs that would easily fit into the firebox. I hauled the wood to the porch, made a huge pile, and stacked it according to size. The principles of the woodstove were simple. For more heat you put in more wood and sat your pot directly above the spot where the fire was the hottest. For less heat you moved the pot away from it. I even baked bread in the oven, though it didn't have a temperature gauge. The bread turned out fallen and a bit hard, but it was worth it for the warmth and good smell.

We'd just finished washing the dishes when we heard a vehicle out on the road somewhere. It sounded stuck and seemed closer than the canyon road. It might even be on the cabin road. The late-November sun had dropped behind the mountain, and the sky was nearly dark. I couldn't see headlights from the porch, so I knew that the car was beyond the creek bed. But whoever was there could easily get out and follow our tracks to the cabin door.

"Stay here," I told Francesca. "I'll try to get them back on the main road."

I put on my hat and coat, grabbed my shovel, and went out to see what was going on. I walked in the tire tracks, across the creek bed to the heavily rutted private road where the revving was coming from. I came over the creek bank slowly, not sure if I wanted them to see me. But when I recognized Ronnie's little Volkswagen high-centered in the ruts, I was more pissed off than relieved.

"How did you find us?" I demanded, yanking open the car door.

"They were going to come anyway," Ronnie babbled. "I couldn't let them go in Rae's heap."

I saw Rae in the backseat with Jonah, and the contempt I felt for her was overshadowed by my sudden concern for the little boy. He was shivering and shaking. He was so pale that he looked blue around the mouth. I leaned in and touched his forehead. He definitely had a fever.

"You're insane to bring him here," I yelled at Rae. "What were you thinking?" I turned to Ronnie. "What were *you* thinking?"

"Where's Francesca?" Rae said sullenly.

Sid spoke from the passenger seat. "It's just a fever."

"And what are *you* doing here?"

"I'm the one who figured out where you were," she said. She actually sounded proud of herself.

"Are you going to let us come in?" Ronnie asked. "The car is stuck."

I was furious with all three of them for finding us, for invading our sanctuary, for blowing our cover, and for bringing a sick child. I took Jonah from Rae. His mother was an idiot, but I wasn't going to punish him for it. He didn't need to walk through deep snow with a fever. I hoisted him on my back and walked back to the cabin.

Francesca opened the door wide, lamplight spilling onto the porch and snow. She was smiling. Happy to see them. I was glad she was so chipper, except that we'd been found by Rae, the person I blamed most for everything that had happened.

"Hey, Jonah," Francesca said, helping him out of his coat. "What's up with you, buddy?" She knelt on the floor and looked into his face. Sid, Ronnie, and Rae stood around them, and a reverent hush fell over the room. It made my skin crawl.

"Bring him over to the fireplace," I said, breaking it up. I rifled through my backpack, looking for the first-aid kit, though I knew that it didn't have a thermometer. I found the kit, and pulled out the acetaminophen. I pushed past the hovering women and laid my hand against his forehead. If I had to guess, I would have said his fever was at least 103. Maybe more.

Rae had taken Francesca's hands and was gazing at her. "I've missed you, Mother," she said.

I took Rae by the arm and pulled her away. "Stay away from her," I growled. I wanted to throw her out, but instead I shoved her against the cabin door. "You were the one who staged that horrid display at Grace Lutheran. You were supposed to be taking care of her. You're no better than a pimp. And now you're using Jonah to get to Francesca. You ought to be ashamed of yourself."

I pushed her down into a chair. She opened her mouth to speak, but I stopped her. "The only thing I want to hear from you is what you gave him for the fever and how much."

She looked poisonous, sitting there like a bratty child. "I didn't give him anything," she said, full of self-righteousness. "I believe fever burns up the disease."

"Right," I muttered. "If it doesn't burn up the kid first."

"You told me you gave him Tylenol," Ronnie said. Francesca sat on the bed and took Jonah onto her lap. She put her cheek against his, and when she looked at me, her eyes were alarmed.

"No, I didn't," Rae said testily. "I said *they* told me to give it to him. They always say to give Tylenol, but fever isn't a disease, it's a symptom. Francesca can heal him, if she will."

Ronnie stared at Rae. "You are fucking insane."

Sid sat on the bed next to Francesca. "Jesus, Rae. He doesn't look good."

My mind worked through the situation. The snowstorm was bad, Ronnie's car was high-centered in the middle of the road and blocking the way. If I was going to take him to the emergency room, we would have to move Ronnie's car somehow.

I measured out the acetaminophen, estimating Jonah's weight and then upping the dose by half, and mixed it into a spoonful of applesauce. I remembered Francesca's baby and toddler fevers, a couple of them elevated enough that we had to take her to the hospital. But all they did was give her a dose of acetaminophen almost twice as high as what was prescribed on our Tylenol bottle at home.

Jonah was limp in Francesca's lap. He took the medicine without complaint and closed his burning eyes. I fixed Sid and Francesca with my most parental expression. "It should take about twenty minutes before his fever starts to go down. In the meantime Ronnie and Rae and I are going to dig out the car."

An outraged gasp erupted from Rae in her seat by the door. Ronnie zipped her jacket and put up her hood without a word. I touched Francesca on the arm. She looked up from Jonah.

"No trippy stuff, okay? Remember how far you've come these last few weeks. Give him a little water. Keep him near the fire, but not too close. If he gets worse, come and get me."

I pulled Rae to her feet and made her come outside with us.

No way was I going to leave her with Francesca. "Hold on to her, Ronnie," I said, putting Rae's wrist into Ronnie's hand. I grabbed two shovels and a flashlight from the porch and the hydraulic jack from my truck.

"How dare you keep me from my child," Rae said. Now she was the indignant mother. She glared at Ronnie, but Ronnie kept hold of her arm.

"You can't make me dig," Rae said defiantly, when we got to the VW. I opened the passenger side of Ronnie's car.

"Wait in there, then."

"No." She crossed her arms in front of her chest. She had no gloves, no hat, and her coat was much too light for the weather. I pushed her into the car and slammed the door.

Ronnie and I began to dig snow away from the front wheels. The snow was light, and the work went fast. The flakes fell steadily, but the full moon shone through the clouds. I fixed the flashlight to a tree branch, aimed on the VW. The spruces were stooped, weighted with fresh snow, and not a single vehicle was traveling the canyon road. All the time I was digging on the passenger side of the car, Rae watched through the window. I could see her white face behind the glass, the scheming in her eyes. Once she tried to open the car door, and I kicked it shut with my boot. Ronnie worked on the other side, and from the look on her face, she wasn't going to let Rae out either.

All I could hear was the sound of our breathing, the shovels making contact, and the occasional thud of snow falling off a spruce. I dug out the back tires, leaving Ronnie to watch Rae up front, until I was able to see where the car was high-centered on its muffler. I set the jack as far underneath the back axle as I could and cranked it up. The car's rear end rose slightly. Rae's alarmed face appeared in the frosted window.

"Ronnie, help me push back here," I said.

A few more cranks and the muffler was clear of the stump. Ronnie put down her shovel, and we pushed, throwing all our weight into it, and the little car popped forward, crashed down off the jack, and rolled a few feet into the shoveled area we had prepared. Rae screamed inside the car.

"You could have killed me," she said, opening the door. Her voice was shrill in the soft meadow.

"Shut up," Ronnie said.

I gave Rae the keys. "Start the car, and we'll push."

She looked suspicious. I realized then just how stupid the woman was.

"Look," I said, "the sooner you start the car and cooperate, the sooner you can go inside and warm up."

So she started the car, turned on the lights, and put it into gear. Ronnie and I pushed. We were just getting the Bug back on the track when headlights beamed up the canyon road.

"Turn it off," I hissed at Rae. She cut the engine and lights. We froze, watching the vehicle come to the turnoff, and waited for it to pass. But it slowed and bounced onto our road. Rae got out of the VW and stood with Ronnie and me.

"Who else did you tell?" I demanded of Rae.

"No one," she said.

"Chester knows," Ronnie said. "He wouldn't come with us. He said it was wrong."

"Well, he was right," I said.

The vehicle bounded and lurched over the ruts, revved in low gear into the riverbed, and then made the wide turn and caught us in the headlights so I couldn't see who it was. I held my breath. It pulled off to the side in the deeper snow, parallel to the VW, and then I recognized Gervais's SUV. He got out of the car. I let out my breath. "Thank God it's you."

"Chester called me," Greg said. "He thought you might be having some trouble up here."

"They're almost ready to head back down the mountain," I said.

The four of us walked single file back to the cabin. Rae was shivering in her inadequate clothes. I tried not to care. She deserved to suffer, after all she'd done. I was sure Jonah's fever would be down when we got to the cabin. Gervais and I would help get the Bug back on the canyon road. Then, because the cabin was no longer a secret, I would have to decide where Francesca and I would go next.

That's what I was thinking when I saw Sid running toward us.

FRANCESCA

She holds Jonah on the edge of the bed, next to Sid, in front of the fireplace. Jonah's eyes are open. They are overbright and burning. He gazes up into Francesca's face, and she looks down at him. Sid's hand picks at Francesca's sleeve.

"Make him better the way you did for Briggs and Cristos." She says it like a challenge.

"It doesn't work like that," Francesca says, but she begins to seek the power. She scans her body for the faint force field of the unborn child. It's an inward pressure she exerts, to fill herself, but the goodness and grace that she has found there at other times are absent now. She tries to conjure it. Her tongue tries to taste it, her ears to recall its sound. But she can't bring it on. It stays outside her grasp.

Jonah is watching her. His breathing is louder and rough. His skin is hot and dry. Heat emanates from him; she can feel his burning skin through the cloth on her arms and thighs and belly.

"It's okay," he says. "You don't have to do anything."

Sid holds a cup of water to his lips, and he sips it. He looks old, trying to bend his neck to the water.

"My neck is stiff," he says, dropping his head back onto Francesca's shoulder. He begins to shiver, yet he is impossibly hot.

"How long since we gave him the medicine?" she asks Sid.

Sid looks at her watch. "About twenty minutes. Can't you do it? Can't you make him better?"

Jonah blinks his eyes. They are so dry that she can hear the lids scraping against his eyes. Francesca takes a breath and lets it out slowly, trying to breathe goodness and coolness into him, but her breath merely blends into the air. So she summons all the particles she's made of. She even summons the child in her womb, the source of all her power. In an avalanche of understanding, she realizes there is no child. Dr. Hadley and Dr. Barrett were right, there is nothing inside of her.

Jonah keeps his old, old eyes on her face. "It doesn't mean you couldn't do it before," he says in a new, thin voice. "It doesn't mean anything." His shivering becomes more violent, so that his teeth knock together. "Maybe you should get my mom," he whispers.

Sid throws on her coat and goes out into the swirling black and white. Jonah's eyes roll up in his head and his arms jerk together. His teeth grind so hard that Francesca is afraid he'll break them. She holds him and searches all the landscapes of herself, finding only dust. She begins to pray, offering parts of herself in exchange for Jonah. She goes to the bottom of her soul, searching for something to trade. But there is no deal to be made.

After what seems like an eternity, the others are there. Someone takes Jonah off her lap. She hears her mother's voice and the voice of the priest, shouting and alarmed, and they are moving quickly. And then she is outside, and she can't get her breath because the cold air sucks it out of her, but she is put into a vehicle, and it moves.

Still she prays, but the only power left to her is the knowledge that Jonah will die. She knows he burned up as she held him on her lap and in her arrogance tried to heal him. She felt his quicksilver nervous system melt and then go hard and dark. She knows that when they get to a hospital, the doctors will try to fix him. They will cool him and fight the infection. But he is already gone.

SID

He was little, but so tough in his own way, you wouldn't think he would be that fragile. God. Most of the kids I knew seemed to be made out of rubber. They survived broken bones and whacking their heads on sidewalks, measles and whooping cough and all sorts of croup and crud. Jonah caught a bug, and it went through him and ate him up. Just like that. The thought of his brain, the awesome braininess of the kid, destroyed by bacteria, made me want to run through the hospital and break windows. The loss of him now and the loss of him later, what he would have been when he was older, made me curse Rae. It made me want to kick and spit at Francesca. It made me want to rake my nails across my own face for bringing them up there, for ever believing any of it. It made me want to take out my knife and cut deep. It wasn't possible that Jonah could die, but he did. And we were all to blame.

His death came fast. One minute they made us leave the

room while they worked on him. Then, in an absurdly short time, they came to us, looking down at their green-bagged shoes, their useless hands folded in front of them.

"The meningitis was too far advanced," the doctor said. "He died before we could help him."

Rae stood up. Her face stretched into a grimace, and she began to howl.

"I'm sorry," said the doctor. The nurse touched Rae, who writhed away from her and into Ronnie's arms.

"Oh, God. My baby," Rae moaned.

"Would you like to be with him?" the nurse asked. She took Rae and Ronnie into the room. The rest of us stayed in the waiting area.

Francesca sat across from me, between Anne and Gervais. Anne had her arm around Francesca. Gervais held her hand. Francesca didn't seem to notice. She stared right through me as if I wasn't there.

"It's not your fault," Anne said to her. "The doctors couldn't do anything. You couldn't have helped him."

I went to the door of the room where Jonah was. I opened the door and stepped inside. His tiny body lay still on the gurney. Someone had already turned off the machines and pulled out the tubes. Rae and Ronnie were standing next to him. A guy was moving around the room, picking up the gloves and gowns and trash from the floor and rolling the equipment away. I couldn't stand to see the guy doing his job, cleaning up after Jonah's death.

Rae was still wearing the ratty fake-fur sweater. Her face was swollen and red from crying. She stood above Jonah and ran her hands over his arms and legs, head and face, as if she would imprint him on her palms. The nurse brought warm water and a sponge, and Rae took it from her and washed him herself. She whispered something as she worked, a prayer in some foreign language.

She started with his face, smoothing the red marks where the tubes had pulled against his mouth. Gently, and with great care, she washed his forehead, so that his hair stood up in little spikes. He lay there, looking as if he'd just come out of the pool or the shower and his mouth was open, as if he was surprised to find himself here, dead on a table in a strange hospital. The nurse brought some towels and a blanket, and I covered the parts that Rae washed, to dry him, to keep him warm.

I had been holding his puppy all the while, and now, after she ran the sponge over his arms, I tucked it into the crook of his elbow, so he would have it to keep him company. So he wouldn't be scared. She washed the whorls of his ears and down his neck to his sharp white collarbones. With aching slowness she bathed his chest, so open and unprotected, washing away the marks from the equipment they had used.

His fingertips were stained with purple marker ink, his favorite color for drawing dinosaurs. Rae washed, but they stayed stained. I dried each finger, marveling at the small nails, one of them torn or chewed below the quick. She squeezed water over the soft, small toes, and then, with great tenderness, she kissed the soles of his feet.

When Jonah was clean and dry and the white blanket was tucked in around him, Rae rocked back and forth, with her arms to her chest, chanting a prayer. The eager, greedy look she'd always had was gone. Ronnie held her and said the prayer, too, and I realized that it was a Jewish prayer. It was long and intricate, but neither of them faltered. They said it the way you say things you learn when you are young. The things that are with you forever.

ANNE

Gervais sat next to Francesca. He held her hand. She stared at the floor, where the snow from our boots had melted into puddles.

"I think you should see him," Greg said softly. He stood and helped her up. We went into the room, the deadly white room with instruments and bright lights and the gurney where the little boy lay. Rae and Ronnie were standing at his feet, crying together. Sid stood at his head. Her eyes darted everywhere, then landed on me, and her chin crumpled.

"I'm sorry," she sobbed. "I told them where you were. They wouldn't have come if I hadn't told them."

She was right. She was partly to blame, and I wouldn't lie to her. Still, when she came over to me, I put my arm around her. She was a child, and she had the rest of her life to judge herself.

Greg brought Francesca to Jonah and touched the forehead of the dead boy. His hand lingered, as if he would make the sign of the cross, but Rae and Ronnie were saying their Hebrew prayer, and he seemed to think better of it. He clasped his hands together instead.

In the weeks we'd been away, I'd come to think of Rae as instigator and traitor. She'd become the person I blamed. But here, in the presence of her dead child, she was stripped to a core of pain that had its own dignity. Her grief made her recognizable.

I wished I could keep despising her, continue seeing her as the source of everything that had gone wrong, but I was seeing something else. I could see that she loved Jonah. Yes, she had made bad decisions. She had put her child after other, more selfish interests. And now she was paying for it.

I was seeing that she wasn't all that different from me.

FRANCESCA

Jonah doesn't look scared. His face is smooth and white, and his forehead is untouched by worry or pain. He doesn't look asleep, as people often say when someone dies. He looks profoundly not there. He is absent. His body is dense and heavy without him inside it, almost the way her own body feels without the new life inside her. She touches her cheek, and it is warm. She touches Jonah's cheek, and it is cool in the way that rocks are cool. She looks at him, and she feels the sprouting of a feeling, just in front of her spine, that Jonah has seen the real mystery. Devotees and healings are illusions. This is the real door to God, and Jonah has gone through it.

She watches her mother and Sid. Sid is clinging to Anne like a small child. Her arms are on Anne's shoulders, and her shirt has slid up her back, revealing her stark white hips where they poke out over the top of her low-riding pants. Francesca has never seen so much of Sid's skin before. Sid has always been shy about showing it, going into the bathroom to change and always wearing long pants and big shirts, baggy pajamas, socks and shoes. The white skin above the jeans is sectioned vertically by rough purple lines, the ends of scars that obviously continue down her legs. Francesca is transfixed by the sight. Sid has always joked about cutting. She is glib and funny and makes it all sound like something that happened ages ago. But the scars are fresh, and they are real.

It's a long night, in which Francesca waits for her mom to make the arrangements. She sits in a chair, and her arms hold the memory of Jonah's dying in them. Ronnie pays the bill and then leaves with Rae and Sid in Gervais's car.

Her mother drops into the next chair as the weak sun rises, casting its watery light into the waiting room.

"Give me a minute, will you, Francesca?" Anne says. She puts her head in her hands and cries softly, efficiently, as if to get it over with.

Francesca can't remember when her mother didn't have life under control. Even during the divorce, she showed no weakness. She always takes care of details and is so strong and quick that it's easy to think she feels nothing. But in the plastic hospital chair, in the strained light of dawn, Anne's shoulders shake and tremble. Francesca moves closer, puts an arm around her mother, and holds her until she's quiet.

Five

ANNE

We stayed at the cabin for two weeks after Jonah died. We made daily runs to see Dr. Hadley. Since Jonah's death Francesca had been getting well fast. Dr. Hadley said it was the medication, but it seemed to me that it was Jonah's dying that had shocked her back into herself.

The plan was to be home for Christmas. So, on December 23 we left the cabin scrubbed and locked and well stocked with firewood, and we headed for town. I drove down our street, and there wasn't anybody outside or near our house. The park was empty. No offerings clogged our fence. We unloaded the car, and I kept looking for strangers, but none appeared. It seemed that the crowds were gone. The public had finally lost interest in us. My daughter was no longer a deity, no longer a miracle worker. And she was no longer a celebrity.

I was on the phone thanking Martin for the use of his cabin when Ronnie knocked on my door. She stood on the porch and wrung her hands together, as if she thought I might yell at her.

"Jonah was cremated," she blurted out. "Rae took his ashes to an ashram in Tennessee. She's going to stay there. She won't be back."

I nodded. I did care what had happened to Rae. My rage at her had burned up with Jonah's death, as had the blame I'd put on Ronnie. I just didn't have the energy to keep it up.

"How's Chester?" I said.

She smiled and blushed like a girl. "He's doing fine."

I couldn't help but smile back. There was something exactly right about Ronnie and Chester together.

Peter and Stacey came home for Christmas. Gervais was leaving town after the holiday; the church was sending him on another assignment. So I planned a Christmas Eve supper for all of us, including Ronnie and Chester. I couldn't remember the last time I had dinner guests, but oddly enough, I wanted to give a party. It seemed right, somehow, to celebrate.

Even so, I was relieved when Greg showed up early to help. I had planned on serving a chicken and a salad and was just beginning to panic that it wasn't festive enough when he came to the door with a paper bag full of mussels and another full of spinach.

"It was a tradition at home. My grandmother made this every Christmas Eve," he said. "I had a hell of a time getting the mussels. Do you mind?"

He sautéed the mussels in olive oil and garlic until they popped open. Then he made a roux in the bottom of a large baking dish, added the spinach and then the meat of the mussels. While it was baking, I washed lettuce and he sliced a red onion for the salad. I liked having him in my kitchen, and not for the first time I wished he weren't a priest.

"Where's the next assignment?" I asked.

"Canada. My home city, Montreal."

"You can't tell me anything about it, can you?"

He shook his head.

"What's it like, being a priest?" I asked.

He laughed. "Usually when people ask me that, what they really want to know is what's it like to be celibate."

I felt foolish. "That kind of sums it up."

He answered quickly, and it sounded like something he'd said a lot of times. "Of course I have sexual desire. Just like anyone. But I made an agreement with myself and the church, and it isn't that hard to keep. It's a choice I made." He smiled his gorgeous smile, and I turned back to the salad, surprised at how much it hurt.

"I'm sorry," he said, his smile fading. "I gave you my textbook response." He became completely serious. "Temptation is real, Anne. It's going to be hard for me to leave you."

He opened his arms, and I went into them, and we hugged. It was a very chaste hug, the hug of a dear friend. He kissed me on the forehead. I hadn't really expected him to leave propriety and suggest a sexual relationship, but there had been the feather edge of fantasy about him, the vague dream of us together. And now I was going to lose that along with him.

We served the mussels with a good bread and the salad and champagne. Peter and Stacey and Francesca were on one side of the table facing Sid and Gervais and me. Ronnie sat at one end and Chester at the other. We ate, we drank, and no one mentioned that we were celebrating the eve of the birth of the last Messiah.

SID

My mom was working anyway, so it wasn't a big deal for me to spend Christmas Eve at Francesca's. Ronnie and Chester went next door right after dinner. Peter and Stacey left early, complaining of jet lag, but not before they had announced their engagement. I expected Francesca to freak, but she didn't. She hugged her dad and kissed Stacey on the cheek. Anne saw them out, seeming a little sad, but being nice. If you ask me, Anne had a serious crush on Gervais. Big mistake. All crushes are a drag, but having a crush on a priest must totally suck.

After the dishes Francesca and I went upstairs to her room. I hadn't slept over since the summer. I got my pj's and put them on in the bathroom. When I came out, Francesca was still in her clothes.

"I know you sold stuff that you took from me."

I didn't say anything, because there was nothing to say. I waited to see if she would tell me to get lost, that she couldn't be my friend.

Her mouth twisted into a smile. "Well, at least I hope you made a shitload of money." Then she got serious again. "Can I see your scars, Sid?"

I wrapped my arms around my middle. Francesca had never let on that she knew about my cutting. I was glad that she wasn't mad at me, but that didn't mean I would show her my scars. Only doctors and social workers ever actually *wanted* to see the scars. Even my mom had never asked to see them. She liked to pretend that they didn't exist. But when I looked at Francesca, I could see that she wasn't getting all weird about it. It seemed that she wanted to see because she wanted to see *me*.

I pulled down the elastic waistband and showed her my right hip and thigh. Layers of scars striped my skin, some of them white and many years old, some of them so fresh that they had scabs on them. The cuts crisscrossed from my hipbone to above my knee, running the gamut from pale pink older scars to fresher red scars and to angry purple wounds. I had a kind of pride in my handiwork. My scars were impressive.

"I don't usually show them to people," I said.

She stared at my leg, taking in the many times I had cut there.

"The other one is just like it?"

"Well, not exactly the same, but similar, yeah."

She kept looking at my leg. She was upset. I could see that the sight of my scars bothered her. She reached out and touched a big red one, which had recently healed over. The air got thick around us and charged up, the way it had when Francesca did her healing thing at the restaurant. Or when the rose bloomed. She pulled back her hand, and the air settled down again.

"Don't do it anymore, Sid," she said. She said it with authority and sadness.

I half expected to look down and see that the scars had disappeared. It would have been so perfect, so fitting, if she could
have taken them away, made my thigh seamless again, just like
that. But when I looked, the history of my pain was still latticed
on my skin. I covered it and patted the cotton over a semi-raw
place.

"Okay, F, I showed you. Now will you tell me something?"

She nodded. A trembling started in my arms and spread to
my hands. I clasped them together and took a deep breath before
I spoke.

"How did you make the rose bloom?"

She looked blank. "What rose?"

I fidgeted. It wasn't possible that she could forget. "Out at
Grace Lutheran. That night. The rose bloomed in your hand. It
was a bud that somebody gave you, and you made it bloom."

Her mouth twisted in a sad smile, as if it were something she
wished she had done.

"Don't you remember?" I said.

She looked sadder yet. "I don't. But just so you know, it wasn't
me. *I* never did any of it."

ANNE

I wasn't sure we were out of the woods yet. Francesca had changed. She was herself, but even quieter and more serious. She still took the medication and went twice a week to appointments with Dr. Hadley, but she was hesitant in everything she did, unsure of herself around people. The only thing she seemed to want to do was practice the cello. She practiced the Brahms sonata now for more hours of the day than when she had studied with Keith. I could tell that she was working toward something. When she asked me to make an appointment with him, I had mixed feelings about whether it would be a good idea, but the cello was her only interest, and I wanted to encourage her. So I called him and set it up.

We arrived at his studio at the appointed time. Keith answered the door. His expression was pouty and disdainful, as always. I was shown to a seat. She'd brought her cello, but I assumed that most of the meeting would be a conversation about resuming lessons.

Francesca didn't even look at Keith. I could see how nervous she was. She was intent on making a point, of showing him how much she'd learned while we were away. I was proud that she wanted to prove something to him. Proud and scared. I was prepared to argue with him if I had to.

She took her cello out of its case and began. She was bowing in a competent way, but even I could tell she was holding back. Her fingers fell short of a note, and it played flat and discordant. She stopped, something the old Francesca never would have done. My heart fell. The old Francesca would have pressed on, playing badly, but determined. She would have gotten through it on sheer grit. For a moment I thought she would get up and we would leave in disgrace, but she repositioned herself and seemed to pull herself together. She began again.

This time the sound carved its way out of the instrument and cut into the air. She found the melody and stayed on top of it, and though I'd heard the Brahms sonata a hundred times in past days, this was the first time I heard echoes and variations and nuances in it. Francesca's face was a smooth, concentrated stone and her body a swaying tree. Her bow drove and coaxed the music from the strings without rush or strain. She seemed to have found control and confidence. She played flawlessly for twenty minutes. Then came the last movement, the most difficult after the tiring first three. The allegro was fast and repetitive. It would be easy to make a mistake. I held my breath. A sheen of sweat appeared on her face, but she remained calm. She vigorously performed the short, strong bow strokes, which, I knew, were supposed to prove her new stamina to Keith. When she finished, her cotton shirt was ringed under the arms with sweat and her hairline was wet so that the curls stood out in a halo around her face. She stood and held her instrument as she would at an audition. The music she'd played reverberated in the room.

The expression on Keith's face was rapt and thrilled. And kind. He was a tough teacher, but he wasn't going to hold a grudge or have a chip on his shoulder. He had just wanted to hear Francesca play the music like this.

"Welcome back," he said.

CHESTER

The memory of the smells was hard to hold. I discovered that since I couldn't smell anger and cancer and lust anymore, I also couldn't remember the way they had smelled. It became difficult to know what I was missing. It was a new world. I slept in a house, in a bed, with a woman. Occasionally I dreamed of people smelling like rust or moth dust, but then I woke up next to Ronnie and the dreams faded.

Her body was a wonder. I loved her white skin and the roundness of her. Her arms, her belly, the orb of her eye were all round. Even her hair was round. I gazed at spiral upon spiral of it on the pillow. She was substantial and firm, my very own earth, and I cleaved unto her. Having never been with a woman, I had no past, drew no comparison and gratefully took the gifts she offered me.

We planted a garden as soon as the crocuses were up. We put in roots first: carrots, turnips, onions, beets, radishes. When the nights warmed up a bit and buds swelled on the trees, we planted beans and cucumbers and lettuce, pumpkins, peas, zucchini. We loved and slept at night under a sound roof with the windows open and the breeze playing above us. Radishes erupted from the ground; peas and beans threw their clinging arms around anything within reach; carrot tops stood next to beets and turnips. On a clear day in midsummer, I lay in the dirt, my face close to the plants, watching them grow. A pair of feet appeared to my right. I rolled over on my back, shading my eyes with my arm, to see Francesca standing above me.

"Mom's making pesto. She wants to know if you can spare some basil and if you and Ronnie want to eat with us." She pinched off a sprig of mint and held it under her nose.

I had a longing then, for the old days, when the smell of holy roses came from her and I was her protector. It hit me like a cramp in the belly, knocked the wind out of me, made me draw my knees up to my chest.

"Are you okay?" she said.

"It will pass," I said. "The basil is over there, next to the garlic."

She stayed a moment, casting her shadow on me. Then she broke off a single mint leaf and held it high. When she let go, it fluttered down and landed in the middle of my forehead. I closed my eyes. The earth tilted and then righted itself. When I opened my eyes, she was gone.

Shortly after that there came a day when I realized that I was smelling deeply, almost in the old way. The smells opened like umbrellas in my head. Cucumbers smelled watery and unstable. Tomatoes were tangy to the point of being nearly synthetic, carrots were strong and quiet and secretive, the green beans were self-absorbed but generous through their roots. I could smell the sugar in the beets and the blunt woodiness of the zucchini.

I didn't say anything to Ronnie; I didn't want to worry her. I avoided people, dreading that the smells of them would begin again. But the garden grew and flowered and formed beans and peas, and I smelled only the plants. The tomatoes went from green to red, and the pumpkins insinuated themselves around their stakes, and still I smelled only sassy tomatoes and sneaky pumpkins.

One day in early September, I went out to the garden and understood that I probably would never again smell the rot or the God inside people. To celebrate I made a bouquet of onions and chard and took them in for supper.

FRANCESCA

She lies in clear, cool water. She can hear her heart open and close, pumping life and blood through her veins. The water pulls the heat from her body and leaves her pleasantly chilled. She floats, happy to have made it to the end of her first week of high school. She smiles, remembering summer and her dad and Stacey's wedding. And Sid, now in honors English, math, and science. She thinks of her mom, and the trip they are going to take, to India, over Christmas break. And the junior philharmonic, where she is second-chair cello.

An ache grows from deep inside her pelvis. The cool water no longer feels good. She pulls herself up, her neck straining to bring the heavy hair out of the water. A fist contracts in her belly, against her pelvic bones. She stands, goose-pimpled and shin deep in the water, and holds a towel to her face. The towel is soft and comforting, and she dries her shoulders, arms, and achy belly. She dries between her thighs, and the towel comes away with a stroke of red, a thick smear of menstrual blood.

It aches to bleed after so long. Even though it has been months since she felt the divine spark in her belly, it hurts to accept the final evidence that she is no more than mortal. She sits back down in the water and watches helplessly as the last of the divinity seeps out of her and is diluted by ordinary bathwater. But she holds on to the thought, close under her heart, that she was once the Virgin. And she is blessed among women.

ACKNOWLEDGMENTS

Many, many thanks to:

Kathy Anderson, for your vision and tenacity and caring. I can't thank you enough. Jennifer Brehl, you're the editor I dreamed of. Thanks for so graciously making me a place at the table. Michael Morrison, Lisa Gallagher, Richard Aquan, Barbara Levine, Debra McClinton, Kelly O'Connor, and all the folks at William Morrow and HarperCollins.

The Rocky Mountain Women's Institute, for your generous support in the early drafts. Tim Downing, Barbara Burns, and Sally Powell-Ashby, for bringing the characters to life onstage.

My dear mud-mates: Kate Vorhaus, Ann Barnsley, Candy Sayles, Carl Stewart, and Darcie Rehmel, I love you guys. Kate Villarreal, for painstakingly reading each and every draft of this manuscript. You rock.

KD, for bringing the music and the old guy back into my life and for telling me to get in the game.

My team of expert advisers, each a treasure: Jerry Jacobson, psychoanalyst and dear friend; Kirk Johnson, paleobotanist and spew-pig master; Father James Martin, for great conversations and insight into Gervais; Alice Belmont, for showing me the passion in Brahms; Kelly, Emily, and Anneka Hallowell for teenspeak and 'tude. Any mistakes or misinterpretations in these areas are entirely my own.

Larry Gold for Evolution as Rube Goldberg.

All the homeless men of Boulder, for collectively giving me Chester.

The many who encouraged, supported, inspired, and sheltered me: Kerry Palmer, Mimi Wesson, Tim Hillmer, Tom Jones, Henrietta Rostrup, Karen Gottlieb, Michael Pietsch, Betsy Lerner, Joyce Meskis, Christine Ashe, Charles Stillwagon, Bette Timm, Laura Svolos, Carli Churgin, Sandy McCleod, Sam Dreyden, Donna Gershten, Meesh Miller, Jim Hill, Kirsten Johnson, Brad and Kim Keech, Brad Gaylord, Lehigh Sheppard, Madhuri Gottlieb, David Goldberg, Deborah Spanton, Jonathan Holden.

Satyajit Ray, for *Devi*.

Zoe Movshovitz, for being my beetle.

Howie Movshovitz, for feeding me and listening. For countless commas and spelling corrections. For growing the garden. For holding me in the dark times. You've given me the moments; you've given me the years.

About the author

About the book

Insights,
Interviews
& More ...

Read on

Samantha Stevens,
Mary Poppins, and
Neem Karoli Baba

The Story Behind the Story

I GREW UP IN THE SIXTIES in Littleton, Colorado, which was then a brand-new suburb south of Denver and decades away from its Columbine infamy. Like other young couples in post–WWII affluent America, my parents set out to make the safest, cleanest, most homogenous place they could to start a family.

What they didn't realize was that their efforts provoked, in most of us, their children, a deep craving for everything they'd struggled to save us from. We craved dingy, nonsterile places to hide and dream, we sought unmanicured nature with its idiosyncrasies and risks. We grew up suspicious of structure and establishment. We found we liked the patina of tradition, any tradition (as long as it wasn't our own), and people who were different from us and our clan. What they had no way of knowing when they built the clean white suburbs was that we needed grit, risk, and "other," even in the midst of clean, safe, and same. We found out we were capable of getting grit, risk, and "other" from anywhere and anything.

In 1964, when I was seven in Littleton, LBJ was in the White House. We were at war in Vietnam and the civil rights and anti-war protests were in full swing at home, but the most important thing that happened to me that year was a new TV show on Thursday nights called *Bewitched*. The show was about

Samantha Stevens, an ordinary suburban housewife, who happened to be a witch. The house and neighborhood on the show looked much like my Littleton house and neighborhood. The housewife, though prettier than most of the moms in my neighborhood, was a fair TV approximation of young suburban housewives. Except that she was a witch. She possessed magical powers. Right there in the suburbs pretending to be like everyone else.

I was thrilled by the idea. She could be anyone, I realized, even someone in Littleton. It occurred to me with all the punch of a life-altering event that Samantha Stevens could be me, or, more to the point, I could be *her,* someday. I desperately wanted to believe it, in spite of the flimsy misogynistic storylines, which, even at seven years old, I knew to be badly written and uninspired. I knew exactly what I was after in *Bewitched*: the possibility of a benevolent superhuman with godlike powers existing in my world. The possibility of a divine one among us.

Being seven, I checked to see if I was magical and had somehow missed that crucial detail. If I had magic powers and didn't know it, I wanted to know it now. I practiced wiggling my nose and tried conjuring the power to move ashtrays across coffee tables, but no matter how hard I tried, I couldn't ▶

66 In 1964, when I was seven in Littleton, LBJ was in the White House. We were at war in Vietnam and the civil rights and anti-war protests were in full swing at home, but the most important thing that happened to me that year was a new TV show on Thursday nights called *Bewitched.* 99

Samantha Stevens, Mary Poppins, and Neem Karoli Baba *(continued)*

make anything happen. The possibility had to be enough to sustain me.

Disney released the movie *Mary Poppins* with Julie Andrews the same year. Here was another role model, another motherly character who possessed magical powers and used them to help the children in her care. Children very much like me. Mary Poppins had an edginess that Samantha Stevens didn't have. Mary Poppins was egotistical and capable of lashing out. She was unmarried and (dare I say it) possibly sexual underneath her maidenly exterior. Everyone around her was awed and afraid of Mary Poppins, and rightly so. She could bite your head off as easily as give you a magical trip through a chalk picture. Mary Poppins and Samantha Stevens had distinctly different styles but it was always clear to me that they were essentially the same: good, fun, magical, motherly women masquerading as ordinary to benefit humankind. In other words, they were divine. And I was hooked.

Seven years later in 1971, when I was fourteen, and the country was tearing itself up over the war in Vietnam, I found myself deep in an adolescent angst beyond anything Samantha Stevens and Mary Poppins could fix. My best friend gave me a book called *Be Here Now* by someone named Ram Dass. I read it with the urgency of a drowning victim grabbing a flotation device. Here was a story of an American man who was disillusioned with success and the establishment I was hearing so

> 66 Mary Poppins was egotistical and capable of lashing out. She was unmarried and (dare I say it) possibly sexual underneath her maidenly exterior. 99

much about but was also disillusioned with drugs and free love and the anti-establishment I was edging toward. *Be Here Now* tells of Ram Dass's journey to India and his subsequent meeting with Neem Karoli Baba, a guru in the Himalayas, who promptly ate a handful of Ram Dass's LSD without any effects at all, thereby proving (to Ram Dass, at least) that consciousness is beyond the body and the mind. Here was evidence of other real people, not TV and movie characters, in search of magic, or divinity. And here was a report of an old Indian man who had the goods. I was convinced that this Neem Karoli Baba really could move ashtrays on coffee tables if he wanted to.

It was all there in the book: miracles and mystery, divine power and yogic practices that were designed to get you there. It was about as anti-Littleton as you could get, at the time. And I was fourteen, with a fertile imagination, ready to soak it all up. Here was plenty of grit, risk, and "other." But being fourteen, I couldn't go to India to find this Neem Karoli Baba for myself. My parents certainly weren't going to take me there. I'd have to wait until I was older. Meanwhile, I did what I could. I read every word of the book many times. I practiced all the yoga and breathing and chanting prescribed in it. I began to meditate. I became a vegetarian. I learned to watch myself in my dreams. Two years went by.

And then I read somewhere that the guru Neem Karoli Baba had died. The news changed everything. He'd died before I could get to India. It was unbelievable, but true. I'd missed him. I'd missed the chance to meet a divine human being. I was devastated. ▶

> " I was convinced that this Neem Karoli Baba really could move ashtrays on coffee tables if he wanted to. "

❝ I finished high school. I moved to northern rural New Mexico and lived on a commune, apprenticed to a potter. I left and went to Italy and then to Minneapolis for art school. I concentrated on getting my BA in graphic design and pushed Samantha Stevens, Mary Poppins, and Neem Karoli Baba to the back of my mind. ❞

Samantha Stevens, Mary Poppins, and Neem Karoli Baba *(continued)*

I finished high school. I moved to northern rural New Mexico and lived on a commune, apprenticed to a potter. I left and went to Italy and then to Minneapolis for art school. I concentrated on getting my BA in graphic design and pushed Samantha Stevens, Mary Poppins, and Neem Karoli Baba to the back of my mind. I worked in a bar at night and went to class by day, and a couple more years went by.

Then I met a man who said he knew a "spiritual teacher" who was so much like Neem Karoli Baba that Ram Dass and his other followers were with her in New York City. As soon as I could afford to, I went to New York to meet this "teacher." I was twenty years old. The scene was colorful and musical. I was told it was "exactly like India" and that the "teacher" was the embodiment of Neem Karoli Baba. His Western devotees gathered at her feet along with a lot of newcomers like me. We chanted and meditated. It was almost like I'd read about in *Be Here Now,* only Ram Dass, I was told, had recently had a falling out with the "teacher." I stuck around anyway. I desperately needed to believe in the "magic" I had found. Anyway, other devotees of Neem Karoli Baba were there and they all said the "teacher" was the real thing. The yearning to find the divine in human form was back with a vengeance.

Being in the community meant giving everything you had to the "teacher." Time, money, privacy, allegiance, mind, and heart. As time went on, the people who had been with Neem Karoli Baba left the scene a few at a time. Dietary and sleeping restrictions were imposed. It got to where we were eating only blenderized salad and sleeping two hours a night. The chores and tasks became increasingly punitive. The sessions with the "teacher" became increasingly about "killing the ego," which seemed to mean making people feel bad about themselves and each other amid a lot of talk about spiritual love.

Shortly after my twenty-second birthday, sick and tired of the scene, I slipped out of the evening session and went to see Woody Allen's *Manhattan* instead. While watching it, I realized that I wanted back into the real world. It was a watershed moment for me.

When I got back to the ashram that night, something new was happening. Everyone was lining up to kiss the "teacher's" feet. It was a command performance. The worth of each devotee was determined by the sincerity of their kiss. I watched and waited, unable to go along with the bizarre drama. I realized in a very profound way that I didn't want to be there. I could see that this "teacher" was neither Samantha Stevens, Mary Poppins, nor Neem Karoli Baba, and I knew I had to get out. I packed my things and left that night. I'll always be grateful to Woody Allen.

So, at twenty-two, I drove across the country in a dilapidated 1966 Mustang, disillusioned, sick, and exhausted from my failed search for the divine. I concentrated on working as a graphic designer. I finished my college education. I married. Life rolled on.

In 1990 I had a child and wanted to stay home with her. At the same time, burned out on the graphic design business, I decided to try something I'd always wanted to do: write novel-length fiction. It was an old dream, to write fiction, and it went back to early childhood, to my *Bewitched* and *Mary Poppins* days.

I was a housewife at long last, but without any magical powers. I was hardly Samantha Stevens, yet once in a while, when I was ▶

> " So, at twenty-two, I drove across the country in a dilapidated 1966 Mustang, disillusioned, sick, and exhausted from my failed search for the divine. "

> " I began to
> learn to follow the
> wisest and truest
> thoughts, and try
> to set them on
> paper. Writing, I
> could very
> occasionally
> touch a genuine
> mystery, a real
> kind of magic that
> I was learning to
> cultivate. "

writing, something almost magical occurred. I began to learn to follow the wisest and truest thoughts, and try to set them on paper. Writing, I could very occasionally touch a genuine mystery, a real kind of magic that I was learning to cultivate. I plodded through my first book five or six ways in as many years, and in the end buried it in the plum orchard out back, not sure if I'd learned anything at all. But I kept writing and living.

Then I got the idea that I wanted to write a book about yearning for the divine; about what people will do to believe in their own salvation. During the six years of writing *The Annunciation of Francesca Dunn* I realized that since I had abandoned my search for divinity, thirty years of moments had gone by. I had experienced the joy of love, the pain of loss, the ties of family and responsibility. People I loved had been born and died. Wars had been fought but peace remained elusive. Political regimes came and went. I had been worn against the sandpaper of my own ordinary life and now, when I wanted to find out what I *knew,* I realized the magic, the divine, had been there all along. It was in my early searches and my disillusionment. It was in my family and friends. It was in the eyes of strangers and in the pages buried in the plum orchard. And ever so gently, as if it was always meant to be, the writing about the yearning took on the essence of Samantha Stevens, Mary Poppins, and Neem Karoli Baba, even as a story about Francesca, Chester, Sid, and Anne emerged. I wrote *The Annunciation of Francesca Dunn* and found in myself a sweet, deep vein where the questions, themselves, are the answers.

A Discussion with
Janis Hallowell

....

How did you come to write this book?

THE PROCESS OF WRITING a novel is, for me, a chance to contemplate at length something I want to understand. When I began working on *The Annunciation of Francesca Dunn* I wanted to find out what was the truest thing I could learn about divinity—and by divinity I mean the state or quality of being divine; the manifestation or evidence of God in human form. Around this time I saw a movie made by Indian filmmaker Satyajit Ray in 1960 called *Devi* that greatly influenced *The Annunciation of Francesca Dunn*. *Devi* is set in India in the 1920s and is the story of a young woman believed by her father-in-law to be the incarnation of the mother goddess Kali. Here was a story of divinity, or perceived divinity, but it was an Indian story, embedded in the Hindu culture of Colonial India. I wanted to tell a similar story of projected deification but set in modern secular America—my *own* culture.

It was 1997 and two people our culture sees as divine or nearly so had recently died: Mother Teresa and Princess Diana. One was widely recognized as a living saint, a nun of the Catholic Church, a miracle worker, and comforter to the poorest of the poor. The other was, in fact, royal and had been elevated to the status of goddess and martyr by the media, and the masses. The lives and deaths of these two women seemed to indicate that my story about divinity in Western culture had to have elements of celebrity, the media, the miraculous, and charisma. Add into the ▶

> 66 The process of writing a novel is, for me, a chance to contemplate at length something I want to understand. 99

9

A Discussion with Janis Hallowell *(continued)*

mix that the great divinity story in Western culture is the story of the Christ child, conceived without sin by the Virgin Mary. Any deification story of my culture would have to take the Christian myth into consideration.

So I had some basic elements to my story: a holy virgin, celebrity, media, miracles, set in modern secular America. Add into that a healthy dose of skepticism and mistrust of all of the above as well as personal knowledge and research into cults, religious followings, and holy people. As I wrote and researched and learned, the story began to emerge. Characters arose and started to tell and shape the story. The story developed and defined the characters, who told more of the story and so it went. And before I knew it—about six years later—I had a book.

....

What changed over the six years of writing the book?

This book, unlike my other attempts at novels, always knew what it wanted to be. The title was there almost from the beginning and it never changed. Once I found the core story about this young girl and the kind of belief it would take to make her "divine," I had a thread to hold onto. As long as I stayed with that core and held onto the thread, the novel pulled me through the writing. That's really how it felt. My main task was to show up, hang on—for dear life sometimes—and stay out of the way enough for the novel to get written. It was an amazing experience, more like remembering or dreaming than like trying to compose. It was the subtle stuff, for instance my understanding of the relationship between madness and divinity that changed over the six years.

Tell us more about the relationship between madness and divinity in the book.

There are two characters in the book with "superhuman" attributes: Chester, the homeless man who has the vision of Francesca as the holy virgin and can smell sickness and emotional pain on people, and Francesca, who seems to perform healings and believes she is pregnant with a new savior. Each of these characters' behavior could be interpreted as being "out there" mentally, or "out there" in a mystical sense. I suspect that each of them has some measure of both. This is one of those things that, in the partnership between writer and reader, the reader must decide for herself. People must read the book and come to their own conclusions about the percentages of delusion and holiness in either Francesca or Chester. There is madness in divinity, and divinity in madness. No matter how we try to sort it out, the frontier between the two remains filled with mirages and mirrors.

The story is told in the first person voices of Anne, Francesca's mother; Sid, Francesca's friend; Chester, the homeless visionary; and in a close third person from Francesca's point of view. Why these four? Why are three told in first person and one in third person?

I wanted to tell the story around Francesca. The structure has that circular quality. She was at the center of the story but because she is the object of projection by so many other people, she can't tell the entire story herself. So the people around her each tell a part. In early drafts Greg Gervais, the priest, and Ronnie, the café owner, had narrative voices, too. But I decided to limit the voices to four. I chose

> " Each of these characters' behavior could be interpreted as being 'out there' mentally, or 'out there' in a mystical sense. I suspect that each of them has some measure of both. "

A Discussion with Janis Hallowell *(continued)*

third person from Francesca's point of view for the fourth voice because the close third is disembodied, ageless, and gives some perspective, as though she is observing herself from above. This voice sounded to me like Francesca's soul voice.

....

Early in the book Anne, Francesca's mother, says that the only God she believes in is Natural Selection. Do you think that Darwinism and Christianity are competing belief systems?

Sure. But the book isn't about Darwinism vs. Christianity. The book is about what happens when people believe something so strongly that it overpowers reason and the truth in front of their eyes. Anne is a paleobotanist and believes in science and Darwin, and so she misses some things that are happening to her daughter because they just aren't in her frame of reference. Chester believes that Francesca is a divine being—to the point that he lets some things slide past his better judgment, and unwittingly puts her in danger because of his belief.

....

Is there a miracle in Francesca Dunn?

This is another one of those things that, in the partnership between writers and readers, falls into the domain of the reader. It was never my intention to write in a miracle. And it's really kind of immaterial whether there's an actual miracle or if things are merely perceived to be miracles. Readers can interpret the events however they wish. ∽

> ❝ It was never my intention to write in a miracle. ❞

Do You Have What It Takes to Be a Divine Mother?

SO, YOU MAY NOT BE HOLY VIRGIN MATERIAL. Sadly, it may have come to your attention of late that you're (a) not really a virgin and (b) probably too old anyway. Not to worry. You may still be a candidate for Divine Mother. Divine Mothers have certain things in common. They all "create" themselves. They all sacrifice in order to serve, they have a flair for what to wear and they all die on the job. Take the fun and easy quiz below to find out if you're likely to follow in the hallowed footsteps of such contemporary Divine Mothers as Marilyn Monroe, Martha Stewart, Princess Diana, and Mother Teresa.

1. Divine Mothers arise out of obscurity. Where were you born and raised?

   A. The "flyover" states
   B. Nutley, New Jersey
   C. Los Angeles
   D. Sandringham
   E. Skopje

2. All Divine Mothers possess icon status and superstar celebrity. Which one best describes your status?

   A. Most of your fans call you Mom
   B. A major discount store carries your line of bath towels
   C. Maybe you slept with the President and maybe you didn't
   D. People besides you think that your sons are princes
   E. You have been beatified by the Pope

Women who nearly made it or Divine Mothers Runners Up

Audrey Hepburn

Princess Grace of Monaco

Jacqueline Kennedy Onassis

Eleanor Roosevelt

the Queen Mum

Golda Meir

Women who may make it yet:

Maya Angelou

Madonna

Queen Elizabeth II

Women who tried and failed:

Evita Peron

Imelda Marcos

Tammy Faye Baker

Your likelihood of becoming a modern day Divine Mother

If your score was:

0 to 8 points—
Not likely, but your kids and cats will love you.

9 to 15 points—
Who are you kidding? But if you stay honest you may get rich.

16 to 20 points—
You're a sex goddess; who cares about the rest of it?

21 to 24 points—
Pretty darn divine, Your Highness.

25 points—
You've made it. Full marks. Now go heal the world.

On the Lighter Side ... Do You Have What It Takes to Be a divine Mother? *(continued)*

3. Divine Mothers have an instinct for the right outfit. What are you wearing?

   A. Your Lantz nightgown
   B. Khakis, a crisp cotton shirt and Felco pruners
   C. A transparent beaded dress, "commando" underneath
   D. Givenchy and a small crown
   E. The nice white sari with blue trim

4. Cameras and ordinary mortals follow Divine Mothers everywhere. What's your following like?

   A. 3 kids, 2 cats, a dog, a hamster and the occasional mosquito
   B. A small but dedicated following, most of whom you pay
   C. Men want you, women want to be you
   D. Everyone with a TV
   E. The poorest of the poor, the angels, and the Nobel committee

5. What Divine Mother archetype do you most want to embody?

   A. Stay-At-Home-Mom
   B. Corporate Diva
   C. Sex Goddess
   D. Royal Princess
   E. Saint

What's your score? Give yourself
   1 point for every A answer,
   2 for B answers, 3 for C answers,
   4 for D answers and 5 for E answers.
   Add them up. Find out how you did, left.

Janis Hallowell
Recommends

**Five films that influenced
Francesca Dunn**

1. *Devi*—Satyajit Ray (1960)
   Ray's classic influenced the story of *The Annunciation of Francesca Dunn* more than any other single work. A Hindu patriarch believes his daughter-in-law is the incarnation of the goddess Kali.

2. *Black Narcissus*—Michael Powell (1947)
   The deceptively simple and exquisite artificiality of the movie influenced the flavor of *The Annunciation of Francesca Dunn*. In *Black Narcissus* organized religion is undermined by the spiritual and sensual.

3. *Mary Poppins*—Robert Stevenson (1964)
   I'm not kidding. *Mary Poppins* introduced to me the possibility of magical or divine beings coming to live among us. In it magic undermines and heals the establishment. Set in 1910 this movie is really about the 1960s.

4. *The Sacrifice*—Andrei Tarkovsky (1986)
   A man literally makes a deal with God. The access to the unconscious mind in this film deeply influenced the essence of *The Annunciation of Francesca Dunn*.

5. *Rear Window*—Alfred Hitchcock (1954)
   As a study of the projections of an observer, this film influenced *The Annunciation of Francesca Dunn*. As a study of voyeurism, it influenced me as a writer.

**Five novels I read in the
last year and liked a lot**

1. *The Last Samurai* by Helen DeWitt (Talk Miramax Books)
   Amazingly brainy and original.

2. *Love in the Asylum* by Lisa Carey (William Morrow)
   Great compassion and wit about mental illness.

3. *All Over Creation* by Ruth Ozeki (Penguin)
   A beautifully written eco-novel full of hope.

4. *Truth & Beauty* by Ann Patchett (HarperCollins)
   A heartbreaking true story about the author and her best friend.

5. *Perfume* by Patrick Suskind (Knopf)
   An olfactory extravaganza.

Web **Detective**

http://www.udayton.edu/mary/
for more on the Virgin Mary

http://www.palace.net/~llama/psych/
injury.html
for more on self-injury

http://www.schizophrenia.com/
for more on schizophrenia

http://www.apparitions.org/
*for a list of apparitions of the Virgin sanctified
by the Catholic Church*

http://www.thehomelessguy.blogspot.com/
*the blog of Kevin Michael Barbieux, a homeless
man*

http://www.gurl.com
comprehensive, interactive site for teenage girls

http://www.csj.org/
for information about cults

http://www.dadsanddaughters.org/
*comprehensive site devoted to father-daughter
relationships*

http://www.nobel.se/peace/laureates/1979/
teresa-bio.html
for more on Mother Teresa

http://www.neemkarolibaba.com/index.ht
ml
for more on Neem Karoli Baba

Don't miss the next
book by your favorite
author. Sign up now for
AuthorTracker by visting
www.AuthorTracker.com.